LEAH FLEMING worked in teaching, catering, running a market stall, and stress management – as well as being a mother of four – before finding her true calling as a storyteller. She lives in the beautiful Yorkshire Dales but spends part of the year marinating her next tale from an olive grove on her favourite island of Crete.

The
Olive Garden
Choir

LEAH
FLEMING

HEAD
of ZEUS

First published in the UK in 2019 by Head of Zeus Ltd
This paperback edition published in the UK in 2019 by Head of Zeus Ltd

9 7 5 3 1 2 4 6 8

A catalogue record for this book is available from
the British Library.

ISBN (PB): 9781788548687
ISBN (E): 9781788548656

Typeset by Adrian McLaughlin

Printed and bound in Great Britain by
CPI Group (UK) Ltd, Croydon CR0 4YY

MIX
Paper from
responsible sources
FSC® C020471

Head of Zeus Ltd
First Floor East
5–8 Hardwick Street
London EC1R 4RG

WWW.HEADOFZEUS.COM

To Brenda T with love and thanks for all those happy days in the sun.

From *The Escape to Paradise Guide to the Greek Islands: Santaniki, Christmas Island*

Off the coast of Crete lies the beautiful island of Santaniki, with its harbour, fishing villages and white sands. The main town is Ayios Nikolaos, known as St Nick's. It is a haven for honeymooners and birdwatchers. The ancient chapel of St Nicholas (patron saint of sailors and all things Christmas) is cut into the mountain rock, with fine frescos inside.

There are exclusive villas to rent in the outlying villages, with a lively British community in residence. The coastal scenery is breathtaking. In spring the central rocky plateau is full of meadow flowers, orchids, poppies and other beautiful species. In summer there are courses in writing, poetry, art and ceramics in the former home of the famous British romantic novelist, Elodie Durrante. A perfect holiday venue for any who are creative in the arts or seeking a quiet retreat from the bustle of city life.

There are regular flights from the UK to Crete in season. A short ferry ride from the lively ports of Chania and Rethymnon will bring you to this charming destination.

I

Ariadne Blunt swept up the bougainvillaea leaves from the veranda of her villa on the island of Santaniki, then stopped to admire the view down the rocky slope of olive trees to the sparkling sea, where the faint outline of the big island glinted in the late September sunshine. Now the summer visitors were returning for school terms in Britain, local activities would start again.

Tonight at the first book-club meeting of the season members would provide a summary of their summer reading or single out a book for discussion, and she wanted them to sit on the veranda in the warmth of sunset.

Looking up, she saw the fledgling swallows peeking out of their nest in the corner. It was always a relief when Hick and Hetty returned to raise two broods before their long flight back to Africa. Their safe arrival each year heralded spring, but it was always a sad moment when the young flew off. Their mess was contained in a bucket, but she'd clean it in case some eagle-eyed member thought it unsightly or unhygienic.

The group consisted of a motley assortment of women, mostly middle-aged and retired, but there was a sprinkling of younger ones, who could be relied on to vary the usual selection of middle-brow literature. As a former bookseller, Ariadne assumed leadership to check any snide comments on choices, but tonight she had something important to say.

It had all started when she'd seen a family coming off the ferry, dressed in tunics and jeans, the women in hijabs, reminding her of the drownings off the coasts of Libya and Turkey. Some eastern islands were swamped with refugees but Crete was too far away for that. Most of the survivors had nothing but what the aid agencies had found for them. Here on Santaniki, she hoped they would be found temporary accommodation and seasonal work, and wondered what she could do to help.

Her thoughts were interrupted by her friend and housemate, Hebe Wilson. 'Shall I set the cups out? It is this evening, isn't it?'

'Yes – I told you so this morning. No apologies yet, so we'll need seven or eight chairs. I thought we might have some wine as it's the first gathering.'

'Isn't the garden looking good?' Hebe nodded in the direction of the path where the oleander borders were still in late blossom. 'Shall I cut some flowers?'

'If you like, but try not to make a trail of dust. I've just swept.'

Ariadne liked everything to look tidy for their guests but Hebe had a knack of spreading clutter, forgetting to wipe up and leaving her gardening tools on the tables. It was only a small villa, among a row of grander ones, of which some were only half finished because of the recession. She sighed. The building trade had collapsed and the glory days of foreigners buying second homes were over. Houses were getting harder to sell. She shook herself. Stop wool-gathering, for heaven's sake! Go and get smartened up, before the early birds appear...

One by one they arrived, clutching book bags. Chloë Bartlett was always the first. in her linen jumpsuit and fancy beads. Nor did she come empty-handed: she was carrying a posy of fresh blooms from her beautiful landscaped garden on a hill-side outside the town.

Then freckled Della Fitzpatrick staggered up the path, wearing skinny jeans and a jazzy top, and behind her little Natalie Fletcher was dressed in black, her thin arms covered with a crocheted shawl.

Dorinda Thorner wore the usual flowery tent, accompanied by a waft of expensive perfume. She would demand the most comfortable chair, on account of her bad back.

Last but not least, and always late, young Mel Papadaki, English wife of Spiro, son of a local taverna owner, would probably get them going. 'I've just read Elodie Durrante's novel, *Under the Cretan Sun*.'

'Did you enjoy it?' Ariadne asked. Once Elodie had been the island's most famous resident and it felt right to honour her with a reading of her novel.

Before Mel could reply, Dorinda butted in. 'I thought it a terrible choice.' She sniffed. 'The sort of torrid romantic nonsense I'm not used to reading.'

'Well, I thought it was brilliant,' Mel replied. 'I'd never got round to reading her before. She writes good sex, doesn't she?'

The others fell silent until Della giggled. 'Trust you to pick that book. She was quite a woman, I'm told. Maybe she'd had a lot of experience in that department. Ariadne, you knew her…'

'I did, and a more generous soul would be hard to find. Her later books were not her best. I think she ran out of steam, but I'm glad you enjoyed it, Mel.' Ariadne didn't want her put down for choosing something light and relaxing. Mel had her work cut out, what with two small boys and a mother-in-law like Irini Papadaki, plus the taverna to help run, when Spiro was away finding work. The taverna was on the square and a popular venue for parties. Ariadne was amazed that Mel had time to read anything. Then she saw that Natalie was hanging back, too nervous to offer her opinion. 'How about you, Natalie? Did you enjoy Elodie's novel?'

Natalie blushed. 'Actually, I've not had much time to read. I've been catering for a house party, but they've gone now. I'll try to keep up with the reading list.'

Ariadne doubted she would ever relax enough to sit down and read anything. She came to book-club meetings for the company, as she did to the Pilates class, which Della ran. At least she always brought a little something with her. This time it was a plate of delicious-looking lemon polenta squares.

'Did you like it, Della?' Ariadne asked.

'Yes, in parts, It's a relaxing read, though I did fall asleep towards the end.'

There were some approving nods, but Dorinda Thorner folded her arms in disagreement.

'We should be reading uplifting fiction that stretches our minds,' she said. 'I don't come here to read smut.' And so it went on, everyone arguing the toss.

'It would make a good film,' Mel put in. 'A real *Romeo and Juliet* story, don't you think?'

'No one would want to film here,' Dorinda replied. 'Think of the expense, and it might stir up old feuds between the locals.'

'What do you mean?' Della asked.

'All that stuff about Greeks fighting Turks.'

'Elodie handled it with sensitivity,' Ariadne argued. 'She did her research well.'

'I think it showed up too much,' Chloë said. 'If you want a good book on the subject read *Freedom and Death* by Kazantzakis. It's long but accurate.'

'Reading's hard when the pressure's on,' Ariadne said, aware that Hebe was half dozing in the corner. Hebe was another who found it hard to concentrate on a book for long, drifting off as the book slid onto the floor.

'I think it's good to have a variety of genres on the to-read list,' Chloë said. 'This wasn't really my cup of tea, but I do have a few books to lend.' She pulled out a pile of paperbacks by prize-winning literary authors, spread them on the table and reviewed each one at length. When Chloë got into her stride there was no stopping her.

Ariadne's eyes glazed over. Chloë liked to take over every meeting, even though no one showed much enthusiasm for her choice, unless it was Kate Atkinson's latest. Time to change the subject. 'Have you finished pulling Elodie's last novel to pieces?' she asked. 'Hands up for wine.' Everyone raised a hand.

'I'll do it,' whispered Hebe, then retreated into the kitchen, where the glasses were already set out beside Natalie's lemon polenta cake.

'It's not village wine, is it?' said Dorinda. 'It gives me a headache.'

You're the headache in this group, thought Ariadne, always criticising, but she smiled politely. 'We had enough of that when Elodie was still alive. I never slept a wink after one of her parties.'

'No, it's Durakis's best,' Della chipped in. 'Anyway, what's wrong with village wine? We have to support local enterprise.' Her support for the local taverna was well known.

'Poor Elodie, we've not been fair. This was her last book, not her best. Still, she was a bestseller and the island owes much to her generosity.' Ariadne wanted the last word. Elodie's magnificent villa was now an arts and crafts retreat centre. She had bequeathed it to the island under the auspices of the Elodie Durrante Arts Foundation. Pilgrim tourists climbed the dusty track to view the small museum devoted to her life and work.

'Do we vote on it, then?'

'No.' Hebe suddenly came to life. 'She was our friend, Ariadne, not marks out of ten, please.' She jumped up and went into the kitchen.

Ariadne smiled. 'We understand, but it is our custom.'

Natalie shook her head. 'Let's leave it as it is. I can't vote because I didn't read it.'

'Now,' Ariadne said, 'I have an announcement to make in a little while but, first, thank you, Natalie, for your delicious contribution.'

She followed Hebe into the kitchen to open the bottles. Hebe was sitting in a chair. The kettle was boiling. She started. 'Sorry, I was day-dreaming,' she said.

Ariadne took a deep breath. Hebe had been so absent-minded lately. Still, there had been a good discussion tonight. Poor Elodie would be turning in her grave at the criticisms of her style: she had always made sure Hebe and Ariadne were aware of her status in the bestseller charts. But her style was old-fashioned, and too raunchy for the older members' modern taste. Perhaps they needed shaking up.

She was pleased to see such a good turnout, now that most of the seasonal visitors were departing. They had their island to themselves once more.

She loved the change of seasons, when the nights drew in early, the air was cooler and even rainy at times. Soon they would change the lacy summer curtains for winter velvets, bring out the woven rugs to warm the stone floors, and gather in the dry olive wood, ready for the nightly fire. Besides all of this, she had plenty of plans for the winter and now was the time to strike.

While everyone's mouths were full of cake, she announced her intentions. 'I've been thinking we should form a proper choir for our Christmas appeal for the refugees, followed by a grand carol concert for the whole district. What do you think?"

'Come on,' said Chloë. 'We'll hardly be the Military Wives Choir.'

'Of course not,' Ariadne replied. 'I was thinking more of a community choir. We've got enough voices to put on a decent show and I have plenty of music.'

'I've not sung since the sixth form, when I got excluded for changing the words of the song we were learning to rude ones. Perhaps we're too old to make a decent sound,' Della said.

'Speak for yourself,' Mel snapped. 'I'm only thirty and I know other younger people who might join in – the couple who run the retreat house, for a start.'

'We need men,' said Chloë. 'Tenors and basses to add depth and tone. We'd sound like a cats' chorus on our own, but it would be good to do something for charity at Christmas.'

'Something jazzy and rock, not just old-fashioned carols,' Della added.

'Oh, but some are so beautiful,' Hebe said. 'I love "Silent Night" and "The Boar's Head Carol". John Rutter's written some excellent tunes.'

'All right, Hebe,' Ariadne interrupted. 'We'll have to make it appeal to everyone in St Nick's, and of course we'll want to show our Greek friends a true English Christmas.'

'They have their own customs. Will they be interested in English carols? Perhaps American classics would be better – "White Christmas" or "Deck the Halls", or even some songs from the musicals,' Chloë suggested, noticing heads shaking.

'We won't know if we don't try, Chloë. Christmas means a lot when you're far from home,' Ariadne replied. She wouldn't be defeated by negative talk.

'Simon and I will be visiting Alexa and her family back in the UK, so you can count us out,' Chloë told her.

'Well, there's St Nicholas's Day on December the sixth. You'll still be here then,' Ariadne said. Chloë always like to set the tone for the group. Ariadne found her a little patronising and negative at times. 'Anyway,' she said, 'think about it. We can rehearse here, in the olive garden.'

'It'll soon be too dark,' murmured Hebe.

'Not in the afternoon. We can use the drawing room when it's wet. October and November can be so unpredictable. I'm relying on you all to chip in and invite your friends – cast the net wide.'

Ariadne sensed hesitation. She'd sprung it on them without warning, but this would be something new. The tavernas hosted karaoke or jazz evenings, but a choir would include people of all ages and abilities. It could form the core of a festive concert, with tickets sold, a raffle, tombola, all the usual money-spinners for a good cause.

When nights were long and daylight shortened, residents withdrew into themselves. This might bring the community together, although Ariadne could tell she had a challenge on her hands, if she was to make her idea anything more than wishful thinking.

Natalie's Lemon Polenta Slices

160ml extra virgin olive oil
200g caster sugar
200g ground almonds
100g instant polenta
1½ teaspoons baking powder
3 large eggs
Zest and juice of 2 large lemons
200g icing sugar

Grease a tin and line it with greaseproof paper. Set the oven to 180°C. Whisk together the olive oil and sugar until pale and frothy.

In another bowl mix the ground almonds, polenta and baking powder. Pour about a third of the dry mixture into the olive oil, add an egg, beaten, and stir well. Then add another third of the dry mixture with another beaten egg and stir again. Add the rest of the dry mixture with the third egg, also beaten, and the lemon zest, then stir thoroughly. Pour the batter into the prepared tin and bake for 35–40 minutes. Test with a skewer: when it comes out dry, the cake is done.

Make a syrup with half of the lemon juice and 50g of the icing sugar: heat them together in a small saucepan until the sugar has dissolved. Prick the top of the cake all over, then pour over the warm syrup and leave it to cool.

Make the topping: mix the remaining icing sugar with the rest of the lemon juice and smooth it over the top of the cooled cake. Leave it to rest, then cut into slices.

2

Sammia Began shook off her headscarf and stared around the stone house with dismay. Maryam, her sister-in-law, had left the room untouched again. In such a small space they must keep things tidy. It was not what they were used to, but it was a roof over their heads. The spacious apartments with high ceilings and balcony windows in Damascus were now just rubble, since the civil war and the bombings had taken their toll.

Thanks to the kindness of strangers, there was just enough space for two families, a recess bench, with a mattress of sorts, and a bedroom for Maryam, Amir and little Karim. There was also an open fire, a well and a sink. The farmer, Yannis, who was also the mayor of Santaniki, had offered them this shepherd's hut in return for Sammia's husband, Youssef, and Amir helping with the vegetable garden by picking tomatoes, aubergines, anything that could be sold at the weekly market. Sammia helped his wife, Toula, with the housework and preparing meals. It was a relief to be occupied, away from Maryam's tears of frustration and grief.

In the flight from Syria, Maryam had miscarried her second child and Karim screamed each time he saw the sea. The ferry trip from the big island to Santaniki had been a nightmare. Distant relatives in Crete had offered them a temporary stay in Chania where Sammia had found comfort in the bustling city and open markets – normality, after so much trauma. The few dollars she had hidden in her brassière had not been looted so she could buy underwear for herself and Maryam. Now at least they had some dignity, beneath the clothing the aid agency had provided. It was hard to be beholden to charity.

A kindly priest had suggested they move to the small island where there would be more work for the men. The tension of the past months had exacted a price from the women – Maryam could not bear to look at Sammia's swelling belly. Inside her, the little one kicked and squirmed, unaware of the dangers he had faced during their escape. At least Maryam had Karim to watch over and distract her. They took him into the hills to play among the rocks and caves and pick scented herbs on the little mountain that rose from the middle of the island. They could sit in the shade, or pick the wild almonds and carobs that grew there. In the hut, they had a sack of dried beans and lentils, with a garden full of vegetables, for stews, and made lemonade from the trees in the grove that Yannis's forebears had planted aeons ago.

Understanding Greek was hard. Sammia wanted to practise her English. She missed her school teaching post, just as Youssef missed his accountancy office. It was hard to feel like a professional person in that humble dwelling. But at least they had life, where others did not.

Her eye fell on the torn wedding photograph, the only one

that had survived the border searches. Its silver frame had been looted. She studied the happy faces of her parents before they had been killed in a bombing raid. Their cousin, Hussein, had been arrested and had disappeared. Amir was a journalist and had known his days were numbered when he had spoken out against the war.

Sammia flung open the wooden door to sunshine, blue skies and silence: no guns, hooting horns or sirens screaming, just the whirring of cicadas in the late-summer heat. Here was peace, but for how long? This was not their homeland and she feared they were tolerated rather than welcome. She patted her stomach and smiled. Her child would be born here, God willing. It was the only joy that stopped her weeping for all that was lost.

3

Natalie Fletcher made her way gingerly to the house the locals called 'The Bunker'. It had been built on lottery winnings, it was rumoured, by a young couple called the Partridges. She was carrying a cake, ordered for a party they were giving, and she wanted to get it to them in one piece.

There was talk among the expats about the prospect of the choir and, as in all small villages, word had spread to Irini's taverna in the square. There, husbands hung out while their wives went to evening classes. Natalie thought it only fair to tell the couple about Ariadne's idea and invite them to join in.

'How daft can you get?' Kelly Partridge sneered. 'It's a stupid idea. You can't make a proper Christmas here without snow and lights, like on Oxford Street. The woman's off her rocker if she thinks I'd join her tinpot choir. We'll be going home for Christmas, won't we, Gary?'

Gary said nothing – he was deep in a computer game.

'I think it'll be rather nice,' Natalie said. 'Not all of us can get back to the UK and I, for one, will be joining.'

'Suit yourself. I prefer the talent shows on TV. That's what I call real singing. How much do I owe you? Can you make us a Christmas cake? My mum isn't too good at baking. I'll take it home with me.'

'I'll be doing a few. They need to rest for weeks to mature so I bought all the ingredients when I was last in Chania. It's amazing what you can get there now,' Natalie said.

'Really?' Kelly sniffed. 'I can't stand the place, too busy and noisy.'

But you're both Londoners, Natalie thought, as she walked back to her own small villa. Kelly and her husband were a mystery: they had turned up three years ago, having built this strange cube-like house, on the edge of the rocks that jutted out into the sea. They didn't associate much with the other expats, instead importing friends from London for parties and holidays. They disappeared from Santaniki for weeks at a time. Natalie was grateful for their custom, though.

The income from her little catering business was more than useful. It paid the rent and gave her a reason to get up in the morning. She loved the aroma of cakes in the oven, of bread and pastry. They soothed her anxious spirit. She couldn't get into the kitchen and start on a batch of bread. While she was kneading dough, her hands could bash out all her frustrations. Coming to the island had saved her sanity. She had always loved Greece in the good old days, when the children were little, watching them racing into the turquoise sea, making castles on the white sands. They had been happy then, but Craig and Candice had grown up into the sort of adults who kept their distance, never phoning much or texting, even.

Don't go there. Think about all those rehearsals and the company in the evenings. She tried to be sociable but preferred providing food for the interminable dinner-party circuit that swung into action once the season came to an end. There was always a dessert to be made. Fortunately she'd taken the Jane Asher cake-decorating course and her little marzipan figurines were in demand. She had an idea for a Christmas nativity scene made with flour paste hardened into sculptures. Would Ariadne find it acceptable for the charity stall they always held a few weeks before Christmas? This year they were raising funds for refugees. She would make mini Christmas cakes and puddings, biscuits, gingerbread men and dozens of mince pies. It would keep her busy for weeks.

She was also giving Mel, from the tavern, lessons in baking and pie-making. Poor Mel could do nothing right for Irini Papadaki. As a university student, Mel's diet had been Pot Noodles and pizza. Her love for Spiro must be under strain when she got only criticism from his mother for being useless in the kitchen.

Greek cuisine was not for the faint-hearted. There were so many vegetable dishes to learn, plus stews, cakes and special pastry, using ingredients poor Mel had never heard of, never mind cooked, but she was a quick learner and a hard worker. Those first years of marriage were special when all you wanted was to please your husband and make a home for babies. They didn't last, though. Tears were dropping into Natalie's dough. How could hers have gone so wrong?

4

Chloë and Simon Bartlett sat on the terrace at sunset sipping G and T and gazing over the immaculate garden that sloped down towards their sea view. The house was one of the oldest villas in the village, bought as a ruin and carefully restored stone by stone, extended at the back and fitted with all the features that reminded them of the original design: ceilings with cypress-wood beams, stone archways into the great drawing room with its fireplace, marble floors and rough-woven Cretan rugs scattered liberally across them. There was a grand piano in the corner, adding grace, but it was rarely played, and a gallery of artwork on the walls.

'Dear old Ariadne she does have strange ideas.' Chloë laughed. 'A choir of oldies trying to re-create their youth singing carols? I really don't want to be party to it but I suppose I should put in an appearance. It is for charity and one must contribute...'

'Hang on! She's about the same age as us so not so much of the "oldies". And you still have a lovely voice,' Simon remonstrated.

'You too, deep bass.' She touched his hand. 'Remember when we sang in the Bach Choir? I couldn't bear to make a fool of ourselves singing to the Greeks. Coals to Newcastle. What will they make of us?' Chloë smiled, recalling the camaraderie of performances in the Royal Albert Hall.

'We have to listen to their music often enough with weddings and baptisms that go on till dawn and tannoys blasting forth. It will do them good to hear us. I'll join, if you like.'

'Would you? Then there'll be at least one male voice,' she said.

'We could ask Clive Podmore. He might like to come. Have you seen him lately? He looks so lost. We ought to have him for supper again.'

'It must be nearly two years since Lucy died but he still looks shell-shocked, poor man. I don't know why he won't go home.'

'Because she's buried here and he can't leave her. They were so devoted. I see him on the headland heading into the hills. He does his daily walk with the dog but I can't even get him to spend an evening with us in the taverna,' Simon said. 'Perhaps if I ask him to join the choir, he'll go for it. That'll make two men and then there's old Colonel Templeton Brown. I've heard him in church but it'll take more than three men to balance you women.'

'Is Arthur still writing his memoirs? He must be over ninety now.' Chloë smiled. 'He was always full of war stories.'

'And as fit as a butcher's dog. He's a military man through and through, but lonely since Caro died.'

'We need youngsters like Mel. She's trying to drum up some of the mothers,' said Chloë.

'We? Be careful, Chloë. This is Ariadne's shout, her baby.'

'But if it's going to happen it's got to be done properly, regular rehearsals, a balanced programme of old and new music and special outfits.' Chloë could see the women in black dresses with bright scarves, red or green edged with tinsel, and the men in dinner jackets.

'Darling, hold back. You know how you can take over...'

'What do you mean? I'm only making suggestions. Look how Gareth Malone got all those communities singing.'

'This is a one-off and we probably won't be here for the concert. Have you heard from Alexa and Hugh?'

'Not a word, but I'll be with her in London at half-term for Christmas shopping. It'll be good to get off the island. It's like living in a bubble, such narrow lives some of them lead.'

'Don't be smug, Chloë. They're here for a reason. They all have their stories.'

'And when you try to get them to open up they clam shut, all running away from something, no doubt, or someone...'

'Or running to this beautiful island. Don't be judgemental,' Simon said.

'I'm not. How can you say such a thing?' Chloë snapped. She was only remarking on what she had noticed. 'Anyway, I just want to help get this thing off the ground..'

'I'm sure you do—'

'I don't interfere. I only make suggestions to improve things.' Chloë was on the defensive now. If something was worth doing it must be done well and she wasn't sure that Ariadne and Hebe were capable of organising a choir professionally. 'Do you think I should have a word with Ariadne before the first rehearsal?'

5

Della Fitzpatrick had pulled out the mats, softballs and stretch bands for the Pilates class on the veranda of her villa, which had a glorious mountain view, but the turnout was thin. All of the usual suspects were either too lazy to come because of the heat, injured or busy elsewhere. Ariadne and Hebe were there, Natalie Fletcher, so thin in black leggings and T-shirt, and for once Kelly Partridge had made an appearance in a new Sweaty Betty outfit with jazzy leggings.

'Got to get in shape for the party season,' she said. 'Too cold to swim in the sea now.'

'The water's warmer than ever this year. I had a swim this morning,' Ariadne said. 'So refreshing.'

Della began the usual warm-up. They exercised in the shade, looking out over the rooftops of the village towards the hills. Her clients were a mixed bunch fitness-wise, but Hebe worried her. Her coordination was clumsy and needed watching. Ariadne was lithe and fit for her age.

Della was feeling a bit wobbly. She hadn't meant to hit the bottle last night but Chloë's choice of book for the next meeting seemed very disjointed and she'd lost interest after fifty pages. It was one of those days when she got the glums. What was she doing stuck on a remote island with winter coming on? She dreaded the darkness, with just DVDs and the World Service during the night when she couldn't sleep. And she must stop buying that cheap vodka.

On every trip to the mainland she ordered her supplies to be delivered discreetly in a box off the ferry. Only the twice-weekly Pilates class kept her sober enough to go through the moves, checking clients' postures and positions. Della had come to Greece for the light, the brightness of its colours, and because it was as far away from Yorkshire, with its grey skies, cold, damp air, and memories, as she could get.

'Right, let's stand and stretch,' she ordered, hoping that the alcohol on her breath was disguised by the peppermint mouth-wash. 'How's this choir of yours coming on, Ariadne? Have we got a line-up yet?'

Ariadne was bending slowly as instructed into the dog posi-tion. 'We've got three men so far and I'll be twisting a few arms in the taverna. I've put a poster up in the village store and the first rehearsal is next Monday in our olive garden. You will come?'

Kelly Partridge laughed. 'You won't catch me there. I've sung in school assembly and then only when I bothered to turn up. Adele is more my cup of tea.'

'I like Alfie Bowe and Russell Watson,' Natalie said, but Kelly pulled a face.

'I'm sure you'd like listening to carols,' Ariadne offered.

'You're joking. That's for kids. You should recruit from the school.'

'I will if I need to, and teach the local children "Away in a Manger",' Ariadne said, not prepared to be put off.

'There you go. A kiddie choir to bring all the parents in and no need for oldies to make fools of themselves,' Kelly replied.

After that no one spoke. Della wanted to crown Kelly with one of the metal knee stretchers. She was such a common piece of work, with her hair extensions, body tanned tangerine and thighs full of cellulite. The girl was overweight and unfit, so there was always a chance she might want a personal trainer. Della knew they had a gym of sorts, a film room, an infinity pool and a view to die for. Such a pity that Kelly had a mean little mouth but a gob as big as the Mersey tunnel. Why they'd come to Santaniki was a mystery. Surely Ibiza was more their style.

You mustn't be unkind, she thought. Who are you to judge anyone? They all know you're no saint but are too polite to comment on your little weakness. *Concentrate! They're paying you for this*. Della showed them some new positions and stretches. *I'll improve the fitness of these punters even if I'm ruining my own*. She couldn't wait for the class to finish so she could settle down in the sun with a large glass of wine. It was not as if she was an alcoholic or anything, but the comfort in a glass was the answer to everything just at this moment.

6

Clive Podmore took his morning walk up the steep cliff path to their favourite spot overlooking the bay where the outline of Crete shimmered in the sunshine. For September it was a fine day for a brisk walk up to the little Agios Nikolaos chapel, which was cut into the rock. There was a bench outside where the pilgrims could catch their breath before it was time to pray and light candles. Here he could chat to Lucy. It had been a favourite pausing point on their honeymoon all those years ago when they had fallen in love with the music of the birds and the crashing waves.

'They've asked me to join a choir, Lucy. What do you think? Last time I sang was at your funeral. That hymn you chose just about choked me. I vowed then never to sing again, but Simon Bartlett called in and insisted I back him up in the bass department. Simon's been such a brick dragging me out to things, but it's not the same being among couples who give me that look. You know – the one that says, "Don't remind me that one day I might be alone like you." They mean kindly, inviting me to suppers and out for walks, but without you it's not the same. How could it be after forty years? Jeremy wants me to come home for Christmas but I'm not leaving you here alone.'

Clive sat back smiling. He was sure she'd be listening out there somewhere. After nearly two years he still felt raw at her passing. Bloody cancer! It had been so sudden and inoperable. She'd faded before his eyes, his beautiful beloved wife.

The villa was empty without her, but seeing everything just as she'd left it was comforting. When he opened the front door, her coat was still on the hook, her dressing-table full of sun lotions and face creams, but the scent of her was fading. Laundry and cleaning lifted the fleeting smells that brought her back to him. It was hard to remove anything that reminded him of their life together. Last Christmas he had shut himself away to watch family videos and write Christmas cards from her list. He'd barely stepped out of the door, despite invitations for drinks and a picnic on the beach.

They had had plans for the garden and for trips all over Greece when they'd retired to St Nick's ten years ago. He'd left his law practice early. Clive was still youngish and fit but now it was as if all the stuffing had been knocked out of him. He felt like an empty shell whose only purpose was living for Bella, his dog. He had thought of ending it all but sensed Lucy would call him a coward for taking the easy way out. In any case, Bella was always at his side. They must just carry on together.

A marriage didn't end when one partner died. There was a great bank of memories to draw comfort from. He tried to keep busy by attending Greek lessons and ordering a good supply of non-fiction to read. There was even a local bereavement group, but he wasn't going to sit down and share his feelings with anyone. His grief was a private matter.

As he walked past the cemetery set apart from the village, he paid his morning call to Lucy's gravestone to check the flowers. He disliked the plastic ornaments that decorated the white catafalques, the family tombs with photographs enclosed in little shrines with candles burning. It was all very Greek. All he had put on the headstone was: *Here lies Lucy Jane Podmore, who loved this place.* There was space for his own name to be added. Father Dennis, the vicar who had a little Anglican chapel in his garden, was kind. Only the other day he'd popped in to see Clive. He was joining the choir, so that made four of them. Dennis was a good pastor. Clive couldn't bear to go into the little church, but Dennis wasn't offended. 'Grieving is a funny thing,' he'd said. 'There's no end to it, but sometimes finding another companion in life can take the edge off a loss.'

No one would ever replace Lucy in Clive's heart, but joining the choir might be worthwhile. He loved carols, especially the more ancient ones. He and Lucy had joined the choral society at university to sing *Messiah* and *St John Passion*. Not that Ariadne Blunt's collection of conscripts would rise to those dizzy heights, but it would be in a good cause and at least it would kill some time.

7

Mel Duckworth-Papadaki was late, having chatted to some of the British girls at the school gate. Stefan and Markos were quite capable of walking to the little primary school along the dusty main street but she liked to spend the time with them. It was early in the morning and the streets were bustling with pickups and scooters dropping off children from the outlying villages and it gave her ten minutes away from Yiayia *Irini*, their granny.

Mel passed a skinny young man walking down the street, one of the group of refugees who had found themselves on the island. '*Yassas, Youssef*,' she called. 'Where are you working today?'

He smiled. 'Cleaning pool for Kyria – Miss Anna,' he answered, in halting English.

Mel knew the newcomers would find it difficult to get work. Life was hard enough for the locals by the end of the season, and there were houses for sale everywhere. Last year three hotels had closed and a tourist shop was for sale. The financial crisis in Greece was hitting the island. Spiro was spending more time in their olive groves and vegetable plot. No one had money for extra labour, except the foreign residents. Cleaning swimming-pools, tidying gardens and chopping wood gave the refugees work, but times were hard.

Youssef always had a cheerful smile and something to do, but for his pretty wife, Sammia, there would be nothing other than occasional cleaning for the foreigners. As for their taverna, how could you make a living from Greek coffee and beer? No one came to dine, except the likes of Chloë and her group. Mel's mother-in-law complained bitterly about lack of trade but they were surviving and tourists were still turning up.

Mel spent hours bottling apricots, preserving beans, making jam and marmalade from their oranges and mulberries to sell to the Brits. Everything came from their gardens and straight to the table. The children fed their chickens and rabbits in the cages. Mel hated what happened to those poor creatures, but that was the way of things – and rabbit *stifado* tasted like chicken in wine, if you shut your eyes.

Youssef and his brother, Amir, lived from hand to mouth. Mel didn't know where they were staying, only that it was out of town somewhere. There was sadness in their soulful dark eyes. What had they suffered to reach the land of the gods, only to find no work, no welcome, no safe haven?

Mel had recruited three more voices for the choir from the English and Dutch expats. She didn't want to be the only person under fifty and a bit of camaraderie would be welcome, now that Irini was in such a bad mood. Mel had forgotten to order extra bread for tonight's gathering of Irini's sewing group. There was a pot of bean stew and a dish of *boureki* to finish for their supper. Mel's job was to clean the tables, check the cloths, polish the glasses, put cushions on the cane chair seats and make sure all Spiro's ancestors in their sepia frames got a good dusting.

She needed to be free to attend the first rehearsal in the olive garden but Irini had a way of giving her time-consuming extra jobs. Now the numbers of tourists were dwindling the taverna opened only for coffee in the morning and supper in the evening: the foreign residents liked the warmth of the olive-log fire in winter and family Sunday lunches. It was still warm outside so daytime trade was thin indoors.

Irini's sewing group was a chance for the local women to exchange family news and have a good moan. Mel was not fluent enough to understand their dialect but she got the gist of the gossip. Chloë called it Irini's stitch-and-bitch club, which was a little cruel. Most old Greek women lived for their home, family and church. This meant spending many hours cleaning and cooking while their men spent similar hours over coffee and games of backgammon.

When the sea was cooling and the weather unpredictable, children were ferried to local tutors for extra study. Mel worried about her own boys' future education. In the old days, island children had left school early to work on family farms and in olive groves. There was no secondary education on Santaniki, and British children were often sent to boarding schools in England. Mel knew that would be out of the question financially, unless her parents helped. She could home-school them in English studies, but when the season was busy it was almost impossible to spare the time. Spiro had taken on extra work building new villas but that market was failing since the financial crisis of 2008 had left Greece deeply in debt and crippled by taxes.

'There you are, Melodia,' barked Irini. 'Gossiping at the school gate again? I want the floor scrubbed and the windows cleaned. I don't want Maria across the road running her fingers along my ledges tonight.'

'Don't forget there's a choir rehearsal this afternoon. Will you see to the boys until I get back?' Mel hoped Irini had remembered.

'Poof! Singing is for children. What is wrong with Greek music?'

Mel tried to smile. 'Nothing at all, but we have our own customs, and singing at Christmas is one of them. The Greek children sing *kalanda* around the houses and in school.'

'Now all they want is foreign music and television. The old ways are disappearing.' Irini sighed.

'It's the same for British children,' said Mel. 'But we still want them to know our traditional carols.'

Irini turned to her baking, leaving Mel to find the mop and make the taverna shipshape for tonight's gathering. Mel loved to sing when she was working, but not in Yiayia's hearing. It was at times like this that she wondered how she had ended up in this backwater, but then she smiled, recalling the night when she had first set eyes on her husband. It had been after finals and she was on holiday in Crete. Spiro was in a line of handsome young men with black hair and beards, wearing black shirts, boots and jodhpurs, dancing and leaping to the hypnotic local music. It was the sexiest dance she'd ever seen and so very masculine in its intensity. Then, shoulder to shoulder, they'd sung ancient Greek mountain songs. She had lingered afterwards and got talking to them.

It had started as a holiday romance but she kept returning to the island, little knowing that his family home was a ferry-ride away. Both sets of parents were appalled at this unlikely romance across the cultural divide, but love has a will of its own.

Their wedding on the island was a thunderous affair of feasting, and as the priest put the customary coronets over their heads and blessed them, she knew she had made the perfect choice. She had no regrets... not big ones, anyway, but they had their fiery moments. They had been building their home when funds had run short, so only the ground floor had been completed: a living room-cum-kitchen, a bathroom and two bedrooms. Everything was surrounded by rubble and builders' mess. She was ashamed of the clutter. When the boys played in other houses with finished gardens and pools, she felt envious. All the same, they were lucky to have a roof over their heads so she knew she mustn't grumble.

All of those disappointments faded when she was in Spiro's arms or when she watched him dance or swim in the sea, so lithe and fit as he played football with their boys on the beach. She loved him to the moon and back, even if he did have some funny traditional ways.

She might have the brains but he had the brawn and the know-how to build them a home. They were a perfect match, she thought now, and no mother-in-law was going to spoil that, or stop her singing in her own language.

8

Ariadne was relieved. It was one of those warm September afternoons as she placed twelve chairs and stools in the garden, more in hope than expectation. Every Briton left on the small island must surely be aware of their project and now she was nervous that no one would turn up.

Her digital piano was connected by a long lead to the house, and the music was clipped carefully together in case of a sudden breeze. Hebe was in the kitchen setting out glasses for the refreshments. They had bought little cakes from the patisserie as neither of them was a reliable baker. Ariadne looked again at her father's watch. There was a lot to get through in two hours of rehearsal.

The first to arrive was Della Fitzpatrick, looking slightly the worse for wear, in a flamboyant sundress with jazzy stripes. 'Hi, am I the first?' Della smiled, her eyes slightly glazed. 'I had lunch in the taverna and thought I might stay on. Who's coming?'

Ariadne shook her head. 'Only the gods know.' Then there

was a crash in the kitchen and they rushed to Hebe. Her hand was bleeding.

'It just shot out of my hand. I'm such a clumsy clot,' she apologised.

Della was quick to clear up the broken glass while Ariadne went in search of a plaster. How many times recently had her friend dropped plates and glasses? She made a note not to let her loose with breakables.

By the time they re-emerged Ariadne was pleased to see that almost all the chairs were filled. There were a few men, including old Colonel Templeton Brown in his khaki shorts and three-quarter socks. During the day he usually wore a slouch hat, but this afternoon he was without it.

Most of the women were in summer dresses. It was one way in which the residents differed from tourists. They dressed for every occasion in pretty frocks, glittery sandals and ethnic jewellery, although Chloë Bartlett was chic in pale linen and glorious necklaces, her hair short, almost boyish, her limbs deep mahogany. Natalie Fletcher hovered at the back in her usual black, which didn't suit her at all. Pippa, the hippie artist, had come with her dreadlocked partner, Duke. As Ariadne surveyed the choir, she felt relieved that there were a few young faces, if not enough men.

'Thank you for coming,' she said, smiling. 'I thought we'd start with a few warm-up exercises to loosen the vocal cords.' She played a note. 'I want you to hum to this.' Nothing. 'Keep going.' There was hardly a sound. 'Please don't be shy.'

This was not working, so she tried another tack. 'This time sing, "me, me, me".' That was no better as everyone was too self-conscious to open their mouths. What to do next?

'Sing something silly,' whispered Hebe across the chairs.

'Okay, how about "Jingle Bells".' She gave them a note on the keyboard. 'You all know the words to that.'

It was a half-hearted attempt but at least there was a sound. They were interrupted by Mel, who was trying to creep in with little Markos on her hip. 'Sorry I'm late, but Irini was too busy to have him.'

Just what I need, Ariadne thought. A howling child. 'Let's try again.' Off they went, a little louder than before. There was a quite distinctive voice among them but she couldn't work out whose it was. The little boy smiled and tried to join in and suddenly everybody laughed, relaxing. Time to try Britten's two-part roundel, 'Old Abram is Dead and Gone'. She managed to get them to repeat it, and when they were sure of it, she divided them into two groups. 'You start, and when I point, the second group follows from the beginning.'

Total chaos ensued.

'I thought we were here to sing carols, not lark about,' a voice called from the back. It was, of course, Dorinda Thorner.

'I take your point, Dorrie, but until we find our voices together we need to warm up. A bit of vocal training never did any choir any harm.' That seemed to shut her up. 'We'll finish today with our first carol. I've copied out the music. Please bring it each time and practise at home if you can. It's a simple one to start with. "Love Came Down at Christmas". The words are by Christina Rossetti.'

She played it through, knowing most of them couldn't read music. She was sure someone would know the tune and sure enough they sang it through. Once again a woman's voice rang out above the rest, like a bell. The little choir seemed to be pulling together at last. 'That was lovely, a great start. I think we'll work well together if we can manage to keep in harmony but we do need more voices, especially men's. Can you think of any others?'

'There's that Gary from the Bunker,' Della said. 'His wife won't have anything to do with us but they're not joined at the hip.'

'I could ask him,' said Simon.

It was time then to bring out refreshments. 'I'll fetch glasses,' said Hebe.

'I'll do it. We don't want any more breakages,' Ariadne replied, then wished she hadn't.

'I can help,' offered Natalie. 'Just show me the cupboard, Miss Wilson.'

'Hebe, please,' she replied, and they went off together, leaving Ariadne to mingle and reassure any reluctant singers.

She made a beeline for Chloë's group. 'I do hope you'll stick with us. I'm sure all of you know lots of carols.'

'Well, I sang in the choir and the semi-chorus at my boarding school but I'm not sure this is for me. It's far too early for singing Christmas carols,' Dorinda piped up, with a sniff.

'But we need your experience to help those who are not as practised and there's a lot of music to get through if we're to make a decent show.'

'I suppose so, but you'll have to blend those voices better. There was a girl at the back you could hear in the next village. Tell her to quieten down.'

'Who was she? Ariadne wondered.

'Who do you think? The latecomer from the taverna,' Dorinda whispered.

So it was Mel's voice she had heard above the others. It had power, tone and quality. She must find out more about the girl who had rushed back to Irini's taverna.

Ariadne was relieved that the little choir stayed on for refreshments. Hopefully this would be the first of many rehearsals in the garden, where the drupes of olives were ripening fast. How she loved its lush greenery and the promise of a good harvest. Yes, it had gone well enough for a first rehearsal but would anybody turn up for a second?

> *Love came down at Christmas,*
> *Love all lovely, Love divine;*
> *Love was born at Christmas,*
> *Star and angels gave the sign.*

9

Clive Podmore sat on his veranda with his sundowner, Orpheus, his rescue cat, and Bella, the dog, snoozing beside him. 'Love Came Down at Christmas'. How strange that singing almost had him in tears. How could he have forgotten its poignancy?

In his final year at university they'd had a candlelit Christmas carol service in the courtyard at the hall of residence. The rector had decided to invite guests to dinner afterwards. There was to be a ball later in the week and Clive had yet to find a partner. In those days there were few women students in his law department when the ratio of men to women was about seven to one.

The guys in the music department brought in some sopranos from the women's hall down the road, and the girls huddled together, unsure of their bearings in that very male college. Clive noticed her straight away. She had a golden ponytail and a dress that shimmered in the candlelight. She looked neat and contained, singing with a serious look on her face, as if the words had a special meaning for her. 'Love Came Down at Christmas'.

Then she'd glanced up and caught his eye. He'd felt a strange rush of sensation. He couldn't wait for the service to finish. He had to know who she was and suddenly had an inner certainty that he had found his partner for the ball. But how to be introduced?

He needn't have worried because she walked up to him, smiling. 'Hi, I'm Lucy. Did you enjoy the service?'

'I'm Clive, studying law,' he muttered. 'I thought you all sang splendidly.'

'Good! Is there supper? I'm starving.'

He escorted her to the buffet, clinging like a limpet to her side. They sat together and she told him she was studying chemistry, with a view to doing research. He noticed the freckles across her nose and that her eyes were almost leaf green.

'Would you like to come to the end-of-term ball – or have you already got a partner?' he asked, expecting to be turned down.

She grabbed his hand. 'I'd be delighted. When? Where? But I'll have to borrow a dress. I'm afraid I'm a bit skint. Lucy in the sky without diamonds.' She laughed.

She'd sparkled at the ball in a deep crimson full-length gown that kept slipping off her shoulders, because it was a size too big. Clive had had a few girlfriends before but Lucy was like no one else he'd ever met.

They danced and he managed some moves, laughing as they clung together. Two weeks later she crept into his room, locked the door and they made love as if there was no tomorrow.

After Christmas she invited him down to meet her family. Clive lived in Sheffield and she in Dorset, but distance means nothing when you're in love. Her father was a well-known actor, who welcomed him into their country retreat as if he was a long-lost son. Her mother lived in London with her new lover.

He had never met a divorced couple before. His parents ran a paper shop and were strict Baptists. He wondered what they would make of Lucy, but when she arrived, clutching flowers and chocolates, they were charmed. What did she see in him? He felt such a dullard.

'Shall we get a flat together?' she asked, at the beginning of term.

Clive was taken aback. 'But my fees are paid for this term.'

'Next term, then?'

'I'm not sure my parents would really like…'

'What's it got to do with them?'

'It's just that…' He hesitated.

'Oh, don't be a prude. I'm on the pill. You don't have to worry on that score.'

But it had overwhelmed him, the rush to be intimate, to be half of a couple 'living in sin', as his mother would say. He'd love to spend days and nights with her but he stalled. 'It's too soon,' he said, and instantly regretted it.

'Suit yourself.' She smiled and that was the last he saw of her for weeks. She just disappeared from his life and he knew he had lost something precious: her spontaneity, her ability to seize the moment and take control. She was unpredictable, quick to make decisions, in a way that terrified his narrow homespun soul.

Clive struggled on as finals loomed. He searched the library in case she was there, hung about the chemistry department, hoping to find her in the refectory of the student union, but she was nowhere to be seen. He wrote an abject letter but got no reply. It was affecting his work. He couldn't study or revise.

How could a girl get so under his skin? He was sure she'd met someone else. It was making him sick. Then, one night, he found himself in agonising pain and was rushed into the infirmary for an emergency appendectomy. When he woke up, his parents were waiting by his bed, clearly anxious. 'Are you all right, son?'

I'm sick, I'm heartbroken and I'm going to fail my exams.

'You've got a visitor.' His mum smiled, turning to the door, and then Lucy was looking down at him.

'Honestly I can't leave you five minutes before you go to pot. Thank goodness your mother told me where you were.'

'You've been in touch?' He didn't understand what was going on.

'We'll leave you two lovebirds together,' said his parents, creeping away. 'You have a lot of catching up to do.'

'I've missed you so much,' said Clive.

Lucy smiled. 'I hoped you might, so I gave you some space to sort yourself out.'

'Will you marry me?' he said, 'After finals, straight away.'

'Of course.' She bent down to kiss him. 'Perhaps nearer Christmas on St Lucy's Day, my birthday. Then we can have that special hymn again. "Love Came Down at Christmas".'

Clive woke from his reverie. The sun had gone. Lucy was his sun, moon and stars, but now there was only darkness in his life because she was no more. How could he carry on without her light? How could he face another Christmas without her?

IO

Sammia Began was feeling restless. It was the farmer's wife, Toula, who suggested she might try the taverna for work. 'Melodia is British. She would be glad to help you with conversation, in return for some light cleaning. Shall I talk to Irini?'

'I'm not sure. I must speak first with Youssef,' she replied, knowing that, with a baby on the way, they would need to buy a buggy and clothes.

That was how she'd come to be working in the kitchen of the taverna with the British wife. Maryam was not happy to be left alone all day, but two women in their small living room was never easy. There was plenty of fruit-gathering she could do, when she took Karim for his daily walk in the hills, and it would need preserving too. There was a little nursery he might attend for a small fee. He should mix with other children and learn Greek. As there were apparently no other Muslim women on the island, Maryam also needed to improve her English.

Sammia was a little afraid of the mother-in-law, Irini. She might be small and tubby, with fierce dark eyes, but she missed nothing, eyeing her at first with suspicion and barking orders, just as Mama Began had done to her daughters-in-law.

Some mornings, at the end of her shift, Melodia would bring out a plastic box of cheese pies filled with creamy *mizithra* and mint.

'I can't.' Sammia hesitated. 'You mean kindly but...'

'No buts. We bake each day fresh and I don't like waste.' Melodia shoved the box into her hand. 'I'm sure you can find a use for them.'

Sammia had a penchant for gooey sweet things and longed to sink her teeth into the syrupy delights. 'Thank you.'

'Don't show them to Irini. This is between me and you. You need fattening up for the baby. Has Youssef got work? Spiro has, when there's a big job on the go.'

'Youssef was an office man but he will turn his hand to anything. He is busy cleaning pools at the moment and chopping wood for the winter stoves.' It was strange making a living from their hands not their heads, standing instead of sitting.

Sammia returned, weary but grateful, to earn a little for the things they needed: a thick rug for the earthen floor, lacy curtains for the windows, and a large tub in which to strip-wash rather than relying on dips in the sea. There was a small rent to pay and bills for food. It was a hand-to-mouth existence but they were surviving.

Talking in English to Melodia made her feel on level ground. The young woman had promised to help her with understanding the Greek alphabet and basic Greek phrases. The more she saw of her, the more she felt she was becoming a friend.

In Damascus they had had many European colleagues who

came to supper. The Begans were not strict observers of their faith, but more cosmopolitan in their beliefs. On Santaniki she might look like a peasant living on subsistence, but talking in English lifted her spirits. Living in exile, being beholden to others wasn't easy, but Sammia knew her parents would have been proud that they had survived and found a purpose, however humble. From now on the only way was up.

11

The flight from Athens was delayed, but Chloë was too engrossed in her book to fret. She would soon be in their tiny flat off Marylebone High Street and her daughter, Alexa, would join her for a long weekend. They would lunch at the restaurant in the Wallace Collection, spend an hour in Daunt's choosing books, then move on to Liberty and John Lewis.

Shopping together was fun. They would see all the decorated shop windows in Oxford Street. Sometimes there was a concert at the Royal Albert Hall and they would taxi from there back to the flat. Alexa was Chloë's only child from her first marriage to banker Charles Anster. Although it had failed spectacularly, Chloë was well provided for. Emotionally, though, she had been in need of a decent job.

She had taken a course in proofreading and started working as a freelance for a London publisher. There she had met Simon Bartlett, an editor, who was newly divorced. He was everything Charlie was not, kind, courteous, old-fashioned, and they both loved the Greek islands. Alexa loved him too.

She was still in touch with her father, but the relationship was always fraught. Charlie was notoriously unreliable. Not that it mattered now, for Chloë and Alexa were close.

Chloë was late reaching the flat, but Alexa wasn't there, which was strange. There was just a garbled message on the answerphone, saying she was held up at work and not to worry as she would meet her mother for lunch the following day.

The next morning was wet and grey, and Chloë felt the change of climate, shivering in her thin quilted jacket and jeans. She breakfasted close to Oxford Street, then tootled around the shops, keeping an eye on her watch.

Alexa was late in getting to the restaurant. Her eyes were heavy and she was wearing a long baggy tunic with scruffy jeans. She had put on weight and looked as if she had slept in her clothes. 'Sorry I'm late – something came up at work. I'm afraid I'll have to go back but I'll be round later.'

They hugged and kissed, but Chloë felt her stiffen. 'Is everything all right? You look exhausted.'

'I'm fine, don't fuss, just a few problems to sort out.'

'With Hugh? I thought you two were solid?'

'He's seeing someone else.'

Chloë shook her head. 'I'm so sorry… You both seemed so happy together last time. What's gone wrong?'

'It's a bit a complicated, Mummy.' Alexa was shaking as she spoke and not making eye contact. Chloë knew only too well the shock of being betrayed by a husband.

'Who is she?'

'Who is he,' Alexa said. 'A guy from the gym, called Jason. They've been seeing each other for months behind my back.' The tears flowed.

Her darling daughter was crumpling before her eyes and Chloë wanted to tear Hugh to pieces for hurting her. 'I suppose he always was a little that way... all that fussing over décor and fitness.'

'Don't be like that,' Alexa snapped. 'Plenty of men swing both ways. This is London. It's just that I didn't guess until it was too late. Oh, let's eat. I'm starving.'

Chloë was stunned by the change in her daughter. All Alexa's usual confidence and sparkle had drained away, leaving her looking older and lumpier. It was like reliving her own nightmare all over again: the shock, the disbelief, the anger and the bargaining. At least Alexa would be spared the arguments over a child.

After they parted, with no plans made for the evening, the afternoon dragged. Why was it no surprise when Alexa phoned, saying, 'Sorry, Mummy, got a call out to Manchester. I'm on the train heading north. Have a good shop and give my love to Simon.'

'Is there anything I can do?'

'No. Please don't interfere. Sorry, I know you mean well, but it's for us to sort out.'

'What about Christmas?' Chloë asked.

'Not sure now, can't think about it.'

'You can always come to us. We were so looking forward to all of us being together.'

'I know, but I can't make plans yet.'

Chloë was trying to reach out to her daughter. 'I shouldn't have come, but we always meet around half-term.'

'I'm not a schoolgirl now, and I should have warned you I might be busy."

'You know that Simon and I will help. You can move into our flat, if you like.'

'Hugh and I will sort this out between us. We're still speaking. I've got to go now. Bye...'

Chloë felt helpless and rejected, held at arm's length while her daughter was suffering, shut out by Alexa's brisk manner. They had hardly seen each other for months and she had been so looking forward to their special time together. Now nothing was turning out as she'd thought. She sighed, recalling John Lennon's famous words: 'Life happens when you're busy making plans.'

Chloë's mothering instinct was powerful and she sensed that there was something Alexa was reluctant to share, which worried her more than anything else.

Suddenly London felt a lonely place, cold, damp and miserable. She completed her shopping list with a heavy heart. What was there to stay for now? At least she could change her flight. No point hanging around when she was obviously not wanted. Time to retreat back to her island in the sun.

12

A riadne and Hebe asked Arthur Templeton Brown for Sunday lunch after church. He was frailer now and unsteady on his pins. With his shepherd's crook, his wispy white hair halfway down his neck, he looked like an Old Testament prophet. They had sherry on the veranda, looking out over the olive garden, which he always admired.

'It'll soon be the harvest,' he said. 'Caro and I loved to help with the shaking down. Nothing like a first pressing of oil. During the war they used to hide the amphoras in the caves but it only worked for a time.'

His mind often drifted back to the old days when he was caught in the battle for Crete. He blamed the defeat on defences being in the wrong place and no one expecting the descent of German paratroopers. Nevertheless the poor buggers hadn't known what had hit them when they'd landed to be hacked to pieces by mountain Cretans. Then he would recount many of his exploits as an escapee. Hebe would hear him out while Ariadne saw to the chicken in lemon sauce and vegetables.

'What did you think of our first rehearsal? It wasn't a bad turnout.' Ariadne was fishing.

''Fraid I didn't catch much of it. I hope we'll be singing the old carols,' Arthur replied. 'I can't stand all that modern stuff Father Dennis likes to punish us with.'

Arthur was old-school C of E. He liked the Book of Common Prayer and sermons lasting minutes, not hours. He always wore a wrinkled linen jacket, a Panama hat and his regimental tie, but lived in shorts, showing off his nut-brown legs. He had been a good friend to Ariadne and Hebe when they first arrived. His wife would often invite them to drinks in their little cube-like stone villa on the main street with its apricot-coloured walls.

He assumed, like everyone else, that she and Hebe were old teaching chums, and Ariadne had gone to great lengths to let the village assume this was so. Their sleeping arrangements were a private matter. They were not out and proud. She often referred to Hebe as a distant cousin, which was not true, but stopped most people snooping.

Now Ariadne remembered the two men who lived out of the village in a bijou villa, Phil and Greg, and wondered if she could recruit them. 'Do you know the lads on the hill?' she asked Arthur.

'The nancy boys? 'Fraid not.'

'I was hoping they might join us. We need more younger voices.'

'You've taken on a brave task, harnessing a bunch of raw recruits. Take my hat off to you, but don't expect miracles,' Arthur said.

'If we get the right balance of voices, you'll be surprised at the result. Look at Gareth Malone.'

'My dear, he could take his pick. You're stuck with a lot of old codgers like me, croaking out the notes. Don't set your sights too high.'

She was making a mental list of choir members, especially the men: Arthur, Simon, Clive, the vicar, Duke, possibly Peter, the director of the Elodie Durrante Retreat Foundation, and perhaps Gary from the Bunker, if Simon could persuade him.

Sopranos were in plentiful supply, altos not so many, but one good tenor, who could hold high notes, and a few decent basses would pull it all together. An orchestra of voices was what she was aiming for. She wanted to surprise the village with their discipline and harmony, and for that she must have youth as well as experience.

After Arthur had left, she paced her sunlit garden with its cacti and yuccas. The last of the plumbago and the oleander flowers were fading, but the scent of rosemary and thyme soothed her. 'Why do you keep doing this to yourself?' she whispered. 'Isn't one big failure enough?'

Word on the Street was set back from the main thoroughfare, but close enough for billboards to guide book-lovers towards it. It had been Ariadne's dream for years to leave teaching and open a decent bookshop, stocking new and second-hand books. A great deal of browsing in Foyles and other shops on London's Tottenham Court Road had given her an insight into what might be required. Hebe would carry on teaching until the shop could support them both. The search for suitable premises took years of abortive trips to buildings all over the country but when she found the wonderful little Georgian house with two bow windows in Manford, she knew her dream had come true.

Manford was a busy working town outside Leeds, a commuter dormitory with supermarkets and independent businesses that, she felt sure, could support a bookshop. There were no rivals, except an antiquarian book specialist. There was a two-storey flat above the premises, in need of repair. Hebe thought it suitable and promptly applied for a post in classics at the new girls' high school. Ariadne and Hebe did their homework with care, budgeting, rents, promotion, internal decoration, shelving. They took advice from booksellers and joined the trade association, but most of her father's legacy disappeared during those first crucial months. Ariadne named the shop Word on the Street, and the launch was a great success, with all the local shopkeepers as guests.

It was sheer luck that Elodie Durrante was on a book tour in the north to promote her new bestseller. Her publishers provided lots of publicity material, and press coverage ensured that queues of loyal fans lined the street to have their books signed. Ariadne was daunted by the tall, striking woman who swanned in. Her hands were covered with exotic rings and her bright scarlet hair was wound into a dramatic coil on top of her head, like a cottage loaf. She was charm itself and signed away, with words of encouragement to Ariadne and Hebe, before she was swept off by her publicist to her next appointment.

It was an impressive start to what they hoped would be a lifetime of bookselling. The first year had seen them in profit, but Ariadne had not taken into consideration what the abolition of the Net Book Agreement would mean.

Now there was no longer a fixed retail price for each book. Within months discount wars were breaking out between rival chains and, worse still, supermarkets could sell mass-market fiction almost at cost, slashing their prices in special offers, prices that Ariadne could no longer compete with.

The impact was immediate. Customers would browse her paperback selection and then disappear to buy elsewhere. They battled on with author events and children's reading competitions. The second-hand section did well enough, until charity shops got in on the act to undercut them.

Unsold stock went back to be pulped. Ariadne slimmed her range, turned away publishers' reps, who were pushing new releases on them. Holidays became a thing of the past – those wonderful excursions to the Greek islands or Spain. Hebe continued teaching, but was unhappy in her new school. Everything was going wrong, and if they didn't find another source of income, Word on the Street would fall silent.

'If only we'd known what lay ahead,' Ariadne moaned as, one by one, they saw other bookshops closing or turning into cheap remainder outlets, selling old stock.

'You weren't to know,' Hebe said, trying to comfort her, but the fizz had gone out of Ariadne's dream.

Some days she sold only greeting cards and wrapping paper. And the accounts files did not lie: they were making losses on all fronts. The business was failing. Ariadne felt so helpless and angry. Sleepless, she paced the shop floor, trying to conjure new schemes to brighten the window display – perhaps they could offer coffee and cake. Fear was making her sweat as her bank balance slipped into the red. She seemed to have a permanent cold, sniffing and wheezing, and was so tired that she didn't eat. Hebe pestered her to see a doctor but 'I'm fine,' she countered.

'No, you are not. This bloody business is making you ill. It's not your fault that the whole trade has changed. It's just about bad timing, so stop beating yourself up.'

'It's all right for you to talk. You have a salary coming in.'

'And a job I hate. The discipline in that school is disgraceful.' Hebe paused. 'What a pair of dolts we are. You know that old adage when things go wrong? "You can lump it, change it or leave."'

'Leave?' Ariadne was horrified.

'What else is there to do? Do you want go bankrupt? At least we own the building. I say we sell up and move to pastures new.'

'Like where?' Ariadne sat down, demoralised. Sensible old Hebe was surprising her.

'We'll find some sun. I'm sick of rain and grey skies. We could go abroad, rent somewhere and start a new life.'

'Have you gone crackers? With what, may I ask? Brass tacks?'

'I have my savings and a pension. You'll have one soon. It could be a great adventure living in a foreign country.'

'You're crazy. Where would we go?'

'Greece, of course! Where else? We love the islands. We can sort out our affairs, cut the losses, gather our resources and vamoose!' She laughed.

'Are you being serious?' Hebe was behaving most oddly.

'Yes, I am. You tried, it didn't come off as we hoped, so we dust ourselves down and start all over again. We've plenty of years to come yet. Let's stop being sober citizens and just scarper into the sun.'

'If only.' Ariadne sighed.

'If only, my arse. What have we got to lose now?'

Ariadne couldn't take it all in. Emigrate? Leave England behind? Hebe was offering a lifeline, crazy as it was. 'Could we really make it happen?'

'Just you watch me,' Hebe replied.

For the first time in months Ariadne smiled.

That moment of madness passed, but the dream did not. It took time to sell the building in a recession, to sort out their finances, to pack up a lifetime of belongings, to find out how to live abroad and not make another mess of things, but they did it, and it was Hebe who organised a half-load of furniture to be shipped to Crete. It was Hebe who sorted out their first rental and found the island of Santaniki, after contacting a friend who'd holidayed there and recommended a good agency to help them with the legalities.

Only then did they discover it was the very island where Elodie Durrante had made her home. When Ariadne wrote to her, reminding her of her visit and their meeting, asking only for advice, the dear woman emailed back, inviting them to stay in her guest lodge until they had sorted themselves out.

It was eighteen months before they packed the old Volkswagen and headed from Hull to Zeebrugge, onwards through Switzerland and Italy to the port of Ancona, then boarded the ferry to Athens. Six days' driving saw them on the night boat to Crete.

Only then did Ariadne pinch herself. 'We've burnt our bridges now,' she said, as they hung over the ship's rail, watching Athens fade from view.

'Nonsense,' Hebe replied, holding out a glass. 'We're beginning a new life.'

As Ariadne was washing up after Sunday lunch, she found herself weeping. Hebe had been so confident and determined then. She had made this new life happen, but now her dear friend, her partner in life, was slower, hesitant, clumsy and oh-so-forgetful. Perhaps she was just getting old. Any other explanation was too scary to contemplate. Perhaps she was just being fanciful and was too full of wine and lunch to think straight, and yet...

13

Gary Partridge was in the infinity pool when Kelly announced they had a visitor. 'It's that bloke from the big house, the posh one up the hill,' she shouted. 'Simon Bartlett. What does he want with us? I expect it'll be a donation he's after. See him off. We're not made of money.'

Gary shoved on his dressing-gown. He'd not even had a shave and was embarrassed to be caught out at this time of the morning. 'Mr Bartlett, nice to meet you again. Do sit down,' he said.

'Simon, please. I expect you're wondering why I'm here.'

'Have a drink – beer, wine or ouzo? Kelly!' he shouted.

'A coffee will be fine, but only if you're having one.' Simon Bartlett looked around with interest. 'Quite a view you have here.'

Gary shot off to find Kelly, who was spinning in the gym. 'Two coffees, love, from the machine.'

'What does he want?'

'Just get us the drinks and then I'll find out.' Kelly was such a stroppy cow at the moment, he thought. When he returned to their lounge, with its white leather sofas and sprawling rugs, armchair throws, fancy cushions, glass cabinets and prints on the wall, it all seemed a bit naff in Simon's presence. He felt nervous, wanting to make a good impression.

'I've just come to ask if, by any chance, you'd consider joining the new choir. We're looking for younger voices and your name was mentioned. What do you think?'

Gary laughed. 'I was an altar boy, but then my voice broke. Karaoke's more my line after a few bevvies. I don't read music. My gran got me piano lessons but they didn't last, not when all my mates were out playing footie.'

'Very few of us can read music. It's just carols and Christmas songs, and all in a good cause. It's in support of the refugees,' Simon continued.

'I'll have to ask Kelly. She's not too keen on…' He paused

Simon smiled. 'She's welcome too, of course. The more the merrier.'

'Can you leave it with me? It's nice to be asked to join in. I'm afraid we do tend to keep ourselves to ourselves a bit.'

'Do you fish?' Simon asked 'A few of us go out fishing and you'd be very welcome to join us.'

Gary hesitated. He got quite queasy in small boats. But it was a kind offer. A bit of male company would be welcome.

Kelly brought in the coffee in cheap mugs and put them down with a loud bang on the glass-topped coffee-table. 'Sugar's in the bowl, but I'm afraid there's no cake. I'm on a diet,' she announced.

Gary nearly choked. Kelly on a diet? What a lie. 'Thanks, love. Simon's asked me to join his choir.'

'Actually it was Ariadne Blunt's idea. She conducts us and provides the music,' Simon said.

'I don't think it's our scene, is it, Gary?' Kelly replied. 'We're not into that sort of stuff.'

Gary felt his cheeks flushing. 'They need more men,' he muttered. 'I'll go if you don't want to. It's for the refugees.'

'Oh, really,' she replied. 'I think they should all be deported to where they came from. I don't hold with it.'

Gary felt ashamed of his wife's opinions. What must Simon, an educated man, think of them both? 'Count me in, but when's rehearsals?'

They drank the coffee, making small-talk, then Simon shook his hand. 'Good show. I thought you might help us.' They made for the door through the large tiled hallway. 'And do thank Mrs Partridge for the coffee. Delicious.'

When Gary returned Kelly's face was a picture of fury. 'I thought we agreed not to get involved in anything local,' she said.

'It's only for Christmas and you could come too.'

'Forget it! I'm not joining those old fogeys, or that funny woman and her dotty sister or cousin, whatever she is.'

'They were kind to us when we moved here.'

'They give me the creeps, dressed like two bag-ladies.'

Gary couldn't believe what came out of Kelly's mouth, these days. She used to be kind-hearted and sympathetic, but lately she'd changed. Had their new-found wealth given her airs and graces? He put it down to her not getting pregnant and two failed rounds of IVF. The old Kelly had vanished and in her place was this loudmouthed sulky madam, who was never satisfied with anything they did. Living out here wasn't the idyll he'd expected. Money can make things more comfortable, but it hadn't shifted his guilt.

If the truth were known, he was in hiding, not from any real crime but from a terrible lie. What would Kelly think if she knew the truth about their wealth? Singing a few Christmas carols couldn't change any of it, but it might sort out his troubled soul.

14

Mel stood on the roadside, watching the procession of schoolchildren waving their blue and white flags and dressed in the national colours. It was a bit of a raggle-taggle affair for Oxi Day: the celebration of the Greek Prime Minister Metaxas's refusal in 1940 to kowtow to the demands of Benito Mussolini and the outbreak of war on the mainland. Today in Greece it seemed more like a day of protest marches against the government, taxes and the general discontent that filled the newspapers, but in the village elderly veterans and the council still considered it a proud affair. She watched Yannis, the mayor, and members of the council marching proudly.

Irini turned her back on the parade. 'What is there to celebrate?' she said.

Mel was missing Spiro. He had valuable building work on the mainland, but it meant three weeks without him – three weeks with only the boys and Irini for company. At least Sammia was a breath of fresh air as she chatted away about little Karim's antics and Maryam. Soon it would be All Saints

Day, when they must picnic at the tomb of the Papadakis family and pay their respects to all the other relatives interred there. Shortage of space meant every so often relatives' bones were removed to the ossuary, to make way for the next generation.

Mel was glad that her own mother lay undisturbed in a peaceful churchyard outside Sheffield. She missed Italian-born Maria, who had come to England as a post-war bride and borne her husband nine children. By the time it came to Mel's arrival, Maria was worn out and nearly fifty. They had also run out of names, so she'd got the daft one: Melody, not Melanie, as most of her friends thought.

Antonio, Paula, Dino, Rosaria, Teresa, Graham, Fred, Julia and then Melody. What a line-up for mass each Sunday. There was little money but love in abundance. A good convent-school education had given Mel a love of learning and music, but it was from Maria that she'd got her voice. Singing opened doors to a university scholarship, but leaving home was agony. She had refused further voice training.

Now she was creating a family of her own. The boys were her joy and she spoilt them rotten. She and Spiro were sticking to two for the moment. She wanted the best for them. Mel's mother used to say a granny should keep her mouth shut and her purse open, but Irini liked to interfere, especially over bedtime.

When Mel was little she'd gone to bed at eight o'clock and stayed there. Here, children went out to eat or visit, often until ten o'clock at night. School was early because of the heat, but Mel wanted them upstairs by eight so she could have some time out of the taverna with Spiro. That was not the Greek way.

As she swept away last night's cigarette stubs and crumbs, the last thing on her mind was tomorrow's rehearsal, so when she saw Ariadne striding towards her, there was nowhere to duck. Was Ariadne going to tell her off for being late? She reminded Mel of Sister Mary Luke, who had taken them for hockey in her size-nine boots: kindly but quick to check any rebels in the ranks.

'*Kalimera*, Mel.' Ariadne smiled. 'Can I have a word?'

'If it's about last week... Afternoons aren't easy.' Mel was quick to reply.

'Not at all – we're lucky to have you. I could hear you singing. You've had training.'

Mel blushed. 'Just a little from the nuns, nothing professional,' she lied.

'Never mind that... I want you to do some solo pieces. You'll be a great asset to our sopranos. I'm afraid some of them are getting to the squeaky stage and will screech the higher notes. I have a few ideas for solo verses, nothing fancy, unless you'd like to sing something special for us?'

Mel was not up to confessing about all the concerts she'd performed in, or her fear of solos – her voice had sometimes let her down. 'I'm not sure I'm up to anything fancy.'

'Did you sing much in choirs?'

'I enjoyed singing around Sheffield and the pubs, where they have their own versions of carols. I love Kate Rusby's music. I might try to cover one of hers, if you like, but they're not the usual carols.'

'We need a variety to please all tastes perhaps even "White Christmas".'

'If only...' Mel smiled. 'I can't get used to a Christmas Day where you sit on a beach having a barbecue. There's been no snow here for years. I do miss a good northern winter with ice and snowflakes, but I don't miss the rain.'

'Melodia,' a voice shouted from the kitchen. 'Where are you?'

'I'll have to go. I'm fine singing in the group, but I'm out of practice, these days. Thanks for asking me, but I can't promise to come to every rehearsal.'

'Come when you can. I can always give you the schedule and sheet music.' With that, Ariadne marched on up to the old colonel's house with what looked like cooked sausages and mash on a plate. '*Yassou!*'

It was a pity so few of the expats spoke Greek, but it was not an easy language to master. Mel did her bit, giving lessons to those willing to try. Some lived in a kind of bubble of Britishness, complaining about the old country yet clinging to a sort of parody of English country living. Sometimes she felt she was caught between two worlds, Greece and Yorkshire. You can take the girl out of God's own county, she mused, but you can't take Yorkshire out of the girl.

'Melodia!' Irini was shrieking like a banshee, in a deep-throated accent.

'Coming,' Mel yelled, through gritted teeth. She knew Ariadne's offer was kindly meant. At least she didn't look on her as a dogsbody. Mel would love to sing solo again, but how would she find the time or the space to try pieces out?

15

The November moon was high above Chloë's house, and now that the olive harvest was in full swing, there was no time for choir rehearsals. Black nets were layered on the ground to catch the drupes and the two young Syrians, Youssef and Amir, were busy raking the branches until the green olives fell. They were then scooped into sacks, ready to go to the olive press in the old mill. It was a yearly tradition that involved all of Chloë's friends.

Chloë couldn't concentrate, though. Her mind was on that abortive visit to London and on the hurt she felt to be kept at arm's length by her daughter. They had texted briefly, but when she'd rung Alexa's apartment there was no answer. It was as if no one was willing to pick up.

'What can I do?' she complained to Simon, in the middle of the night, over yet another cup of camomile tea.

'Just leave her to come to you when she's ready. Don't push any more. Alexa's a big girl and very capable.'

'It's all very well for you to say that, but a mother knows when her child needs help.'

'Alexa will find help when she's ready. Go to sleep now, or you won't be fit for harvesting.'

'I'll make a list of groceries for the harvest supper.'

'You do that... and then try to relax.' Simon turned onto his side.

The supper was a big thank-you to all the friends and locals who had helped them bring in the harvest. There would be bottles of olive oil for them all, in due course. Their olive groves were terraced up a hillside, blessed by sun and rain in turn. Chloë was hoping for a decent quality with an intensity of flavour and colour. Bread dipped in olive oil was a meal in itself, the very staff of life. With a ripe tomato the size of a tennis ball and a little feta cheese, who could ask for more? Tonight would be a feast.

Half of the choir would be coming, and Simon had invited the couple from the Bunker Much to his surprise Gary had come to their last rehearsal and helped with the harvesting, but not his wife. No doubt she would join in the celebrations.

It was always a relief when the olives had been gathered and pressed. It was a milestone on the way to Christmas, and who knew when the rains would come and spoil their outdoor living? The catering was mostly farmed out. Irini would send a great vat of bean stew and lamb ribs roasted in rosemary oil. Natalie was making *galaktoboureko,* a sort of Greek custard pie, and *baklavas.* There would be decent Cretan wine, as well as lemonade made from their own lemons.

Tired as they all were, this was a good evening – if only Chloë felt more cheerful. There was just time for a shower before she dressed up, as was the custom. The guests arrived promptly, appetites whetted by hard labour. The night was mild and citronella candles twinkled in glass vases along the trestle table, which was covered with a white cloth and decorated with the last of the garden flowers.

The Blunt sisters, as she called them, were always early, wearing their usual bright tops and linen trousers. Most of the men came in chinos and coloured shirts but there was a nip in the air so jumpers were at hand too. Natalie, dressed in her usual grey and black, slipped into the kitchen as Pippa and Duke arrived, bringing homemade raki. Phil and his partner Greg appeared with Della, who wore a wonderful ethnic caftan encrusted with beadwork. Last to arrive were Gary and Kelly Partridge.

What was there to say about her get-up? A low-cut skinny top showing cleavage, ripped white jeans, and all two sizes too tight. There was enough gold jewellery to set up a stall in a souk. Why did some expats wear so much gold? Greek key necklaces, jangly bracelets and gaudy rings, but worst of all were chains round thick ankles, and toenails in horrendous colours.

Chloë smiled, imagining her Home Counties mother sniffing with superiority: 'Common as muck. In my day those anklets were worn by ladies of the night standing in the doorway after closing time.' Styles changed, so she mustn't be too snooty. Kelly just hadn't the height or the figure to pull off the ensemble. 'Stop it,' she murmured, feeling sorry for the girl, who looked so tanned you could hardly see her features. She'd pay for that later. The Greek sun took no prisoners.

Chloë was more of a pearls girl. Pearls saw you through any occasion, from weddings to funerals. They were discreet and classy, but not good with sun cream and the conditions here.

A young designer from Athens lived outside Agios Nikolaos and made exquisite little pieces, earrings, torques, using natural stones, polished and set in gold or silver. Tonight Chloë was wearing a rainbow necklace of stones linked by a gold chain over an asymmetric white linen tunic and matching trousers.

Out on the terrace, guests mingled, sitting down to enjoy their first taste of this season's oil. Chloë insisted Natalie leave the kitchen to take an empty chair next to Clive Podmore. She reckoned two lonely people ought to be able to make conversation together. On the opposite side sat Arthur, the old colonel, invited every year to make sure he got a decent meal and some company. Chloë could listen to him for hours, just as she had done to her own father in his latter years. She was relieved to see everyone eating and drinking, chatting and enjoying themselves.

'Hey, what are we singing next?' chipped Duke to Ariadne. 'Reckon we could do a rehearsal here and now. I've brought my guitar.'

'Young man, I've not decided, but something nautical for St Nick's Day, which isn't far off. He's the patron saint of the island."

'And prostitutes...' someone whispered.

Ariadne didn't hear and continued, '"I Saw Three Ships Come Sailing In"?'

'"What Shall We Do With the Drunken Sailor"?' Della shouted, now well into her cups.

'"Sailing"... I love Rod Stewart.' Kelly was equally inebriated and laughed.

'It's not a carol, love.' Gary nudged his wife but she was in full flow.

'Who wants to sing boring old carols? What about them songs from Sister Sledge or Boney M? Anything but dirges.'

The table pretended not to hear. Gary looked embarrassed. 'Drink some water, Kelly.'

'Some girls don't know when to stop,' remarked Dorinda Thorner, within Kelly's hearing, and her husband, Norris, nodded in support.

'Who're you calling a drunk, you old bag?' Kelly stood up and knocked into the table, sending wineglasses crashing onto the floor.

'Now look what you've done. I'm taking you home.' Gary pulled her away. 'My apologies. I'll replace the glasses.'

Chloë was quick to reassure him: 'They're from the pound shop in Chania, easy come easy go.'

'How can such a nice young man get stuck with such a slut?' Dorinda continued. Although Norris and Dorinda Thorner were stalwarts of the English chapel, they were a surly pair. Norris objected to Ariadne's choir, saying Advent was a time for preparation, not singing. Carols should not be sung only before Christmas Day. His wife defied him, not wanting to miss out on anything going on in their community.

'If you can't say anything nice, then shut up,' Della replied.

The atmosphere was turning hostile to the Thorners. Chloë shot up to smooth things over. 'Simon and I are so grateful for all your help today, and to Youssef and Amir, without whom we would both be on crutches. So let's toast them. Lift your glasses to Youssef and Amir Began. *Epharisto poli*, thank you both.'

The men were sitting politely at the top of the table drinking lemonade, while the guests stood to toast them. It was getting late and the oldies looked tired. Phil and Greg volunteered to escort the colonel home, Della offered to do some washing up and Natalie darted round collecting leftovers. 'Do you mind if I put these in a box for the lady who rescues dogs?' she asked.

'I'll help you,' Clive offered. 'Julie does a great job rescuing strays.'

That set off Dorinda again. 'There are far too many flea-bitten dogs and cats on this island,' she said, preparing to launch forth about lack of spaying and how puppies were dumped in the rubbish bins at the side of the road.

Chloë was in no mood for another of her rants. 'Take what you want, Natalie. Dorrie, can you bring in the water jugs?'

When they had all gone, she sat surveying the empty table with Simon. 'We could have done without Kelly and Dorrie.' She sighed.

'Poor Gary didn't know where to put himself. All is not well in the Bunker,' he mused.

'Don't ask me to do marriage guidance,' Chloë said.

'I wouldn't dream of it, but she's not a happy bunny. Looks a bit lost to me.'

'You always see the best in people.' Chloë clutched his arm. 'It's getting cold, let's go in. Katarina can clear the kitchen when she comes tomorrow. I'm past it.'

'What's a good party without a bust-up?' Simon said. 'If we'd been Greek, guns and knives would have been out by now.'

'Thank goodness we British know how to behave.' Chloë yawned.

'Now there's a loaded comment. We can be as bad as anyone

else in the world when our boots are filled with Satan's brew. Remember, I was once a good teetotal Methodist with parents in the Band of Hope. Drink was the ruin of many a man and woman.'

'And now we're singing in the chorale of chaos. Ariadne has her work cut out to make us a jolly band of Christmas cheer.'

'Up the stairs, woman, before you fall asleep on your feet.'

Chloë kicked off her glittery sandals with relief, knowing everything could wait until tomorrow. She wished she could feel more enthusiastic about the choir, but it was Alexa who kept her tossing and turning all night.

Recipe for Natalie's Greek Custard Pie
(*Galaktoboureko*)

Serves 8–10

65g fine semolina
200g sugar
65g cornflour
6 eggs, beaten
1 litre milk
12 sheets filo pastry
130g butter
Zest of 1 lemon, finely grated (optional)

For the syrup
250g caster sugar
200ml water
A few drops of rose water (optional)

Preheat the oven to 170°C.

In a bowl stir together half of the semolina with the sugar, cornflour, eggs, lemon zest, if using, and blend well.

In a large saucepan heat the milk almost to boiling point, then whisk in the semolina mixture slowly. Continue to stir, gradually adding the rest of the semolina. Do not let it boil or the mixture will curdle. Set it aside to cool.

Melt the butter. Use a little to grease a deep baking dish, then line it with a sheet of filo to hang over the edge. Brush the pastry with melted butter, then repeat with 5 more sheets.

Pour the semolina mixture over the filo and cover with the remaining sheets, brushing each one with melted butter as you go. Tuck the edges into the baking dish, then brush the surface with melted butter. Mark squares on the top of the filo, then sprinkle with a little water.

Bake for 45 minutes in the lower part of the oven.

Prepare the syrup: over medium-high heat, bring the water and caster sugar to a boil. Turn the heat to low and stir constantly until the sugar dissolves completely and the mixture is clear, approximately 3 to 5 minutes. Add the rose water if preferred. Remember – the longer you boil it, the thicker the syrup will be when cooled.

Remove the pie from oven and, while it is hot, brush the surface with melted butter. Let it cool. Pour the warm syrup over the pie, then leave to cool.

16

Ariadne woke early to make her annual pilgrimage up the rocky path to Agios Nicolaos chapel to light a candle for Elodie Durrante's birthday. She left Hebe snoring in bed, exhausted by last night's gathering. Now Ariadne needed time to sit and think.

The old chapel smelt of damp walls, candle wax and incense. There were the usual *tamata* – silver plaques of feet, faces, arms hanging before the icons in gratitude for some miracle of healing or in pleas for recovery. The frescos were still bright in the semi-darkness, Our Lord always placed in the centre, with his mother and Nikolaos on either side, as depicted in a Cretan-style icon.

Kelly Partridge's drunken jibes had hit home. Was she being unrealistic? Would her choir come together in harmony or just make a series of amateurish attempts to stay in tune and time? Then there was Norris Thorner, denouncing any carol singing before Christmas Day. He disapproved of Father Dennis joining in, but Dorinda was coming though. She liked to have her voice heard.

The last rehearsal had been promising, but time was running out for learning new stuff. Better to keep things simple.

Young Gary had a good tenor voice and seemed pleased to be in the group. Simon was keeping him company. It must be hard living with a discontented woman, who had everything and yet nothing. She thought of how Hebe and she muddled along financially and yet were happy with their own company, even though Hebe was always tired, these days, and not so steady on their walks.

They had first met at a boarding school nearly forty years ago. Hebe had taught classics and sport, while Ariadne was head of English, with music thrown in. Both had Greek first names, which amused them, and loved music. Their friendship gradually evolved into a deepening love for each other. Ariadne's father was glad she had found a soulmate. He saw nothing wrong in their relationship, but Hebe's parents wanted nothing to do with Ariadne, threatening to inform the governors that this unholy alliance was a bad example to vulnerable girls. Ariadne had had no choice but to give in her notice and move elsewhere.

Now they shared a small house. People in the street assumed they were relatives and only the postman knew otherwise. Theirs was a loving relationship, as good as any marriage, she thought. Now all these things were possible, civil partnerships, marriage, with provision for pensions. Ariadne had made sure Hebe was included in her will and Hebe had done the same so their futures would be secure. They were happy to stay as they were, without signalling their special relationship to all and sundry.

Yet Hebe's mind was wandering again. There was always a

niggle at the back of Ariadne's that Hebe was not herself but she did love the choir and she could accompany the singing flawlessly. It was worth all the effort to see her smiling and joining in.

Once this day was honoured and little prayers of gratitude offered, it was time to head down to Elodie's retreat house to collect clothes from her neighbours for the refugees appeal. Alison and Peter, the young couple who managed the house, were both in the choir and offered some baby clothes. It seemed appropriate to visit them on Elodie's birthday. Without the author's help and generosity, Ariadne and Hebe would never have settled so well, and Elodie's presence still seemed to permeate the house. A large oil painting of her hung in the entrance hall. She looked every inch the matriarch with a chest full of pearl ropes, alert, critical and imperious, a latter-day Queen Mary.

There had been a few men in her life who had come and gone, no doubt inspiring those daring intimate scenes of sexual variety. Years ago they had been shocking, if always relevant to the developing story. Now they must seem quite tame. Elodie had known how things stood between Hebe and Ariadne, but she was cosmopolitan enough not to care. They provided inspiration for her writing.

Ariadne loved Elodie's studio, set in the garden, surrounded by roses, white jasmine and plumbago, red, white and blue. It still held a tang of tobacco, and Elodie's favourite heavy Guerlain perfume clung to its walls even after all these years. There was a desk piled with pens, for everything had been handwritten, an old Imperial typewriter, a clutter of notebooks, and photos in silver frames. There were red and black Cretan rugs on the floor and a large office chair for her generous rump. Elodie used to laugh about her derrière: 'Writers' bums are prone to expanding into soup bowls not teacups,' she would say.

Ariadne could see her now, sitting there, smoking, trying to figure out her next idea. A shelf of first editions lined the wall and there was a hint of damp that worried her. The room needed regular airing and heating in the winter, or everything would become foxed, perhaps even worse. Now Elodie's house was filled with artists and craftspeople. The kitchen had a communal dining area, and the large cypress-beamed drawing room was a comfortable place for discussions and readings. Peter and Alison were there on a year's contract. Their children were in the village school, alongside Mel's boys. They lived in the service apartment with its own courtyard and pool.

All of this was a far cry from Elodie's humble origins as Gladys Pickvance from Ashton-under-Lyne, the daughter of mill workers, but with a canny knack of telling stories to anyone who would listen. Those yarns had turned into paid clips in magazines and the rest was history. Of her pen name she'd said that 'Elodie' had come from a gravestone, and the surname from the music-hall artist, Jimmy "The Schnoz" Durante, whom her parents loved. How she raised herself from such circumstances was a mystery, but pictures of her in youth showed a startling woman, with a figure that would have attracted attention.

Her success was due to her dedication to writing and to her performance as a diva on stage when being interviewed. Gladys had ceased to exist, and in her place came Elodie, with no family ties, no children. Books were her children. Stories were set in exotic locations full of drama, romance and dazzling heroes. Her life was her writing and the occasional man, who lightened her life until the next book was due.

Elodie exuded glamour and in her latter years nothing was stinted. She invited guests from the literary world for holidays. Ariadne once glimpsed a very good-looking man, who, the old colonel whispered, was Patrick Leigh Fermor, responsible for the capture of the German commander of forces in Crete during the war. He had once walked from France to Constantinople as a boy and had written travelogues in wonderful prose. They read all his books but never saw him again.

How she furnished a home in the grand style was the talk of the village, as donkeys laden with antiques climbed the hill out of town. Most of the valuable items had now been auctioned to equip the Foundation Trust, although Elodie seemed still to hover over all of the proceedings. A pool and an outside bar beside canopied loungers gave guests a luxurious rest after a hard day's creation.

Alison and Peter were sorting out materials for a workshop for the local children. 'We're making little boats for St Nicholas's Day and some for the Christmas decorations. It's the custom to place them on the table in honour of the saint.' They were just simple shapes to be painted in the blue and white Greek colours but Alison was experimenting with some wall hangings, stencilling boats onto fabric.

It cheered Ariadne to know that young families were carrying on local traditions. 'Can you make some Christmassy bits to sell at the charity bazaar?' She was impressed by what she was seeing. 'Good luck. Will you be coming to choir tomorrow?'

Pete smiled. 'One of us will be there but the other will have to look after Katie and Archie. Afternoons aren't brilliant for childcare.'

'I know, but everyone seems to be so busy in the evenings, what with bridge, drama group, Greek lessons and entertaining,' she explained. 'I do need your young voices to give us some zing.'

It was like herding sheep, trying to get everyone in one place at the same time, but she had learned another trick from watching Gareth Malone. Perhaps it was time to split them up, let them rehearse in their own homes. Now it was getting dark early and chillier in the olive garden she would book the community centre to claim the date for their St Nick's concert and the Christmas carol service. The Anglican church was only the size of a large garage, and with Norris on the warpath, she didn't want to land the vicar, Father Dennis, with a dilemma. So much to do and so little time left, but she was more determined than ever to make this event a night to remember.

17

Clive put a bowl of leftovers on the veranda of Natalie Fletcher's little villa. He didn't want to intrude but the smell of baking wafted through the open window. When she waved and invited him inside he didn't hesitate.

'I'm preparing a batch of Christmas puddings – it'll soon be Stir-up Sunday, so I'm getting ahead with my orders. I'll let them soak in rum,' she said, smiling shyly.

The scent of spices and fruit took him back to his childhood when Mam had made her recipe, with carrots and nuts and a splash of brandy for Christmas Day. He was allowed to lick the bowl if he was home from school. It would boil away, steaming up the windows for hours.

'I'm having a coffee. Have you time for one? Natalie offered.

Time hung heavy on his hands and he sat down. '"Never miss an opportunity," Lucy used to say.'

'You must miss her. She was always so lively.'

'But she was no cake baker. We always bought our Christmas

cake,' he replied, remembering his wife grabbing most of her shopping on Christmas Eve when they'd lived in Leeds.

'Thank you for the leftovers. Julie's so grateful. She's got ten dogs to feed.'

'Do they get walked?' he asked, wondering if he should volunteer.

'Not easy as she can only take two at a time. Her neighbours are complaining about their barking at feeding time. Bless her, she does her best. I would offer, but they're too big for me to handle safely,' Natalie said.

'Perhaps I could take one or two out with Bella down the lane, on leads, of course, and you could take a little one,' Clive suggested.

'That's a kind thought, but just at the moment I'm busy with orders,' she replied, not looking at him.

Nice try, whispered Lucy, in his head. *This one's too jumpy even to think of being seen out with you, darling.* Clive flushed at his boldness. Natalie seemed so hesitant socially – getting her to open up at the olive harvest supper had taken an hour of gentle probing and small-talk. It was as if she felt she had no right to be among them. He knew nothing of her history. Was she divorced or single? There was no wedding ring on view. She had the sort of pale look that some middle-aged women faded into, with wisps of fine mousy hair greying at the temples, and wore a wishy-washy top with black leggings – and she was so thin. Did she not eat any of her concoctions? Clive wondered. A good Yorkshire meal was what was needed. Her clothes reeked of the cigarette smoke that had lined her face over the years. Natalie must once have been quite a looker, with fine bone structure and dark blue eyes. How had she landed up here alone? He noticed a picture of two children under a fridge magnet. 'Yours?' he asked.

She smiled. 'Craig and Candice, yes, but that was taken ages ago. They're both grown-up now. Craig is in New Zealand and Candy in Scotland, married to a farmer.' Her face lit up as she spoke. 'And you?'

'Just the one, Jeremy. He's married but no children yet.' This was safe territory. The big question lay unanswered. Why was she living here like a hermit in widow's weeds? '*Siga, siga,*' said the Greeks. Slowly, slowly. He pulled back from asking anything more.

'Lucy and I came here on honeymoon. It stayed in the back of our minds so we kept returning. She loved the light.'

'I saw one of her paintings in Chloë's house. She was very talented. I did try the art class here, when I first came, but I'm no good at anything creative,' Natalie said.

'Cooking is a great art. Look at the success of *The Great British Bake Off* on TV. Your custard pie was a big hit last week, just like the Greeks make it.'

'Don't tell Irini. Mel gave me the recipe behind her back. Greek pastry is an art all of its own,' Natalie added.

'There you go. Your talent lies in a different field. Were you in catering back in the UK?'

'Oh, no.' Natalie turned back to her mixing bowl. 'Nothing like that. I was just a housewife.'

How many times had Lucy jumped on that remark? 'You run a household, cook, clean, see to children, shop, organise the budget, and make sure others get to school, the dentist and work on time.' This was not the time to put forward his wife's views. 'You must have been kept very busy, then,' he offered.

'I suppose so.'

'Then I mustn't hold you up. I'll be on my way and thanks for the coffee.'

'Any time,' she said, smiling. 'Kind of you to call.'

Was that an invitation? There was just a glimmer of pleasure as she spoke, a shy lowering of her eyes, almost girlish in its appeal. 'I meant what I said about dog-walking. I'd be glad of some company,' Clive said.

'I'll have a think but not yet… See you at choir tomorrow, though?'

'Oh, yes. I'd forgotten. What is it we're doing now?'

'Not sure, but Ariadne will be knocking on your door if you don't turn up.' This little touch of humour gave him hope. Natalie Fletcher was a mystery and he was intrigued.

That's more like it, Clive. You've wheedled something out of her, whispered Lucy's voice in his ear. She could have charmed confessions out of a priest, given half a chance. Would she mind if he took an interest in the little hermit with the mixing bowl?

18

Gary was finding the atmosphere in the Partridge house hard to shift. 'Perhaps we should get a rescue dog, Kelly,' he said, as they lay on the loungers, catching the last of the autumn sun. 'Simon says they need good homes.'

'You mean a dog instead of a baby? Is this your way of saying we've no hope of ever conceiving?' Kelly didn't look at him. 'Simon says this, Simon says that...'

'He's a good bloke and I like him.'

'Well, I don't like his stuck-up wife, all airs and graces,' Kelly replied.

'You didn't exactly show yourself in the best light at their house, love.'

'I never wanted to go to that bloody supper,' she whined. 'You're never away from the choir these days. I thought it was going to be just the two of us here.'

It was time to deliver some home truths. 'Trouble is, you're not very good company at the moment. If only you'd find some friends and make an effort.' Gary was trying to chivvy her. It wasn't working.

Kelly stomped off back to the kitchen to open a bottle of wine. 'Want some?' she shouted.

'It's a bit early for me,' Gary said, sensing a storm brewing. 'I'm sorry you're so miserable. If I could conjure up a baby for you, I would, but we have to accept it's not looking good. You get so tense. The doc said there was nothing wrong with either of us. Sometimes it just happens this way.'

'So it's all my fault, is it, for not fitting in? We didn't come here to fit in, but to enjoy ourselves and conceive. I want to see that specialist in Heraklion again. There has to be a way. Perhaps it's time we left this sodding island and went home.' Kelly sipped her wine with a look of misery on her face.

'Back to London?' This was news to Gary. 'I thought you liked St Nick's?'

'You can get sick of a place. There's nothing to do here, no nightclubs, shops. I don't know why we ever came.' Kelly glugged another glass of rosé.

Gary sighed loudly. 'There's no pleasing you lately. I'm going to see Ariadne to collect my music. I'd forgotten how a good sing can lift your spirits. You should try it.'

'I prefer my spirits out of a bottle, thank you very much. You go off to join your poxy choirboys. I don't care.'

Gary was losing patience with his wife. He couldn't do right for doing wrong and he wanted to escape the dark cloud that seemed to hang over them these days.

Ariadne was printing off carol sheets, paper spilling all over her kitchen table. Gary leapt to catch them as they fell. 'Looks like we've got a lot to learn!' He laughed.

Hebe drifted in from the garden and frowned when she saw him. 'That's my job, printing off the carols,' she said to Ariadne.

'I know, dear, but last time you got a bit muddled and we had to throw them all away. Come and sit down. Gary's come to collect his music.'

'What will we be practising this week?' he asked, aware that Hebe was glaring at him.

'"The Twelve Days of Christmas" with actions. It should be fun. You know the one, "a partridge in a pear tree".' Ariadne paused. 'Oh, you must know it by heart,' she added, seeing the look on Gary's face.

'I do indeed,' he responded. 'Only too well, with a name like Partridge. I used to get called Birdie at school.'

'Did you really? How is your wife? She looked very anxious to me.'

'Kelly's a bit under the weather, women's stuff,' he replied, not wanting to reveal to strangers the true reason for her misery.

On his way home he stopped off for a coffee at Irini's, watching Mel busy herself in and out of the kitchen, carrying bottles for the fridge. If only Kelly had a friend like Mel or Della, instead of hiding in the villa, reading magazines and watching TV. Their idleness weighed on him, and "The Twelve Days of Christmas" was the last carol he wanted to sing. It brought back memories of the bullyboys in the street pinning him against the wall, 'Sing for us, Birdie Boy.' He'd once had a solo in the school choir before his voice had broken. He'd hated that grammar school and the purple and grey uniform that stood out against the usual browns and dark blues of the comprehensives.

It was all his gran's fault for making him sit the eleven-plus and, when he'd got a place, parading him around as the boy wonder of Cardigan Street. Yes, he was bright enough to hold his own in the class, but on the way home he was waylaid by their neighbour's lads and given a thumping or worse. He hated school for that reason, hating his gran even more, when she made him join the church choir at St Aidan's with all the old men and girls. Gran had delusions of grandeur, on account of having it rough, with Granddad being out of work, then leaving her for the woman up the road. Gary had never known his mother, something about being knocked up by a soldier and left holding a baby, which she'd promptly handed over to her own mother before scarpering. It was not the best start in life.

Then there was the question of his name. Gran was called Elsie Garfield Partridge. Garfield Partridge was his name but only Kelly and his passport knew this secret. He had been Gary from the moment he'd entered infant school. 'Garfield' was part of Gran's plan to make something out of his unfortunate start in life as an illegitimate orphan. He was destined to be a success, a cut above the other babies in the street. Nothing was too much of a sacrifice. She'd sent him to a private kindergarten a bus ride away, where he mixed with children way above his station. He got invited to parties in large houses on the outskirts of town, with big cars and gardens the size of recreation grounds. Gran took him on the bus and walked around, waiting to collect him when the time came. He had the best clothes and play outfits.

How she funded it he never knew, until one day in his early teens, he came home unexpectedly from school to find her in bed with a stranger. It dawned on him then why the neighbours sneered at them. She was a prostitute and his education was funded by her trade. He felt angry, ashamed and confused by this discovery. That was when he went off the rails, failed his exams, got excluded from school for drinking, cautioned by the police for stealing bikes, scooters and finally cars.

It was his probation officer, Stuart Gordon, who stood by him and noticed that he was good with computers. He found Gary a job, goodness knows how. If ever he had a son, Stuart would be his name.

He tried to make Gran promise to give up prostitution and stop making him into what he was not. She took offence and shoved him out of the house to fend for himself. It was Kelly Marie Keogh who came to his rescue, funny little Kelly, who loved him for who he was. He'd known her for years as a friend and once fancied her big sister, Bernie, but Kelly was the one who stuck by him.

That was when he worked out that, before her, no one in his fractured family had really loved him. Gran had praised him for achieving her dreams but never cuddled him. He recognised you could be dirt poor, yet have a loving family. Gran did her best, by her own lights, but it had all gone wrong between them.

Kelly had brought him down to earth, helped him to find himself, to take on responsibility and have fun. He had wanted to give her the moon and stars. Their wedding was a simple affair, and Gran didn't turn up because the Keoghs were Catholics. They took a cheap package holiday to Greece and fell in love with the heat, the colours and the food of the islands. Of course, going to live there was just a fantasy until

19

Natalie looked out of the window: yet another day of heavy rain. The doors rattled with the wind, the golden sunset and silver sea transformed into dark sky with rolling waves crashing onto the harbour. It wasn't a day to go walking but for baking. Natalie counted her orders. Ten Christmas puddings, three gluten-free, four pint size and three minis, six Christmas cakes, regular tin size, and six jars of mincemeat. She must remember to add on her labour and the cost of the Calor gas: every penny counted at this time of year. She wanted to send a nice parcel to Candy and her husband with olive oil, soaps and an embroidered linen tablecloth.

She still hadn't got over Clive's invitation to go walking with him. It was a bit of a shock to know he had picked her out as suitable company. 'I'm not good at socialising,' she had wanted to say but didn't, sending him away wishing, no doubt, that he had never asked her.

She looked down at her sticky fingers while mixing mincemeat – apples, spices and dried fruit. The scent was intoxicating.

She liked to temper the mixture in the oven. It helped to pre-serve and soften the fruit before she put it into jars. Time to sit down with a soothing cup of mountain herb tea.

Natalie looked down with a sigh at her finger, still dented from where her wedding ring had once lain. No point in pre-tending she was still married to Rick... It was more than three years since he... 'Don't go there,' she said. 'Do your humming.' Whenever she thought about that time she forced herself to hum the tune from *The Archers*: tum-ti-tum-ti-tum-ti-tum... It forced her back into the moment and away from things she could never change, but it was hard.

Was it only two years ago that she'd arrived with a suitcase of cookery books, waiting to receive a half-load of cooking equipment, bed linen and a bicycle?

Everyone said Natalie was a good homemaker, a clever cook, a pleasant neighbour but then it had all changed and she knew she never again wanted to see Glenholm Close, with its circle of detached houses, pristine front gardens and clipped box borders.

Her friends had thought her mad to up sticks and seek sanc-tuary on a Greek island. Craig had tried to understand, but he was still in shock at what had happened to his family and felt she was deserting them. The bereavement counsellor said she must nurture her wounded self and, if and when she felt ready, perhaps move away from the memories. Their home was not easy to sell, once its tragic history was known, even though it was redecorated, wiped clean of the terrible events that had shattered her world. There was no choice or the bank would requisition it... Tum-ti-tum-ti-tum... She pushed away the image in the back of her mind. They whispered that

Rick's death was some accident gone wrong but she knew different. No one would prise that knowledge from her here. It was in a sealed box locked inside her mind.

Rick's public death had left a terrible mark on her: shame and guilt but most of all anger at being left to deal with the mess he'd left behind, police, coroner's court, solicitors, estate agents, newspaper enquiries, her children's grief, prying neighbours and, worst of all, the bank's demand for their home.

The result was an inability to swallow food without bringing it back some time later. She didn't deserve to feed herself, but was marvellous at feeding others with delicious, nutritious, wholesome recipes. Preparing food was time-consuming, full of textures, colours and aromas that permeated her kitchen, lifted her spirit and filled her day.

Now there were other distractions: Pilates and yoga classes, Greek lessons, the book club, and the choir that she was enjoying far more than she deserved to. In St Nick's she felt safe from judgement, but this came at a cost. Distance must be maintained. If they knew her history it would be Glenholm Close all over again.

Be careful what you say, what you do, mingle but don't mix and, most of all, don't ever get involved with anyone again. This was the daily mantra she murmured as she did her exercise routine. The less people knew the better. Who would want a bankrupt widow in their midst?

20

Sammia was busy unpacking groceries onto a shelf when there was a knock at the door. Toula, the farmer's wife, stood outside with two jars of jam. 'Can I come in?'

'Of course, but Maryam is out with the boy.'

'Kyria Sammia, I hate to say this,' she stuttered, in broken English, 'but you must go.'

'Go where?' Sammia wondered if there was trouble somewhere. She didn't understand.

'We have a son, Aristotle, in Athens. His work is ended and he wants to return with his wife and girls... back here.'

'That is good. You will be pleased to see him again.'

'*Popopo* – you don't understand. They need a house. Yannis must give them this house. Ari is family. I'm sorry.'

'We have to leave?' At last Sammia could see the embarrassment on Toula's face.

'I am sure someone will let you have rooms. I will ask for you.'

Sammia sat down with shock. 'But it is winter... Where can we go?'

'We can give you another week to pack up. You have kept the house so tidy and clean and made it very comfortable, but we cannot let our son be homeless.'

Sammia rubbed her belly. 'I have not long to go now. I was hoping my baby would be safe here.'

'I'm sorry.' Toula shook her head. 'It is this terrible time, all over Greece. People have lost money, work, homes. You have friends in Chania?'

'They have no rooms or work for us, but I understand how it is. We will find somewhere.'

Toula held out the jam as a peace offering.

'Thank you, Kyria.' Sammia felt cold as she tried to retain her dignity. It was not Toula's fault that Fate had turned so cruel. Family needs must come first – but so sudden an eviction! How could she break this news to the others, just as they had settled in? Karim was making friends and had played with them on the beach, as children do. Youssef and Amir were busy. Perhaps Melodia would help them, but Sammia didn't want anyone to know about this. They had faced much worse but the timing was so very wrong. She knelt on the prayer mat. 'What do we do now?'

21

Ariadne was busy printing sheet music and writing out the different parts for each section to practise and share. Thank goodness for *The Oxford Book of Carols* she'd found on the bookshelf and some online verses. The abilities within the little choir were mixed, and trying to sort out singers from squeakers took all the tact she could muster. Dorinda Thorner was one of the worst offenders, with a voice like a foghorn. Ariadne hoped the woman would get a cold and lose her voice before their first performance. Mel hadn't turned up again, and Phil and Greg were away on a cruise.

How was it she could never get a full choir to rehearse? The colonel never missed. His voice was frail but he could read music, and Simon chivvied him along if he lost the page. Gary was a surprise with his rich tenor, and Clive was a regular too.

After their first rehearsal of 'Silent Night', Arthur had stayed behind for his usual tea and cake. Tonight his rheumy eyes looked far away. 'Penny for them, Arthur,' she joked.

'Singing that carol took me back, way back, Ariadne, to a time I'd almost forgotten.'

She knew reminiscences were on the way and she hadn't time tonight. Hebe was wanting to listen to an audio. Ariadne had neglected her of late, caught up as she was in planning the choir's first performance. All the same, there was something in the sadness on his face that made her sit down to listen.

'You know I was in the battle for Crete. It was an absolute shambles in the end. We were taken prisoner, marched over the White Mountains and back again, barefoot and bloodied. Then, as prisoners of war, we were shipped like cattle through Greece to Germany and on to a stalag in the middle of nowhere. Believe me, it was grim, with starvation rations, and that first winter we had nothing but thin blankets and not a pot to piss in,' he said.

'I'm sorry,' Ariadne replied, no longer wanting to stop his flow.

'We were stuck there from 'forty-one to 'forty-four. I thought I'd go mad but we organised ourselves with classes and lectures, even made a secret radio. There were art workshops – anything to take the mind off our misery and sense of defeat.

'I think it was in 'forty-two or 'forty-three when the Red Cross parcels turned up trumps with tins of food. Life perked up after that, but we were still corralled in miserable huts.'

Ariadne could see Arthur was lost in his own world, a world she could only imagine. 'I'll make another pot of tea and you can tell us all about it. Hebe will want to hear your story too.'

It was coming close to Christmas and Chip Woods was preparing the pantomime with the chaps who could act a bit and play the fool. No doubt Sid would do his drag act, playing a full-blown queen. Didn't need any practice with that. Arthur was not much of a drama buff or a musician but they scraped together enough pianists and brass-band enthusiasts. The Swedish Red Cross donated instruments to make a decent enough sound for their Christmas show.

The padre was drawing up a choir for the carol concert. No one was in the mood at first. How could you celebrate the birth of Christ in that miserable place? They were far from home, knowing that in England people would be roasting chestnuts round the fire, enjoying a Christmas dinner with all the trimmings, despite rationing. At least the Allies were on the move eastwards. Perhaps the war might be over before Christmas, but more likely next Christmas. Being a prisoner, or a kreigie, as they called themselves, was a bore. For some it was time to learn, prepare perhaps for a new career. For others there was always the fear that those at home had forgotten them and forged new lives in their absence. Letters from home were treasured. Arthur found it hard to write to his wife. He didn't want to upset her, so he lied through his teeth.

'We're fine, treated well. Don't worry, darling, I'm fit and well.' Even as he wrote, his nose was streaming with a feverish cold.

The goons here weren't too bad but there was always the odd sadist who liked to beat the shit out of any poor sod who stepped out of line.

'We have to make an effort,' Chips cajoled his volunteer entertainers. 'A bit of Christmas cheer helps lift the spirits so let's decorate the place with paper chains, cut strips off all our papers, make flour paste and hang them from the rafters.'

They were given a branch of pinewood and Bert, who was

a metalworker, beat out the cleaned Red Cross tins into strips that he twisted with a curve on the top. 'This is real tinsel.' He showed how his handiwork could hang on the branch. The effect in the light was good. It was all very makeshift but at least it took up time. Time was the killer: the busier they were, the better.

When Christmas Day came, they were given a proper dinner for once: Vienna sausages, potatoes and a chocolate pudding, with biscuits and cigarettes. For once there was no curfew and they were allowed to wander freely in the compound. It was an ice-cold night, but above them, the stars twinkled and Arthur thought of Caroline and of how the same stars were lighting up her Christmas. Out of the silence and chill came a lone voice singing 'Silent Night' and they all listened, stunned by its beauty. Then another voice was repeating the tune. 'Stille nacht, heilige nacht, alles schläft...' One of the guards, his voice cracking with emotion. Here was another man missing home and family, sharing the moment with us.

'How beautiful.' Ariadne found she had tears in her eyes. 'That carol will always be special to you.'

'Oh, yes,' Arthur replied. 'It was the last time we were there at Christmas. While the Russians were heading west we were made to walk towards them in the depths of winter. A cruel death march. We were ill shod and clothed. Only the strongest of us made it through. Poor Sid, Chips Wood and many others were left in the snow.' He could say no more.

For a while no one spoke.

'War is a terrible thing,' Hebe said.

22

It was too wet and windy for singing outdoors. The olive trees bent into the gale as the weather set in from the north. The village community hall was booked for the rest of their rehearsals, and Ariadne thought it was time to put the choir in the right order with sopranos, tenors, basses and altos in clumps, leaving the front chairs for soloists.

The first in was Dorinda Thorner, placing her considerable bulk on a front seat. She was the last person Ariadne wanted blasting away into the ears of their audience. Arthur called her the 'Iron Lung'.

As the choir filtered in, Ariadne looked on in dismay as a phalanx of Dorinda's cronies took up precious space, leaving Natalie, Della and the others with good voices to sit further back. Then Mel arrived, late, with Duke and Pippa. Ariadne had not put out enough chairs. 'I'm sorry, ladies, but would you mind moving back a line so I can let the young ones sit in the front. Mel is singing a solo verse for us so I need her there.' Ariadne smiled sweetly. It had taken much village wine and persuasion for Mel to agree to this. It was important not to make her sit at the back. She would be nervous enough, Heaven knew why when she had the voice of an angel, but Dorinda was not for budging.

'I was here first. She can sing from the back and still be heard.' She sniffed.

'I think not.' Ariadne tried to smile. 'Better to get the blend right from the start. The young voices need to be in the front.'

Big mistake. Dorinda rose, followed by her friends. 'Norris was right to warn us about desecrating Advent. You all want to hear the sound of your own voices. I'm not going to wait to be insulted. It's age discrimination.' She pushed back her chair so that it clattered and fell, then stormed out, like a prima donna.

Ariadne was now short of voices. Nothing for it but to bluff it out. 'Let's get started on "Mary's Boy Child". We need a few modern carols to give variety. Mel, would you take the verses and we can all join in the choruses.'

'"Long time ago in Bethlehem…"' Mel's lovely voice rang out into the rafters and the chorus followed. It was a joyful tune with Caribbean rhythms, but sounded a bit flat and stiff.

'Let's give it more bounce and sway. Let yourselves go a little more,' Ariadne suggested. That only seemed to make things worse and there was no balance in the harmony. Dorinda's dramatic exit had shocked the choir. Now everyone was self-conscious and unresponsive. If only Dorinda hadn't arrived first. Should she go round and apologise? Like hell she would. The woman could stew in her own juice, but Ariadne knew she'd made an enemy, someone capable of denigrating all her efforts. Time was running out to find new voices. Once again doubts flooded her resolve. Was the choir a big mistake? Was she being too ambitious? If she backed down and called off the concert, it would not be too late.

'What shall I do, Hebe?' She sighed as they put away the chairs in the hall. 'Have I made a big mistake?'

'I think you're doing splendidly, love. Just keep rehearsing. We'll get better, I'm sure.'

Ariadne couldn't sleep for going over their programme. The choir wasn't gelling as a team. Something was missing. They congregated in separate groups, males, females, youngsters and oldies. A good choir was a vocal orchestra, needing fine tuning, belief in itself and good leadership. In her teaching days she had honed the girls into making a beautiful sound. What was needed was a confidence-building exercise, but what?

23

Mel was humming 'Mary's Boy Child' to herself as she prepared their evening meal. Word had gone round the expats about Dorinda's defection. What a fuss about nothing. If they didn't want to sing, so be it, she thought. Those who were left could make a decent stab at it. Sure, the oldies were a bit stiff, preferring traditional carols, but she was enjoying singing again and sensed her nerve coming back as a soloist. She was hanging out washing on the first dry day for a week when Ariadne appeared, looking worried.

'I'm sorry for the debacle on Tuesday. I should have labelled the chairs, but what's done is done. I just wish we could get a group feel to our concert,' she said.

'I know what you mean. We need to loosen up a bit and get a party atmosphere to some of the numbers.'

'Mel, you just gave me a brilliant idea. Why don't we have a bit of a do, a social, a *glendi*, as the Greeks call it, get everyone relaxing together, talking, mixing? Would Irini agree?'

'Leave her to me. I could teach you some of those pub carols I told you about.'

'Pub carols?' Ariadne had forgotten this.

'You know, I told you – around Sheffield they like to sing their own versions of carols to special tunes, with a pint around a pub fire. It happens every year. Get a few bevvies inside them and you'll be surprised. We could put on village sausages and mash, with a fruit pie or two.'

'Sounds delicious, thank you. It's such a relief to have a young person's view on things,' Ariadne said.

'Hang on, I'm not that young!' Mel laughed 'If we're going to sing, we'll do better if there is a sense that we're united.'

'My thoughts exactly, but what shall I do about Dorrie and company? I don't want to cause offence. We're such a small community.'

'Forget about them and their small minds. Let's make them green with envy at our success.' Mel had no time for Dorinda Thorner. She was a first-class complainer, critical of everyone, a gossip – in fact a total sleazeball. Her cronies were not much better. They never dined at the taverna, preferring the smart Italian restaurant up the hill, Fabrizio's, with its linen table-cloths and napkins. Irini and Spiro hadn't had a good word to say about Fabrizio's attempts at Greek cuisine. When he'd tried them on the menu, her spies had said they were neither one thing nor another.

'Irini will be pleased to have the gathering.' Once Ariadne had rushed off, Mel slipped into the kitchen to let her mother-in-law know they had a booking. 'It'll be a real knees-up.'

'Then we must book Giorgos, the lyre player. I will do *boureki* and chicken souvlaki with lamb ribs.'

'Would you mind if we cooked British? I was thinking more of village sausages, potato mash and gravy for a change,' Mel suggested.

'What do you mean "for a change"? This is a taverna, not a chip shop. They will have what I cook, or nothing.'

'I was going to do it myself with a little help.' Mel felt the first stirrings of an earthquake.

'Who owns this restaurant? I am not in my grave yet. You will have to wait many years to get your hands on my kitchen, young lady.' Irini's voice thundered through the door and along the street. 'It's bad enough half the village being taken over by foreigners wanting their own dishes, turning their noses up at good Cretan cuisine. We are famous for our Mediterranean diet. We live long on baked vegetables, olive oil, oranges and lemons, and now my only *nifi* chooses to insult me. Maybe we are now a poor country with all the taxes... Look at this!' She shoved a bill in Mel's face.' How can we pay it? No one has money for dining. No one takes their pickups from the *plateia* for lack of petrol, cigarettes. Everything costs, but your lot up the hill have money.'

'But I didn't mean—' Mel interrupted her flow to no avail.

'It was a bad day when my son brought a stranger into our family, a girl who can only cook chips.' Irini was now erupting like lava overflowing.

Mel knew she had blundered. The direct approach had been a mistake. She should have slid the suggestion in sideways, so Irini felt she was making all the decisions herself. 'I'm sorry,' was all she could say.

When Spiro came home that evening, he arrived into a stand-off. There was an awkward silence in the house. Mel spilt out her side of the argument to him while Irini was simmering in the kitchen. The poor guy was stuck in the middle, like a UN peacekeeper 'At least there are no plates smashed,' he said, with a smile. 'Mama has a point, Melodia. This is her business.'

She knew it was difficult for him to take sides when he wanted to please them both, but now she needed his support. She pulled him out into the street. 'I only asked for village sausages, not a wedding feast. Honestly, I'm trapped between a rock and a hard place. I don't want to cause offence – and I thought she'd be glad of the custom. Without the foreign friends, we'd have no business at all.'

'It's not that bad, is it?' Spiro smiled, ruffling her hair.

Mel couldn't resist his boyish charm but this time she poked his chest with frustration. 'Have you seen the books? The cost of goods off the ferry, the tax we have to pay now. When did we last take a penny from the business?'

Spiro flung his head back and sat down pulling out his worry beads and twirling them round, trying to make his point. 'But we live off our land, not the taverna. No one has much, these days. We have our health, our children, a roof over our heads. Not like some refugees.'

'They come of their own wish. We did not invite them. It is none of our business.' Irini had joined them, overhearing the argument, standing close to her son, who could do no wrong in her eyes.

So much for the Greek love of strangers, *zenophilos*, Mel thought, but said nothing. She stalked off. Sons and mothers, what could she do? 'Will I ever be good enough?' she said later to Spiro, as she stoked up the log fire. 'Irini won't let us hold a *glendi* here in British style.'

Spiro listened to her frustration. 'You gave her grandsons. You are part of this family now. She misses Papa. Find another place for your party, the community hall or one of your choir members' houses. Some of their villas can host a big party. Come here, don't be upset. Mama is proud of our cuisine, that's all. '

'I never thought I was offending her. I don't understand. Why it is such a big deal?' Mel sank down on their sofa, leaning on his chest. 'Pubs in England are always hosting parties.'

'This is Santaniki, not Sheffield. We do things in our own way.'

'So I gather.' Mel sighed. 'I'll see Ariadne and explain the idea is off.'

'Not off, just needing another venue.' He plonked himself beside her and kissed her. 'Let Mama simmer for a little while. You never know, she may change her mind.'

'Pigs might fly,' Mel muttered to herself, but this storm at least was over.

'What you say?' Spiro looked puzzled.

'Nothing. Just a storm in a teacup and it'll pass.' When would she ever understand the internal dynamics of this family?

24

Ariadne was tearing down to the harbour when Mel caught up with her on her way back from the fish stalls. 'Glad I've seen you. There's going to be a slight problem with—'

'Yes, yes!' Ariadne couldn't concentrate. 'Have you seen Hebe?'

'Not on the street, no. Is there a problem?'

'It's just that she went out for a walk and it's over an hour and she's not back for her breakfast. It's not like her... Do you think she's fallen somewhere?'

'Does she have a regular route?' Mel said.

'Along the harbour to watch the boats coming in, just a stroll, nothing strenuous, no cliff paths, unless I'm with her.'

'Do you want me to come with you? I can get help.'

'No, no – I'll manage. She's a bit forgetful some of the time. You carry on and I'll be fine.'

'If you're sure. I just came to tell you our party will be better in someone else's home. Irini is not keen—'

'Another time, Mel. I must get on.' Ariadne left the girl

standing, as she marched along the harbour. The cafés and the ouzerias were boarded up. The wind was raising quite a swell and there was more rain in the air. Where on earth had the silly woman got to? It wasn't the first time she'd wandered off, forgetting the time. Ariadne tried not to be cross with her, but she had so much to do now. Mel was saying the party would not be in the taverna. Why not? She had no time to think about that now. Perhaps Hebe was talking to a fisherman, or sitting on a bench, gazing at the view across to the main island. It was not a morning for lingering. Was she even wearing her anorak? Oh, Hebe, where are you, dear? Don't keep worrying me like this. Then she saw a familiar figure doing his morning jog. 'Gary, have you seen Miss Wilson? Hebe?'

He stopped. 'No, I don't think so. To be honest, I'm listening to my music so I don't notice much, but if you go on this way, I'll head homewards and see if she's up in our direction.'

But she never wandered that far. Ariadne felt uneasy. There was no sign of Hebe along the shoreline and she walked home, half expecting her to be sitting at the table, or on the veranda searching for her. Then the landline rang. It was Gary Partridge.

'Kelly found her. She's fine, just a bit cold so Kelly's making tea and toast. I'll run her down to you.'

'No, I'll bring the jeep and collect her. Thank you so much. It's such a relief.'

Ariadne jumped into their old jeep, its canvas roof now on, and raced up the bumpy track towards the villa they all called the Bunker. She had watched it being built but had never been inside. What was Hebe doing up that track? When Ariadne arrived, there she was, eating toast, oblivious to the concern around her.

'I can't thank you enough.' Ariadne was breathless.

'Sit down,' said Gary's wife, still in her dressing-gown. 'Lucky I was looking out the window and I saw this lady wandering, with no coat on. It didn't look right, so I followed her. Is she okay?'

'She gets forgetful from time to time,' Ariadne replied

'She looked very lost to me, didn't know where she was. I've never seen her up here before.'

'Hebe, where were you going?' Ariadne asked, but there was a faraway look in her eyes, as she smiled.

'Birdwatching, I think. Do I live here?'

'Birdwatching? Without your binoculars?' Ariadne was puzzled.

'I wanted to see the sea eagles.'

'But there aren't any here, dear. That's in Scotland.'

'Do I live here?'

At her confusion no one spoke.

'Mr and Mrs Partridge found you.' Ariadne looked round the large kitchen, with its granite tops and ceiling-high cupboards, wanting to change the subject. 'Isn't this spectacular? And you've a panoramic view of the bay. You must be enchanted by it.'

'Not in this weather. It's so grey,' Kelly replied. 'Excuse the dressing-gown. I like to have a long swim now we have a heated pool. Gary, warm up the coffee for the lady. Would you like to look round?'

'Ariadne, please,' she said, and guided Hebe through a sequence of spacious rooms, dining room, drawing room, study, a TV snug, all with marble floors and Persian rugs, like an Oriental palace, but nothing that suggested they were lived in. 'Soulless' was the word that came to mind. 'What a wonderful house and such views,' she said.

Kelly smiled. 'We rattle around a bit, but we do have friends over from the UK for parties.'

'Talking of which,' said Ariadne, 'my idea for a choir party has fallen through. Mel's mother-in-law's not keen. Poor Mel, she wanted to have a singsong there.'

'We could do it here,' Gary said, turning to his wife.

'Are you sure?' Ariadne was thrilled.

'Any time. We've no visitors booked, have we, Kelly?'

'It would be just a social for choir members and their friends. This would be the ideal venue, if your wife is willing?'

Kelly was looking shocked. 'I'm not a cook,' she said.

'That's not a problem. Natalie and Mel will help, and we could have a faith supper where everybody brings something. All you would need to do is open the door. But don't feel you have to.'

'We'll be delighted to host it, won't we, Kelly?' Gary was searching his wife's face for a response.

'I suppose… yes, it'll be okay.' Kelly didn't look too enthused.

Hebe clapped her hands – 'A party, what fun!' – but Ariadne was no longer feeling cheerful. 'I'll take this wanderer home,' she said, and they made their exit down the steps. 'We shall look forward to coming again, and if I can do anything to help… I'm hoping to get all the choir mixing. It won't be long before our St Nicholas's concert. Bye for now and thank you so much.'

Hebe was silent on the way back. Ariadne was worried that

she hadn't known where she was. Watching birds in Scotland? She could have slipped and fallen on rocks, or worse. For the first time Ariadne realised that Hebe mustn't go walking alone. Perhaps it was just her mind flitting from one thought to another. Tomorrow she'd be back to her old self. What she needed now was rest and the normal routines of the day. But something wasn't right.

25

Chloë was thrilled to hear her daughter on the phone. 'How are things?' she asked Alexa.

'I'm fine.'

'I was just planning our flights for Christmas. Shall we come to you first?'

'Not a good idea. We're selling up and I'm flat hunting.'

Chloë sighed. So the separation was final. 'So soon. You could use our flat for as long as you need.'

'Thanks, might do that, but I must find something of my own.'

'You sound very stressed. Why don't you fly out to us for a week? It's quite lively over here at Christmas time.'

'Mummy, I don't feel lively. I'm better off left alone this year. I have friends I can visit. Christmas is off, as far as I'm concerned.'

'But we'd love to see you,' Chloë pleaded. She longed for things to be as they once were.

'Mummy, don't fuss. I'm just not very sociable at the moment. I need my own space to think things through.'

'But we've acres of space here and we do miss you,' Chloë persisted.

Silence at the other end.

'I'd better go now – got a lot to do. Love you.' Alexa's phone clicked off.

Chloë sat on the floor and cried. Why won't she let me in? What's going on? She looked around her workroom, then pulled out a carved wooden box, spilling its contents onto the floor. She began picking up old cards and photographs. 'You were such a lovely baby and a joy to hold.'

Here was her pink baby weight card from the clinic, the plastic wristband worn when she was first born. There was a glowing school report, her baptism certificate and a rosette from that win at the gymkhana. A school photograph, with her gorgeous curly hair scraped back under a straw Panama hat, made Chloë smile. 'Why did you have to grow up and marry the wrong man? Just as I did, I suppose. You were looking at the handsome external bits of him rather than into his true heart.' Only later had Chloë found out that Charlie and she had very little in common... *Except you, darling. Once you were grown there was nothing to cling to. But you and I were always together, sharing so many holidays, trips and memories. You're my beautiful golden egg, who hatched and flew the nest straight into the arms of Hugh.*

Perhaps if Muhammad wouldn't come to the mountain, it was time to book a flight and turn up on the doorstep. You'll have to face me then, Chloë thought. She jumped up full of excitement with her idea. I'll spend Christmas with you and it'll be like old times. Simon can stay here and sing. He'll understand – he always does. Nothing here that couldn't be missed when she was needed elsewhere.

26

Sammia helped serve the vegetable stew, while the men sat staring into the fire. Maryam was busy settling Karim, then returned to join them. 'I know a place we can go.'

'Where's that?' Amir said, twirling his amber beads.

'We can go to the cave, where we played with Karim. He likes it up there.'

'Are you mad, woman? It's winter. Caves have no doors or windows,' said Amir, laughing.

'Come and see for yourself. You can fix something. No one will bother us there. It's large enough to divide into two. We can make shelves out of the rocks. We can build a firepit. There is fresh water from the stream. We will be warm and private. If they don't want us here, we can live out of sight.'

'It's not like that,' Sammia argued, knowing that Toula had no option but to let them go.

'Oh, but it is. We are strangers who do not speak their language. There is a long history between Greece and Turkey.

They view us as the enemy within. I see how the old women look at us in the village.'

Maryam was angry, but Sammia could not let her vent these old arguments. 'That's not true. Irini and Melodia are kind to me, and Spiro finds work. We should be grateful.'

'They give you leftovers and you should be resting, not working, not standing. We have everything we need to bring up to the cave, pots, rugs, bedding. I say we go at night, vanish. There will be no rent to pay and no one to shove us out. Amir?'

He shrugged. 'Youssef has asked around, but there's either nothing going, or they don't want us as neighbours. Maryam is right. We go until we find somewhere decent.'

'We could ask the English priest and the other residents on the island.' Sammia did not want to give up the effort to rent a proper home.

'No!' Youssef shouted. 'We do this ourselves. Tomorrow we go and see this cave and make our decision then.'

27

Della Fitzpatrick came into the kitchen with a tongue like rush matting. Two empty bottles of her favourite Durakis red wine stood by the sink. Could she have emptied them herself last night? Surely not. The scary thing was that she couldn't recall doing so. Perhaps she had had a visitor.

Now there was a full day of Pilates and a session of reflexology, but who with? She consulted the wall chart to see that Kelly Partridge wanted a session in the afternoon. Hell's bells! I must have a shower, drink a litre of water and sharpen up. Why do I keep doing this to myself?

If only she could face an evening alone, without the comfort of alcohol.

You're a right one,' she said. 'A practitioner is only good if they're nurturing themselves.' If she was drained and tense, how could she guide others? That was not nurturing, it was punishing. She had the moves, the knowledge, but no longer the enthusiasm. Classes paid the bills but nothing altered her mood.

It was always the same at this time of year. She just had to get past December and when the New Year came it was a relief: a new start, a diet, a detox. Dry January... She could just about manage a month, or almost, until Burns Night when the Scottish residents held a shindig. Somehow she must get through the morning class and face young Kelly. 'You are a fraud,' she muttered to herself, 'a bloody shambles, but you mean well.'

Kelly was early. It was her first session. 'I've heard about reflexology, that it's good for pregnancy. Do you think it'll help me conceive? I've been reading up about it online.'

Della smiled. 'It can help some couples, but we need to look at the whole picture. You understand the principle that the feet are full of nerve endings and by working on the energy pathways we can rebalance your whole body.'

'Just by tickling my toes? I don't understand,' Kelly said.

'It's not as simple as that. I need a full history of your health and can't promise anything, but we can work on your energy levels and blockages.'

Kelly was impressionable, desperate, and one unhappy young woman. Della felt a surge of pity. All that money and luxury but two failed IVFs. Did she really want a baby, or was she feeling deprived at not having one to show off?

Della felt herself tensing. This was too close for comfort but she knew she must put her client first, forget her own feelings, and give the girl a good session. All her own senses and experience must go into the task of reading Kelly from her feet upwards. The girl's bitterness and anger were almost palpable. Yet, to her surprise, Kelly relaxed and fell asleep to the New Age music of Michael Hoppé, which always helped things along. Della let her wake naturally. 'You may feel a bit woozy and tired. You went deep and that's good.'

'So what did you find?' Kelly asked, sipping a large glass of water.

'Everything feels in working order, some imbalances around your glands and bowels, but nothing serious. A few regular sessions may help you relax even more.'

'You know Gary's got this choir do. He set it up without consulting me, but I suppose I should do my bit. Why did you join?' Kelly was curious.

'Because I like singing and helping others in need. Life here is pretty privileged when you see the poor refugees with nothing but the clothes they stand up in.'

'They shouldn't come here, then.'

'It's not that simple, Kelly. We can only imagine what some of them have had to endure. Rape, imprisonment, starvation and betrayal. They want their children to have a better life. Isn't that what we all want?'

'How many children do you have?'

'Just the one, but he died.'

'Oh, I'm sorry… All I think of is holding a baby in my arms. It's just not fair.'

Della felt she must labour the point. 'Life isn't fair, especially for those who are hungry and homeless.'

'I suppose not. I've never thought of it like that. Gary says I need a tea strainer in my mouth. I speak without thinking.' They both laughed. 'Can I come next week? That was a very strange sensation. Not a bit what I was expecting, but it was nice.'

'Good. That's what we like to hear. Don't worry about the do. We'll all help for Ariadne's party. She just wants the choir to mix socially as well as in rehearsals, and it's very good of you to lend us your home.'

After Kelly had left Della sat down, drained but shocked at her blatant lie. How could she say she'd had a child when she had never allowed it to live?

28

Clive could hear Lucy's voice in his ear again: *That won't do, you look like you're dressing for a funeral, not a party.* She was chuckling at his attempt to look smart. She'd always chosen his suits, co-ordinating his clothes as if he was colour blind. He had trimmed his beard, put on the lotion that Lucy had bought him for Christmas. It smelt of sandalwood and smoke and always made him feel smart.

Bella knew he was going out for the night. She gave him a sad eye, knowing she always got a treat before he closed the door. He intended to walk up to Gary's home, but halfway there Simon and Chloë stopped to give him a lift.

Chloë was carrying an enormous bowl of fruit salad, covered with clingfilm. 'We'd better be on our best behaviour tonight. We don't want to ruin their white leather sofas,' she said.

'Chloë! Don't be mean. It's good of them to have us, and Gary's a decent chap.'

'Sorry.' She laughed.

Clive felt sad, hearing the familiar banter between a couple who knew each other's foibles. Chloë was quick to make judgements, but kind in other ways. Simon was solid as granite. Lucy had liked them both.

Clive dreaded going alone to this sort of occasion but there would be a crowd of them mingling, and he hoped he'd see Natalie out of the kitchen for once. She hadn't taken up his offer of a walk, but Lucy teased him: *Faint heart never won fair lady.*

How could she make a joke of this? No one would ever replace her. Yet there was no harm in a bit of female companionship, was there? *You only live once, so don't waste time wool-gathering,* he heard Lucy whisper in his ear. If he took up her suggestion, he might lose that voice in his head. While he was alone, she reigned supreme.

'Here we are – and what a house. It's an interesting shape. Old Arthur says it's like a bunker on the Atlantic Wall defences and that terracotta stucco is so last year.'

'Chloë!' Simon exclaimed. 'Enough.'

There were candles in jars up the steps to the portico where two stone lions were guarding the door. Inside Clive found a large drawing room humming with voices. Ariadne was checking out the piano while Hebe hovered, passing round little canapés. He could see the Reverend Dennis in a corner with old Arthur, who was wearing his crumpled linen suit and a cravat. Phil and Greg were chatting to Duke and Pippa, who was wearing an outrageous floaty garment that looked like real silk. Della was hugging her glass, but there was no sign of Natalie, so Clive found his way to the kitchen where she was helping. Mel had a large tray of village sausages. Natalie looked up and smiled. For once she was not wearing black, but a pretty floral dress and glittery sandals. Her hair was not scraped back but loosely falling on her shoulders, and she looked ten years younger.

'Can I help?' he offered. A job would help him to mingle.

'Tell them grub's up,' Mel announced, in a broad Yorkshire accent.

'Is Spiro not here?' Clive asked.

'No, we had no babysitter. It's Irini's night out.' She shrugged. 'The choir isn't going down well with her, for some reason. Greeks versus Brits, I fear.'

'That's a pity,' said Natalie. 'I do hope they come to our concert especially for St Nicholas's Day. We're hoping to have a little ceremony.'

'What sort?' Clive said.

'Wait and see.' Natalie smiled. 'Now go and call the crowd in.' She was being bossy and he liked it.

'Aye aye, Captain!' he replied, and winked at her.

'Did I see that? You and him?'

'Nonsense, we're just good friends,' Natalie replied.

The food was delicious, washed down with good wine, and after the fruit salad and chocolate cake, Ariadne got up to speak. 'On behalf of the Christmas choir, may I thank Gary and Kelly for their generous hospitality? It's been good to meet up, other than in rehearsals but we must sing something for our hosts. How about "I Saw Three Ships Come Sailing In"?'

The choir gathered in its usual shape and Hebe played a chord to set them off.

Clive thought they sounded not at all bad.

Then Mel came forward. 'I'd like to sing one of Kate Rusby's carols. Do join in. It's called "Sweet Chiming Christmas Bells".'

It was a jolly tune and soon everyone was joining in the chorus. He noticed even Gary's wife was singing. The party was going much better than he'd hoped, but he had yet to get Natalie's attention. He intended to walk her home, but he was stuck in a corner with the vicar and Simon.

'I've got an awkward situation,' said the vicar. 'Norris Thorner has made it clear that there are to be no carols at the Advent service. He says it's not in keeping with the solemn aspect of Advent. Christmas carols must only be sung on Christmas Day and afterwards.'

'But we always sing "O Come, O Come, Emmanuel" and "Joy To The World". What's the problem?' Simon asked.

'They helped fund the alterations to the vicarage garage long before my time. I think he regards it as his duty to have a say in whatever is going on.'

'Good job they're not here tonight, then. Perhaps it's more about his wife leaving the choir over that misunderstanding,' Clive said.

'Ah, yes, you've got a point. Our main concert is in the community hall and they can stay away if they choose,' said Simon.

Father Dennis hesitated. 'It's just that the season of goodwill is coming soon, so I'll try to find a compromise.'

All this fuss over carols, thought Clive, amused. 'I don't get it.'

'There's a lot of churchmanship around all this. Some believe carols are pagan in origin. They arose from medieval dances and perhaps earlier rituals, so we have to let them have their say.'

'What's wrong with a bit of singing and dancing?' Clive did not understand.

'Nothing at all,' said Father Dennis. 'But for some if it's pleasurable it may be sinful...'

They all smiled.

'Sad but true,' he continued. 'Advent used to be a period of preparation and fasting, which in earlier times meant they saved their meat for a feast day, killed a pig on St Thomas's Day and gave a meal to the poor. Winter was harsh in those times and meat was only for the rich. The singing and dancing went on until Twelfth Night. Blink, and it was Lenten fasting before Easter. This was a cycle of feast and famine for some, especially the poor.'

Ah, well, thought Clive, none of my business, except there had been a suggestion that the choir would sing at the Advent-candle-lighting service. As the party began to wind down, Clive made his way to the kitchen to see Natalie out, but she wasn't there.

'Natalie left a while back, but you might catch her up.' Chloë was loading plates into the dishwasher. Clive shot out of the door, after saying thank you to his hosts. If he jogged, he might catch up with her. He saw a figure in the dark with a flickering torch. For once the sky was clear and full of stars but it was chilly. 'Natalie!' he called, and she turned round.

'Oh, it's you... I'm on my way back now.'

'But it's quite a trek in the dark. I was going to ask you to let me walk you home,' he said.

'That's kind, but I'm fine,' she replied, not looking at him.

'Wasn't it a good party? Ariadne's idea was great and the food was delicious,' he said.

'Mel did most of it.' Natalie carried on walking.

'I thought you looked splendid tonight. It was nice to see you wearing colour.'

'What's that supposed to mean?' she snapped.

'I noticed you wear black a lot.' Clive sensed trouble.

'What if I do? It's nobody's business but my own. I'm a widow, and every widow wears black in Greece.'

'I'm sorry. Did it happen a long time ago?' he asked.

'Long enough, but you never get over these things.'

'They say time heals but I'm not sure. I think you carry your loss for the rest of your life.' Clive was trying to soften his faux-pas.

'It depends on—' Natalie broke off. 'If you don't mind I'd rather not talk about it.'

'Sorry, I seem to be getting off on the wrong foot.' Clive hesitated.

After that there was a deafening silence. When they came to Clive's villa, he suddenly blurted out, 'Would you like a coffee?'

'No, thank you, I'm tired,' Natalie said. 'I prefer to walk the rest by myself. Good night.'

Clive stood by his drive, stunned by her sharp reply. He had got it all wrong. The woman didn't want company. She had made that very clear, and he felt foolish and embarrassed for trying to pursue her. 'Now look what you've made me do, Lucy, I did try.'

Not hard enough, she whispered. *Don't be a wimp. Natalie has her reasons. Find out what they are.*

29

Natalie clattered her dishes as she angrily put them into the kitchen cupboard. Why had she been so rude to Clive Podmore? He was only trying to be friendly, if a bit too friendly. She had noticed the way he looked in her direction with those sad eyes and it made her blush. Mel hadn't missed a trick when teasing her about him. He was quite handsome for an oldie, Mel had said. 'I like his beard and he's fit for his age. You could do far worse.'

'I'm not interested in relationships of that sort. Have we got enough plates?' Natalie was desperate to change the subject. Was it obvious to the rest of the choir? Cruel to be kind was the order of the day. He was offering her friendship and a chance to meet up, not a proposal, but she'd thrown it back in his face for his own good. If he knew her history, he'd not be so keen to ask her out. *Tum-ti-tum-ti-tum*, she hummed. It was too late at night to go down that dark Memory Lane. She was tired and feeling guilty about rebuffing him.

Natalie knew how much Clive missed his wife, living alone

with his dog. She'd seen how joining the choir had brought him out of his solitary shell. He had a good strong bass voice, the sort that anchored the beat of the choir. Mel was right. For a man of nearly sixty he was in good shape and she had just knocked him back. How could she face him again?

What's wrong with you? Why can't you let this opportunity blossom whichever way? He was right that those black and grey colours did nothing for her looks, but it felt like a good disguise. Tonight she had pulled the pretty Masai dress out of her wardrobe and made an effort. Look where it had landed her! Compliments, an escort and an offer of a nightcap!

Some women of her age would have taken his hand off for such attention… and a sneaky part of her had wanted to respond.

Now Natalie lay in her cold bed, wide awake. No amount of mountain tea would make her relax. She sat up and put the light on to reach for her journal. If she wrote it all down, it might put her worries on the page and stop them racing round in her head.

She had met Rick Fletcher at a disco. The girls from the office had a night out each month when they dressed up to the nines and danced round their handbags. One by one they were picked off and Natalie found herself dancing the night away with a guy in jeans and a leather jacket, who drove her home on the back of his Honda.

He worked for his father's business. He had the darkest eyes and there was Greek somewhere in his family gene pool. Friday nights with him, and her life was changed for ever.

They became inseparable. He liked to see her dressed up, bought her earrings and other presents. Rick liked to help her choose her outfits. Looking back at the photos, she saw an overdressed doll with shoulder pads, big hair and Princess Di-style dresses with flouncy collars. But, then, it was the eighties.

Everyone liked Rick. Her parents thought him kind and generous and were happy when he put a diamond solitaire on her finger. The girls at the office in Preston were envious, now her future was secured. He didn't like her going out with them too often, and once Craig was on the way he preferred her to stay at home. They didn't entertain much, or mix with the neighbours in Glenholm Close, so with two small children, Natalie sometimes felt isolated in her own home.

Rick would phone her during the day to check where she was. They did the big shop together at the weekend. Natalie was glad of playgroup meetings and a chance to chat to other mums, but she felt as if her brain was rotting away.

There was an evening class at the local college called Entertaining: Cookery for Beginners, which appealed, but Rick wasn't keen. 'We don't entertain,' he argued. 'A waste of time.' But she replied she needed some time to do something for herself.

'You're home all day by yourself,' he said.

'That's not the same, not with Candy and Craig at my heels. I can't even go to the loo without them banging on the door. I'd like a chance to do something different for myself.'

She wore him down, but he sulked when she signed up for the course. Then, when she tried to get to the class, he was late home from work, pleading a delay because of extra paperwork.

This meant she had to get the children to her mother, pushing the pram for miles and getting a bus back, just to be in time for the class.

Natalie loved those classes, learning Cordon Bleu techniques, pastry with fancy French recipes. She shared a bench with Martin Fox, who was a teacher at the secondary school. They had a laugh when their dishes collapsed and sometimes the group went to the Red Lion for a drink afterwards, but that had to stop when Rick found out. One night she was late coming home. He lost the plot, yelling and waking the children.

'What's so wrong?' she said. 'I'm doing this for us. You like the dishes I bring home.'

In response he smashed the plate on the kitchen floor in a tantrum. 'I forbid you to go again. A wife should be here with her family.'

'Rick, it's only one night a week. Can't I do anything without your say-so?'

'You are my wife and you promised to obey.'

'Those are just words in the prayer book. Surely today men and women are equal partners in a marriage.'

'My mother never left home, except to shop and go to church.'

'I'm not your mother, Rick. This is not the 1950s. Times have changed.' It was then she saw the rage in his eyes. 'I'm sorry to be late, but I do enjoy the classes.'

'Who is this Martin you work with?'

'Just a teacher from St Mary's. He's a very good cook.'

'Is he married?'

'He's a bachelor and lives in Haig Street.'

'So you're pally with him. Does he buy you a drink?'

'Oh, Rick, please, I'm tired. I just go to improve my cooking. It relaxes me. Don't begrudge me a night out. I'm stuck in all day. Let's go to bed.'

That night he was rough with her, as if he was taking out his frustrations on her body. After that there was little finesse in their lovemaking. He did let slip, though, that Fletcher's Automotive Accessories was struggling. The competition was undercutting their prices. His father was considering retiring, leaving Rick to salvage what was left of the business or join another firm. No wonder he was on edge.

Natalie found the classes a lifeline and Martin a shoulder to cry on. He was calm and a good listener. There was never anything sexual between them, which she found puzzling at first. He was like a big brother and she loved the after-class drinks, until one night she found Rick in the bar, staring at the group in fury.

'Come and join us,' she called, but he refused to budge. His mother must be babysitting. Surely he hadn't left the children alone. Natalie began to panic. Surely not! She shot to her feet. 'I'm coming now. Who's got the children?' she asked.

'They are fast asleep in their beds.'

'You left them alone?'

'If my wife goes gallivanting, why shouldn't I?'

'Rick, how could you? What's got into you?'

'I wanted to see this boyfriend of yours,' he replied.

'He's not my boyfriend.'

'You looked very pally to me.'

'Surely I can have friends of my own. We're not joined at the hip. How do you think up all this rubbish?' Suddenly

Rick felt like a stranger to her. This was not the man she'd married but a jealous lover who had left his children alone at night.

After that, how could she go to the class? It was then that Natalie felt trapped while Rick took every chance to check up on her. There was no one with whom she could share her misgivings. Was he having a breakdown? Where had the happy-go-lucky guy in blue jeans gone? She put it all down to stresses at work.

'Let's have a good holiday this year,' she suggested. 'We deserve it. Two weeks in the sun.'

For once he jumped at her idea, booking them an expensive package to Crete. Away from home, Rick relaxed back into the man she loved. Everything about the holiday was perfect, the food, the villa, the sunshine, far away from the grime of their home town. But holidays end, and another term beckoned for her evening class. Natalie signed up, without telling Rick, and arranged for her mother to babysit. If Rick was going to play tricks again, she was ready for them.

It was close to December and the end of term, and the gang of would-be cooks decided to hold a Christmas party at the college. Their lecturer decided who would cook what for the celebratory meal and they decided to invite friends or family to sample their delights. Natalie was proud of her decorated fruitcake, putting the finishing touches to it at home. 'You will come, Rick, won't you, to see what we've cooked for you all?'

'I don't want to spoil the party. You two lovebirds will want to be on your own.'

'Oh, not that again! How many times have I told you? Martin's just one of the gang. Stop making things up. You're getting paranoid! Loosen up – come and meet everyone for yourself.'

'All I can see is that on Thursday nights you dress up to the nines, let your hair down, put on make-up and it's all for him!'

'Rubbish! It's the only time I get to take off my pinny and change out of dirty jeans after gardening. When I go to class, I'm Natalie, not mother, laundry maid, gardener, nanny, little more than a duster. I don't think it's a lot to ask, is it?'

'You prefer them to home and family.'

'When have I ever neglected you all?'

'You're not the woman I married,' Rick said.

'Nor you the man. You've changed. What makes you think I'm having an affair?'

'Because I see no love for me in your eyes. You close your eyes when we make love. You've gone cold, saving your heart for this Martin.'

Natalie carried on dressing. She couldn't take any more of his twisted arguments. 'I'm not going to listen to this any more. I'm going out now and when I get back, we must sort this out once and for all.'

The party was fun. Natalie got them singing. Martin insisted on driving her home, because snow was falling. When she got through the front door, all was quiet in the darkness, but Rick was nowhere to be seen. She raced upstairs to check on Candy and Craig who were dead to the world.' Rick!' she shouted. He might be in the garden, having a smoke. It was then she smelt fumes coming from under the garage door. There was no light on in there.

'Rick!' She opened the side door to a waft of exhaust fumes and saw the pipe. The rest was a blur. Rick was in the car and it was locked. She smashed the window to release the lock, but she knew, in that moment, it was too late. What happened next was fumbling for the phone, dialling, rushing to a neighbour, knocking them up, carrying the children into someone's car, away from the house. It was a policewoman who handed over the note on Rick's lap. The writing was clear, then grew fainter, until there was only a dribbled line.

I know you're going to leave me for that guy. I can't live with the thought of you loving another man. I thought we would be together till the end of time. I hope you know what you have done to me. Then his script faded away.

Natalie sank into oblivion after the doctor gave her something to help her sleep. It was two weeks before Christmas. Presents were hidden in the wardrobe, and there were cakes, mince pies ready to share. Her mother took over the children, who were silent and confused. Natalie curled up in a ball, knowing she had killed her husband. It was all her fault. Why had she never told him that Martin was gay? His partner, Will, had joined the party that evening. They lived together in Haig Street.

'If I'd told him, he'd still be alive today,' she confessed to the local priest, Father Pierce. 'It was my only bit of power. I was angry at how he controlled every aspect of my life. I wanted to make him jealous. How will I live with such guilt?'

'Rick was depressed about his work and anxious to keep up your standard of living. He wanted to control everything around him. You mustn't blame yourself.'

Natalie couldn't agree. 'I left out the one thing that would have made things right between us. I withheld it for my own satisfaction. I'm so ashamed.'

'Ah, the sins of omission, the if-onlys that haunt all of us for the rest of our lives and blight any chance of future happiness. Don't let this tragedy colour your life. It's a closed door now and staring at it won't change a thing. You run the risk of missing other doors that will open across the hall.'

Natalie didn't want to hear his compassion. It was too soon for any forgiveness.

The coroner's inquest made an issue of the letter's contents. She denied everything, not wanting Martin's name in the press, but the muckrakers made much of the news. Martin resigned and moved away. Natalie was left to sort out the mess and bring up the children as best she could. When they grew up and moved away, she fled to the sanctuary of the Greek island where no one would ever know the truth of her betrayal. Clive could be no part of her future, kind as he was. Her punishment must be to stay alone.

30

On Sunday morning Ariadne sat in their little Anglican church, Agios Pavlos, feeling peeved that the Thorners did not want the choir to sing. When it came to taking communion, she sat back, refusing to budge. How can I when I'm not at peace with my neighbour? It would be hypocritical to kneel beside them, the very couple who were thwarting her at every turn. They were lucky to have this little chapel made from a stone-built garage and an extension at the back with a stained-glass east window depicting the dove of peace at its centre. Peace. She sighed. If only…

The Advent service was always special, she recalled, thinking of the boarding-school girls parading with candles in paper cones, singing 'O Come, O Come, Emmanuel', their sweet voices echoing in the lofty school chapel. It heralded end-of-term ceremonies, reports to be written, the Christmas party with country dancing, and marked her growing closeness to Hebe Wilson.

Hebe was not feeling well and hadn't got up. Attendance

was thin and she guessed some of the choir had stayed away to make a point but that was yet another mean thought. Why had the Thorners such a narrow idea of worship? Why couldn't they see another point of view?

The world was full of joyless souls who preached, 'Only we have the truth,' or, worse, killed in the name of their faith. The sort who thought the earth was flat or created in only six days, who refused blood transfusions for dying children on some interpretation of Biblical texts. Don't go there, woman, it will only raise your blood pressure. She sighed.

Advent was the coming of light in the darkest part of the year. The coming of a child into the world who would preach love and peace to all people. *Comfort ye, comfort ye, my people*. She loved *Messiah*. Perhaps one day they would be able to sing extracts, perhaps not. Theirs was just a little Christmas choir, but it had brought folk together, and she smiled at the success of the party at Gary's monstrous villa. It was so ostentatious and out of keeping, yet had provided space for them to meet. Why am I so critical of others? Gary and Kelly were kindness itself when Hebe had been lost.

Sitting in the chapel brought home to Ariadne that she was no better than the rest, with her own prejudices. Growing up knowing you were out of sync with most women was not easy. Having to conceal your pashes on other girls and teachers, trying not to disappoint a mother who was planning your future wedding to Harry Fellowes, a dear friend from childhood, being unable to explain how you felt to her about regular marriage, and hiding the fact that Hebe was her real soulmate. Only after her mother's death had she been able to tell her father the truth.

Thank goodness times were more tolerant. No more talk of being an invert or queer or a pariah in society. The sacrifice of others had opened the door to recognition that some are born different and love comes in many forms. Was it written in the blood or genes? Whatever, no matter. It is what it is.

At last the Church of England was recognising that there were clergy of many hues, some in civil partnerships, others staying celibate. She had never openly stated her true relationship with Hebe. Simon and Chloë suspected perhaps, but had said nothing. For some it was still 'the love that dared not say its name'.

Elodie had provided Hebe and her with a safe haven. The dear warm soul was a woman of the world who held no prejudices. Ariadne missed their talks. A mill worker's daughter had grown into an international star, generous to a fault, imperious at times if someone stepped out of line. Elodie could sniff out a fake at fifty paces: would-be writers who wanted her to read their manuscripts and give them ideas for their novels, hangers-on who wanted to feed off her fame. Tough as old boots, Elodie ditched them with a stare. On the other hand, she was such an encourager. 'Ariadne, don't let what others think get you down. You are who you are. Live it and love it. Don't be afraid to come out, as they say now, when the time is right.'

Yet she was afraid, even in these laissez-faire times. There were the Thorners of this world, who would condemn her and Hebe as unchristian, unnatural and beyond the pale. As she stared up at the stained-glass window, with the dove shining through the sunlight and the wall hanging of the nativity scene, all donated by Elodie's estate, she thought of Mary watching her strange boy growing up, moving away, gathering crowds and enemies, and of his terrible end. Courage comes in many forms. Watching and waiting to lose your son must have been hard: who was she to grumble at her lot?

St Nicholas's Day was coming up in a week's time. Peter and Alison at the retreat were making little boats to be launched into the sea and the choir would sing in public for the first time under the stars. On the darkest days of the year there would be candles to cheer, wishes to write down and carols to sing together. Ariadne's prayer book fell open at Psalm 133: *Behold how good and how pleasant it is for brethren to dwell together in unity.*

In her wandering thoughts she had lost her place. If only everyone could sing from the same hymn sheet.

31

Sammia watched the rain cascading down the hillside from the shelter of the cave entrance. Youssef joined her. 'No work today in this downpour. This is not the life I wanted for you. It makes me ashamed. Perhaps would have been better not to have come here.' He rested his head on her shoulder.

'The rain will pass and we'll find a proper home,' she replied, touching his hand to reassure him. 'You've worked wonders here to make us comfortable and dry. Look around. We have a firepit and griddle, plastic sheeting on the floor and in the entrance. The rugs are dry. You made a table from wooden boxes, and benches to sit on. We have a tub for Karim to have his baths and plenty of dry wood. It's not so bad.' She was trying to lift their spirits.

'Huh!' snapped Maryam. 'It's not so good, but it will have to do.' She sulked in the corner.

Amir was worried about his wife. 'She won't go out.'

Sammia had noticed that her sister-in-law refused to leave the cave, except to do chores or play with her little son. They didn't want to reveal where they were living and it was hard to wash – they took turns to strip-wash behind a makeshift curtain. She feared that everything smelt of damp or smoke, but there was a launderette in Santaniki town that they could use when desperate. Sammia was warm in the taverna and was grateful now to bring back leftovers to heat over the fire. Youssef bundled washing on the back of his scooter and Sammia dealt with it during her breaks at work.

They had pooled all their resources to equip their dwelling. They had a curtain on a pole to divide them at night. Karim slept in his buggy. It was not ideal but they had warm blankets and big cushions. Supplies were kept in tins and a dustbin to keep them dry and safe from any insects. They had a container of fresh stream water that they boiled. Everything had been smuggled to the cave under cover of darkness. They had a lantern, an oil lamp and candles.

Word must have got round now that Aristotle had returned to the farm with his family but no one mentioned it at the taverna, and Sammia pretended they had found rooms further out of the town.

There was not much to be proud of in all this, except the dignity implicit in being beholden to no one. The one worry she had at night was that her baby would be born in a cave. The Christians took pride in the humble birth of their Christ, but stable scenes on the icons were one thing. The reality was another.

How could they be reduced to this? She could see the shame on her husband's face as he returned each night, weary. He had not been born a labourer, and none of them had been used to slumming it until they had fled Syria. Was this the will of

Allah, a time of trial to be endured, for the good of their souls? Sammia prayed that the Compassionate One would find them a way forward.

32

Ariadne peered up at the chapel on the hill, wondering if Hebe could make the trek up from the village over the wooden bridge. The water ran off the hillside in a channel, then flowed out to Mistrali beach and into the sea.

Recent rain had filled the often dried-out riverbed into a steady stream. Then there was a steep path up to the little chapel of St Nicholas. It was 6 December, his festival day, and troops of Nikoses and Nicolettas would come to bless his icon and wish each other *chronia polla*, or many years. There would be offerings, candles lit, and Father Michaelis would be saying prayers. As it was on a weekday the lighted procession would come later, but the little chapel flickered with hundreds of tiny Christmas lights.

Ariadne wanted the choir to sing something nautical, since St Nicholas was the patron of seafarers and ladies of the night who plied their trade in the back-streets close to harbours and ports all over the world.

Peter, from the retreat, brought the little paper boats for

the children and anyone else who wanted to light a candle and pop in their own wishes.

Hebe would be better off staying on the bridge and enjoying the flotilla of little boats bobbing on the stream into the sea. Ariadne did not want her out of sight. There were moments when she seemed so lost, complaining of a headache. It was time to see Dr Makaris again, to have her checked over thoroughly, and if that meant a trip to Heraklion Hospital on Crete, then so be it. Something wasn't right. Perhaps she should pop her own wish for Hebe's health into one of the little boats.

The turnout of residents at dusk was decent enough and this time they didn't sing a carol, but that famous of all sea hymns:

Eternal Father, strong to save,
Whose arm has stayed the restless wave…

Who could complain about that? she thought, as the choir gathered together, singing in harmony. The sound wafted over the gathered crowds and she hoped it would carry down into the village.

Father Michaelis was quite happy to let them perform outside the church, where stars twinkled above them. There were benches by the chapel for the weary to sit awhile and catch their breath. The chapel twinkled in the darkness, set high to catch the last of the sunset, but tonight it was windy and cool. Ariadne was glad of her Puffa anorak, excited by their first public performance. She sensed it had gone well.

Chloë climbed the path with Simon and Gary, hugging her secret to herself. Tomorrow she would take a flight to Athens, then fly on to London to surprise her daughter. She would tell Simon later, not wanting him to throw cold water over her plan. Alexa was her child and something was wrong: she could feel it in her bones. Her daughter needed her, whether she knew it or not. She might be grown-up, but in Chloë's heart she was still her baby girl.

Coming to visit the chapel felt like a pilgrimage. She would light a candle and pray that her journey would be blessed and fruitful. She had even written a little wish to slip into a boat. To her surprise, even the Thorners made an appearance, standing on the bridge, not prepared to join in except for the hymn.

Fairy lights illuminated the path up the steep slope, but Simon had insisted that Arthur, the colonel, stayed on the bridge with Hebe and some of the older villagers. Peter and Alison gathered the children, ready to set sail. It made a great photo opportunity so Chloë fished out her iPhone to capture the moment.

Clive Podmore read out a brief history of the Bishop of Myra, who threw gold in at a poor man's window to enable his daughters to be married, not sold into prostitution. His mission angered the pagan leaders and he was arrested and tortured for his faith. He died in 342, but his life and generosity transformed him from bishop to St Nicholas, to Santa Claus, to Father Christmas in northern Europe. Clive knew that soon it would be St Lucy's Day. It would remind him of happier seasons, when his wife was alive at his side.

The wind whipped up a chill and it was a relief to sing the hymn. Then everyone made their way down to the bridge at the side of the stream, where Peter and Duke had created a sailing yacht out of scraps of wood and cloth lit with tea lights. It was a moving little ceremony, with people placing their wishes in flimsy paper vessels and letting them go, perhaps in memory of lost ones. Wishes must be unspoken, but Clive heard Peter's son telling old Arthur, 'I want more Lego for Christmas.'

What wishes went into those little vessels? They all followed them down to the water's edge and the choir sang their second piece, 'I Saw Three Ships Come Sailing In'. Then the boats were off down the stream, some collapsing, some sailing on upright, quite a sight, but now a strident voice rang out: 'Who is going to collect all these metal tea lights when they end up on the shore as litter? It's very thoughtless to pollute the stream with paper and metal,' said Norris Thorner.

'Don't worry, Norris,' said the vicar. 'We'll fill a sack with anything we find. I think our choir is responsible enough to do that. It was a lovely idea of Peter and Alison to help the children to see that light can only shine like this in darkness.'

Chloë could hear the tension in his voice, as he soothed ruffled feathers. Why did Thorner have to raise objections to a simple ceremony and spoil the atmosphere?

'Wine and cake at the vicarage,' the vicar's wife announced. 'Before all of us freeze to death. I fear the wind is bringing rain on its edge. Hurry, before the deluge hits us.'

Chloë knew the little lights would soon be blown out, the paper would sink and drown the wishes in seawater, but it was the gesture that mattered. It would be a while before sun and warmth returned to the island. Tomorrow she would be flying back to yet more cold and rain, but it would be worthwhile to see the surprise on Alexa's face. Tomorrow she would find out the truth about her daughter's troubled life and she couldn't wait.

Gary Partridge paused, looking out into the darkness. What the hell am I doing here, singing hymns, floating boats, scribbling a wish on a bit of paper? I must be mad leaving Kelly sulking. We should be sailing on a cruise, not doing such a silly thing. But Gary's heartfelt wish was for his childhood sweetheart to conceive. What had that vicar said as they put the wishes into the little boats tonight? 'Ask, believe and receive.'

Could he really ask for a child to be born, when he carried such guilt in his heart? Their lives were built on sand, not rock. Sooner or later he must confess his secret. Perhaps only then could his wish come true.

33

Overnight the wind grew into a storm, battering the olive trees, rattling doors and tiles, whipping up the waves into great rollers. For two days the rain lashed onto the houses, pouring into the roads, and the stream turned into a torrent, funnelling down through the gullies until they overflowed and the main street became a rushing flood. Parked cars rose and floated down to crash into the barriers. It was not safe to leave the house. The power soon cut out so the citizens of St Nick's were lighting candles and oil lamps, piling up dried olive wood to fuel stoves and fires.

Chloë looked out of the window in despair. How could she make the ferry in time to catch her flight to Athens?

Simon stood behind her, his face full of concern. 'You're not thinking of going out in this?'

'I have to get Athens. I told you, I'm booked on the evening flight to London.'

'Just look at it! We have no power. No ferry will sail in this. Be sensible, darling. It was a nice idea, but no one in their senses will go anywhere until the storm subsides. Remember two years ago, when poor Giorgos's brother got swept away by floodwater and drowned, trying to rescue his car.'

'It's not fair!' she cried in frustration. 'Why now? It was dry until yesterday. I don't understand.'

'How long have we lived here? This is the season when it can rain as much as it does in Wales in just a few weeks,' he said, putting his arm round her. But she shook it off. 'The winds from this direction are unpredictable. It's winter and even our jeep won't tackle the track. I'll make a coffee while you unpack. You're going nowhere in this deluge. Why not wait until the power comes back on, phone Alexa and invite her for Christmas? Say you missed your London get-together and would love to see her. Keep it light and breezy. If she makes her excuses, then accept that she's a big girl now. Let her do the running.'

'But I have to know what's going on,' she argued.

'Do you? Why? She's her own person, not a child. You can't force her. That's the quickest way to lose her.'

'It's all right for you to talk. She's not your child!' That was unkind, but Chloë was in no mood to be appeased.

'How can you say that after all these years? I love her as my own. Think about it. Send an email. We don't own our children. They have their own lives to live.'

Chloë knew he was right, but she wasn't going to give him the satisfaction of admitting it. 'Sometimes you can be very smug,' she snapped. 'I'll change my flight, but I have to go.'

'If you must... but don't forget we have the carol service to rehearse.'

'They'll have to manage without me. Alexa is far more important than Ariadne's whimsical choir.'

'But she's put so much into it – we mustn't let her down now.'

'My daughter comes first. I have to see her.'

Simon sighed. 'Suit yourself. Go if you must, but I think you're making a big mistake.'

Chloë sniffed and took herself off in a huff, staring down at her overnight case in despair. When would the wretched storm blow itself out? When would the power come back? Why were the elements against her?

The storm raged on and on. The mayor of St Nick's declared a state of emergency, as the floodwaters rose. The power did not come back over three more days. All travel plans were cancelled. Chloë's suitcase was unpacked. She was going nowhere.

34

Mel was mopping up the flooded floor of the taverna. Water had rampaged through the kitchen and dining room. It was full of rubbish and mud, and Irini was having a fit of rage at the gods for ruining her business. Spiro was away again, stranded at the ferry port by the storm. It was just the two of them against the damage. Irini was crying in frustration. 'Look at this mess. How can we cook after this?'

'It's not touched the cooker , the water will drain off and we can mop out. There's still the old bread oven. We can use that while the power's out. Besides, no one will be wanting to leave their house. It'll pass, you'll see, just a flash in the pan.' Not strictly true, of course. This was a storm and a half.

'I don't understand. What flashes in the pan?'

'Just saying, Yiayia.'

'I'm not your *yiayia*.'

Mel bit her tongue in frustration. Here she was trying to help and Irini was criticising her effort. If only Spiro was here, but as usual he was finding work on Crete. She missed him. The school was closed and the boys had no TV, only board games and Lego to play with. Now she could hear them squabbling. Any minute now one would appear, crying, telling tales on the other. How could she be in two places at once? Two days of this storm and no sign of it lifting. She dared not let the boys outside. It was time to find something for them to do.

Mel found paper and drew the shape of an angel with wings. They had colouring pens and she showed them how to copy the shape, cut it out and colour it in. 'We can make an angel tree,' she said.

'Where do the angels live?' Stefan asked.

'In our hearts, or anywhere people are kind, but they like to come out at Christmas time to brighten things.'

'Have you seen an angel, Mama?'

'I don't think so but they can come in disguise, can't they, Yiayia?' Mel gave Irini a look that said, Please don't let me down.

Irini lifted her head from her cleaning. 'Ah, yes, angels are all around us but sometimes we miss them. The holy saints see them and give them errands, like putting presents in little boys' stockings if they are good. They are God's messengers. One of them told Maria she was going to have a baby boy, who is our Christos.'

'That's right.' Mel smiled. 'They are all around us, so you make as many as you like. Colour them in neatly and I'll help you cut them out.'

That would keep them quiet for a bit, but there was so much to do. She sang the chorus from 'Sweet Chiming Christmas Bells' to cheer herself up and then a Greek *kalanda*, learnt from YouTube to please Irini.

'You have a good voice, Melodia. Not a Greek voice, like Melina Mercouri, of course, but a pleasant sound.'

Praise indeed from her mother-in-law. She smiled.

'Do you believe in angels, Melodia?'

'I'm not sure, but we could do with a few of them to help us clean up.'

'Have faith. They will come, if we pray hard enough.' Irini crossed herself fervently and looked to the grey sky for an answer.

Natalie, Della and even Sammia turned up to help with the mopping out. Not quite the angelic hordes Irini was expecting, but mere humans who had their uses, even if one perfumed the air with the scent of an ouzeria. Della had hit the bottle again. Who could blame her after this depressing storm? If it didn't stop soon, they would need Noah's Ark to rescue them.

35

Ariadne settled down to write their Christmas cards, bought online from their favourite charity Freedom from Torture. It was such a worthy cause, supporting dispossessed and traumatised refugees.

The shutters closed off the worst of the rain. It was as if the little villa wrapped itself around them to protect them from the ravages. Lamplight was so soothing and the olive wood logs gave off the scent of summertime. There would be a deadline to reach for posting and now there was nothing to do but write to all those far-off friends, waiting to receive jolly cards that decorated the mantelpiece and dangled from string across the beams.

Hebe was happy signing cards, but Ariadne noticed her signature was wobbly and sloped on the page. She said nothing, seeing that she was engrossed in her task. They sipped ginger wine and nibbled the last of the shortbread biscuits that Natalie had brought to choir practice. The programme of carols and readings was almost complete. The hall was booked. Della and Natalie were in charge of making a seasonal mulled wine, mince pies and ginger biscuits for their guests.

There could be no rehearsal this week and she prayed the community hall was not awash with floodwater. Thank goodness it was set up high from the *plateia*, next to the marble war memorial, with the names of the fallen from the Cretan Wars of Independence, the First and Second World Wars and those of local Resistance members who had been executed; their names adorned many of the streets in the village. They asked the mayor, his councillors, Father Michalis and his family to the concert, and pushed leaflets through every door, inviting the Greek citizens to join them.

This venture was all Ariadne's doing, so the concert must go well, as a gesture of friendship to all on St Nick's. She felt guilty that so many of her compatriots lived in a bubble. It was important for them to know they were guests here, not imposing their Britishness on a culture centuries older than their own. People like the Thorners did not see it in that way. They saw their right to live here as a given, their right to practise their faith and customs as if the locals did not exist. That caused resentment in the likes of Irini Papadakis, putting Mel at times between a rock and a hard place.

Soon there was a pile of envelopes waiting for stamps but they could wait until the storm abated. How would her olive garden survive the battering wind? All her pots would be knocked over, but at least they were sheltered under a stone wall. In a strange way she was comforted by the rattle of doors and shutters, by the flickering firelight, the kettle on the Calor gas hob. It reminded her of winter storms in Yorkshire after the war, of being huddled by firelight while Papa read to them from *Pickwick Papers*. All things pass, and so would this. She smiled. It could have been worse: an earthquake or an avalanche. They had light, food enough and warm beds. They were thrice blessed.

36

Clive woke on St Lucy's Day remembering their wedding all those years ago, but there was no time to be morbid. There were trestle tables to be raised for the Christmas charity bazaar in the marketplace and he had promised to give Simon a hand. Since the storm had abated, everyone was clearing up the mess in the streets, seeing to their flooded buildings and, as if to compensate, the day dawned like a summer morning with blue skies and warmth that meant the stalls could be set out in the *plateia*. It would be like a Christmas market, with decorated stalls and the smell of glühwein in the air.

The vicar was going to dress up as St Nicholas for the children, in a little tent, with Alison's children as elves. Artists from the surrounding villages were bringing their crafts to sell. Proceeds from renting out stalls would help to raise funds for their refugee appeal.

There were so many creative residents across the island – wood turners, sculptors, artists, jewellery, while local people made cosmetics and salves from mountain herbs and honey.

The few winter visitors who had survived the storm flocked around the square looking for Christmas presents and souvenirs. It was always a lively day and it helped Clive to forget when Lucy once had a stall selling framed pictures made from sand and shells. She had created seahorses, fish and landscapes from the things she scavenged along the shore. She'd also sold frames covered with tiny shells, which were very popular. Clive's pathetic artistic attempts were not fit to sell, no matter what his art teacher said.

Chloë was preparing the photography stall, selling cards and framed landscapes, while Hebe drifted round, talking to friends. Taverna Irini was open for business, selling souvlaki on a grill. There was a bustle of chair stacking for the local band concert, cars arriving with boots full of crafts. *I hope you're watching, Lucy. It was your idea to set up this event all those years ago. Happy anniversary.* Then he saw Natalie struggling with a tray of bakes and went to help. He had made no gestures in her direction since the night of the party. He was embarrassed that he had misread her interest, but that wouldn't stop him being neighbourly.

'Thanks.' She smiled. 'I don't want to drop anything. The festive baklavas are straight from the oven.' The delicious aroma was overwhelming.

'I'll have to buy one of your pasties before they're snapped up,' he said.

'I'll save you one,' she said. 'Isn't it looking festive? Did you put all this together?'

'Only with Simon, Phil and Greg's help. Those two always come down and give us a hand,' he added. It seemed natural to scatter the praise around.

'Could you give Della a hand with the glühwein?' she whispered. 'Otherwise most of it will find its way down her throat and not into the cups… Sorry, I know that sounds mean.'

Clive chuckled, nodding. 'Don't worry, I'll keep her sober. She's so generous. When Lucy was ill, she came to do her feet and sat with her to give me a break. You don't forget those kindnesses, do you?'

They stood together, staring out over the market. 'Of course, it's St Lucy's Day,' she said. 'It must be hard.'

'You get used to it,' he replied, not looking at her. 'You must know how it feels.'

'My marriage was not like yours. It got complicated towards the end.' She gave him a sideways glance. 'I'm afraid it left a bad legacy.'

'We're all left with feelings hard to explain to others, regrets, missed opportunities.' Clive didn't want to pry. It was good she was sharing this with him.

'You made Lucy happy… Rick and I…' She paused. 'For us it was different… Oh, look, there's Father Christmas!'

Clive made his way to Della's tent. There was a vat of decent village wine, scented with cloves and cinnamon, oranges floating on the top, a pile of plastic cups and a cashbox.

'God! How I hate these Christmas jollies,' Della muttered. 'Christmas in Dingley Dell it is not. Why are we pretending we're still in Yorkshire?'

'Because it reminds us of home and church bazaars.'

'I have no desire to remember my home in Hunslet, thank you very much. Our Christmases were a farce: the Sunday-school party, flicking jelly on the spoon with paper hats and crackers, Mum and Dad fighting. It was a bleak few days for us kids, and our only presents came from the Sally Army. They meant well, but there was never a toy I really wanted, a Cindy or a toy sewing-machine or a trip to the pantomime at the Grand. God, I sound like a miserable git. Sorry.' Clive could see her cheeks reddening. 'I need a drink…'

'I'll get you a coffee, then,' Clive offered.

'Thanks. It's just this season. It's not a good one for me, but we have to do our bit, or Ariadne will be cracking the whip. I wish I had her energy and she's years older than me. Hebe's not looking so good, though. She seems to have shrunk.'

Clive hadn't noticed anything about Hebe, except that she dithered a lot more than before. Still, they were all getting on a bit. He made his way to Irini's bar, where Mel was turning over the chicken souvlaki sticks. She shouted to her mother-in-law, 'Greek coffee,' then asked Clive, '*Skieto, medrio* or *glyka*?'

'Not sure. It's for Della.'

'Definitely strong, then.' Mel winked. 'Or she'll be capurtled by lunchtime, poor sod. She's such a good Pilates teacher. I don't know why she drinks so much.'

'Perhaps she's lonely,' Clive offered, knowing how the whisky bottle tempted him on a bad day.

'She's never out of the bar and there's plenty of Greek men who give her the eye. She ignores them. You don't fancy her, do you? She needs sorting out.'

Clive was shocked. 'Not my type.' He laughed.

'I know who is, though.' Mel winked.

'Cheeky beggar!'

'That's a Sheffield lass for you. Tells it how it is.'

Clive scuttled back to Della with the coffee, smiling. Whatever did Mel mean?

Natalie's Festive Baklavas

For the syrup
500g sugar
2 tablespoons lemon juice
2 tablespoons orange blossom water

For the baklava
200g pistachio nuts, plus 50g extra, finely chopped
175g hazelnuts
1 teaspoon mixed spice
500g filo pastry
375g unsalted butter, melted

You will need a large roasting tin, oiled and lined with baking parchment overlapping the sides.

First make the syrup. Put the sugar into a pan with the lemon juice and stir over a medium heat, slowly bringing it to the boil. Boil for about 2 minutes, then take off the heat. Stir in the orange blossom water, then transfer it to a jug and leave it to cool in the fridge.

Preheat the oven to 190°C. Blitz the 200g pistachios and hazelnuts in a blender. Mix in the spice.

Now layer up the baklava. Take a sheet of filo pastry, lay it in the prepared tin and brush it with melted butter. Continue with the filo, brushing each sheet with the melted butter, until you have used half of the packet (about 7 sheets). Scatter over the spiced nut mixture and press it down so that the pastry and nuts are compacted together. Brush the top with melted butter. Now place a sheet of the remaining filo on top and brush with melted butter. Continue until you have used all of the pastry. Press down firmly, then brush the top with melted butter.

Cut the baklava into diamond shapes before you bake it or it will crumble.

Bake for 45 minutes, turning up the heat to 240°C for the final 15 minutes.

Take the tin out of the oven and pour over the cold syrup. Let it cool, then turn out the baklava and sprinkle with the finely chopped pistachios.

It will keep in a tin for up to 4 days, if you can resist...

37

Della knew why they'd sent Clive to share the mulled-wine tent. Everyone knew she was a lush, but no one spoke out of turn to her. For that she was grateful. Many of the residents were middle class, polite, but she knew several ate and drank too much. She'd watched them fatten up over the years, but Christmas was the worst season.

It was a drag to pretend she was enjoying all of this, but it was for a good cause. That was what kept her in the choir and the book club, teaching Pilates and doing foot massage. Knowing she ought to keep up her training didn't help. It meant going over to Crete. Perhaps when spring came...

Standing in the market square was hard on her feet – she was out of condition – but then a record on the tannoy pulled her down into a black hole of despair. Someone had a load of British and American slushy Christmas songs and up came Johnny Mathis singing 'When A Child Is Born'. His languid tones rang out across the square and Della clutched her stomach. Not that... not those words. She wanted to rush away from those memories, but she must stay at her post. It brought back all those years in the eighties. Every detail of those days rushed back to her.

It was a summer of festivals, a summer of love, and she was living in a psychedelic caravan with Luke, a boy she'd picked up at the Who gig. He was heavily into the scene, cannabis, anything that took him to where the world was a blur of hope and oblivion. They were a good crowd to be with. She was working in a candle shop, selling beads and ethnic goods, hippie cottons and cheesecloth shirts, surrounded by incense. Della had left home, school and all the restraints of Yorkshire to live in this commune of sorts. It was out in the country close to Hardcastle Crags near Hebden Bridge. They were not gypsies or travellers, just dropouts from the nine-to-five, leaving behind restrictive conventions.

Luke was a fraud, a schoolboy from a landowning family in the Yorkshire Dales. He wore silk shirts from hippie market stalls and velour jeans, and smelt of incense and weed. She thought it was love, adoring his body. He liked to swim naked in any lake or river. Wild swimming was what they called it now. He lay in the sun unashamed. In his company she lost all her Catholic hang-ups about sex and sin.

One day a young man arrived in a suit. He was Luke's elder brother, Ivo, demanding Luke return for his parents' silver wedding anniversary celebration. 'Put on this dinner suit,' he ordered. 'I don't want you looking like a tart in front of them. Mummy will be so pleased to see you. Don't let her down this time. She thinks you're working in London.'

'I'm not going without Della.' Luke clutched her hand in defiance.

'Then get her something decent to wear.' Ivo looked her up and down with a sneer.

'I can dress myself perfectly well, thank you,' she replied.

Rachel in the shop kitted her out in a long velvet smock with batwing sleeves and put her long hair up in a braid, dotted with fake pearls. She wasn't going to let him down and was curious to see just where he came from.

'Smile and say nothing,' Luke said. 'Tell them you work in a boutique. You look gorgeous.'

Ivo came for them in a large estate car. He looked them up and down.' You'll do, but no hash in the house or my car.' He was such a supercilious snob, so different from Luke.

The grandeur of their home was a shock – it belonged to another world she'd hardly known existed: it was almost the size of the house in *Brideshead* on the telly, with a huge lake and a fountain. There was a field full of expensive cars and women in evening gowns, studded with real pearls and jewellery she'd only ever seen in magazine adverts. 'I can't go in there,' Della whispered. 'It's not for the likes of me.'

'Yes, you will. You're my girl.' Luke hugged her. She knew then that they could carry it off, but her hands shook as she and Luke made their entrance into the marble hall, which was lined with busts and gargantuan flower arrangements. It smelt like a florist's shop.

'Darling Lucas, how wonderful to see you at long last.' Hermione Fuller-White clutched him to her ample bosom. 'And who is your little friend?'

'This is Della.'

'Cordelia, actually.' She added her full baptismal name. It sounded posher. They were whisked away by Ivo, who looked at her as if she were shit on his shoe.

'Don't think you can have a future with my brother,' he said, taking her to one side. 'Lucas will come back into the fold in due course.'

Della knew Luke couldn't stand his old life, with its snobbery and rigid standards, so she smiled sweetly. 'Fuck off, wanker!' The look on his face said everything.

Their life together continued in bliss, but winter was coming and they found the caravan leaking and damp. Luke still took his daily swim, but one afternoon he didn't return. When it got dark, Della grew afraid and persuaded the rest of the camp to go looking for him. Later the following morning, a gamekeeper found him floating at the edge of the river. Her lovely boy had drowned.

His family came to take him home. The anguish on his mother's face never left Della. 'What lies, all lies!' she cried, seeing the state of their caravan. 'How could he do this to his family, living in this den of drugs? You should be ashamed of yourself, young lady, leading him into a life of debauchery,' she snapped at Della.

Ivo stood back smugly. 'We want nothing more to do with you, or your lot.'

It was a smart country funeral, but none of the commune were invited. Della went anyway. She stood by Luke's grave, defiant to the last, but they ignored her, leaving her to throw a bunch of rosemary onto the coffin in remembrance of the good times they had shared. By then she had her own secret. She was nearly three months pregnant and desperate. She had no idea how she was to live with the only part of Luke that was left.

Della's parents were horrified and didn't want to know. The caravan, without Luke, held no charm. Her biggest mistake was writing to his parents to tell them she was expecting their grandchild. By return she received a solicitor's letter informing her that the Fuller-Whites had no desire to acknowledge the baby. They wanted no contact with her, suggesting she was a money-grabbing whore. Enclosed was the promise of a thousand pounds with an address for a clinic that would 'take away' the problem. She would receive the cheque after she had attended and proof had been supplied that the abortion had taken place.

Such a sum was a life-changer. She could start afresh and get training. Why not just have the money and be allowed to keep the baby? It was nearly Christmas and it was time to make the momentous decision. Della knew it was a mortal sin to submit to an abortion and that kept her awake. Her only excuse was that she was a lapsed Catholic. The rules did not apply to her, did they?

There was no one she could share this with, no friend she trusted enough, not even Rachel in the shop. She sobbed all the way to the clinic in the Georgian square in Leeds. How could she destroy a life? But how could she keep a child with no home, no money and no support? Della went through that door and killed any chance of happiness for the rest of her life.

Afterwards she went into the Merrion Shopping Centre and heard, on the tannoy, Johnny Mathis sing 'When A Child Is Born', knowing she had made the worst mistake of her young life. In doing that, she had betrayed Luke and the love they had shared. By ignoring her deepest faith in the sanctity of life, she felt she had been cast into darkness. She wanted to die, but the will to survive is strong.

The money was released. Della went to college to educate herself, slept around, hoping to bring another life into the world but with no luck. That was why she hated Christmas. It reminded her not of new life but of death, of darkness not light, of guilt and weakness. How could she ever be forgiven?

Later, when she got home, Della wept. She reached for the bottle, giving herself up to oblivion.

38

Ariadne was standing by a roaring fire in Chloë's drawing room and on the table a pristine embroidered cloth was ready to receive plates of canapés. It was the book club's annual party. Champagne was cooling while the members carried in dishes of salmon mousse, filo pastries, pakoras and sweets for their feast.

'Business first,' she announced, wanting them to make their Christmas reading recommendations before indulging in the goodies and getting too sloshed to do anything but gossip.

Hebe had another of her bad heads and wasn't up to joining them. Ariadne had insisted they must make an appointment to see Dr Makaris in the morning. Tonight everyone was dressed up for the gathering, because the weather was unseasonably warm after the terrible storm.

It was going to be another mild Christmas, she thought, barbecue weather, picnics on the beach, but part of her longed for crisp frosty-morning walks on the North Yorkshire Moors, and the little cottage near Helmsley, with just the two of them enjoying a simple dinner, after Midnight Mass in the old stone parish church.

'Penny for them, Chloë,' said Dorinda. 'I thought you might be going home to your daughter. We're off tomorrow to see our new grandchild, Poppy, and all the family. You can't beat a proper Christmas in England, can you?'

'This is our home now,' said Chloë, curtly.

Ariadne felt a sudden chill in the air and changed the subject. 'What has everybody brought to read?' she asked. No one spoke, not wanting to be first. 'A Child's Christmas in Wales by Dylan Thomas,' Della offered.

'Oh, not that again,' Dorinda muttered. 'We seem to have it every year, or Laurie Lee's *Cider with Rosie*.'

'I brought a poem, "Snow" by Louis MacNeice,' Natalie said. 'It's only short, but it catches a winter atmosphere.' She read it beautifully.

'Thank you,' Ariadne said, with relief. 'That was lovely.'

'But it's really not about Christmas, not like T. S. Eliot's "The Journey of the Magi".' Dorinda sniffed again.

Ariadne was finding it hard to shut her up.

Saved by the doorbell. 'Sorry I'm late.' Mel walked in, out of breath. 'Irini's got a cold and I had to wait for Spiro but I've brought some Greek Christmas bread.' It was a large spiced loaf, decorated on the top. 'It's very traditional here and this is Irini's recipe,' she added. 'I've got my piece from Elodie Durrante's novel, *The Winter Bride*.'

'I hope it's not full of sex again,' Dorinda said. The others exchanged glances and rolled their eyes.

Ariadne was sick of the woman's complaints. 'Elodie wrote

about Christmas in the country. I've seen some of her journals. She could be very poetic at times. Don't judge her by her later work. I, for one, will be glad to hear it. Santaniki owes so much to her generosity.'

One by one they read their pieces, some short, others a bit tedious. She could tell they were all dying to hit the dining table. It was then that Simon burst in.

'Ariadne, your house is on fire! Your neighbour smelt smoke and saw flames in the kitchen!'

Everyone jumped up to make way. 'Oh, my God, Hebe's in bed. She's taken one of her sleeping pills. If the smoke gets to her—' Ariadne screamed.

'Don't worry. Clive, Norris and the neighbours called the local fire station. It's well equipped for forest fires. They're at the scene now.'

Ariadne's villa was downhill, closer to the shore and the harbour. She could hardly breathe with panic – darling Hebe. At least the house was unlocked. No one needed to lock their doors here.

'It'll be all right.' Simon tried to comfort her, and Chloë wrapped a shawl around her shoulders. 'Get into the car – it'll be quicker.'

The fire engine was blocking the drive. Hoses were pumping water. The mayor and farmer, Yannis, was among the volunteers, busy dousing the building.

'Hebe! Where's Hebe?' Ariadne shouted, over the noise of the engines. 'Hebe?'

Clive rushed over. 'She's okay, safe. We got inside and pulled her out, but she's a bit confused. It was lucky I was walking Bella at the time and saw the flames.'

Ariadne's only thought was to find Hebe. The house could go up in flames, as long as Hebe was safe. 'Oh, my dear,' she cried, seeing her partner sitting in Clive's lounge, her hair dishevelled and smelling of smoke, her pyjamas covered with a man's dressing-gown.

'Is this a dream?' Hebe asked.

'No, love, there's been an accident. The decorations must've set the house alight. Clive and Norris got you out.'

'Where am I?'

'Next door. It's going to be fine.' Ariadne patted her hand, shedding tears of relief that her beloved Hebe was safe.

Yannis and Spiro came to say everything was under control and mostly contained in the kitchen and living room.' Big mess, Kyria Ariadne.'

Everyone stood around, shocked, as all the rugs and smoky furniture were laid out in the olive garden. The windows were blackened and downstairs was uninhabitable, but the staircase was intact. Ariadne knew things could have been far worse.

'We've been upstairs and checked the rooms,' said Clive. 'Your office was untouched and your bedroom.'

'I didn't realise you had only two rooms upstairs,' Norris interrupted, giving Ariadne a funny look as he turned away.

'You're coming with us,' Simon insisted. 'We've plenty of bedrooms. The clear-up can wait until morning, I reckon.'

'We'll help,' offered Della and Natalie.

'I'll come down to look at the damage again in the morning,' Spiro said. 'I can bring Youssef and his cousin, Amir, to help.'

'You're so kind, all of you. I can't believe it – our home is in ruins.'

'Homes can be rebuilt,' Clive said. 'Lives cannot. Norris, your house will be empty. Aren't you off home tomorrow?' he added, as Norris was walking away with Dorinda.

'Sorry, but we don't want their sort in our home. There was only one bed in that house, you know...'

'So what?' shouted Della.

'You know what that means,' Dorinda replied. 'Those two aren't just friends. We've been deceived by them pretending to be relatives. It's disgusting.'

'What is disgusting is your narrow-minded view of the world. This is the twenty-first century, and there are many kinds of love,' Della replied, wagging a finger at them in fury.

Dorinda puffed herself up. 'Not according to the Bible. We don't hold with such unnatural intimacies.'

'Oh, go to Hell, you poker-faced hypocrite!' yelled Della. 'What do you know of life? You make me sick.'

'The feeling is mutual. We all know what you are, missy.' Dorinda dismissed Della with a flick of her hand. 'A drunkard through and through.'

'And you are a fat-arsed killjoy, who wouldn't know fun if it jumped up and bit you.'

'At least I don't prop up a bar, or live in a den of drinkers and sodomites, who show little respect for this season of Advent.'

'Come away, Dorinda. The less said the better. These people don't know how to behave themselves.' They stormed off down the track to their villa.

Ariadne had heard all of this, but was too choked with

smoke and exhaustion to respond, even to get anything from upstairs.

'Bed for you two ladies. Hebe doesn't look well,' said Chloë, ushering them away from the scene.

Hebe looked at their house. 'How did that happen? I woke with such a headache. I made myself some tea downstairs... I can't remember.' Her words drifted away.

Ariadne felt sick. Hebe was forgetful. She might have lit a match and left it. If only she had been there to supervise. It was then she realised all the Christmas music had been in the living room and her digital music centre was destroyed. Downstairs was a mess of charred remains. Christmas and their reputation lay in ruins.

'Come along. Things will look better after you've had a good sleep.' Natalie took Ariadne's arm and led her away, like a child.

Ariadne knew that nothing would look better in the morning.

Natalie's Christmas Bread Wreath

For the basic sweet dough
500g plain flour
A pinch of salt
175mls milk
28g dried yeast
110g butter
110g caster sugar
2 eggs, beaten

For the topping
Butter and caster sugar
50g raisins
1 teaspoon cinnamon.

To decorate
Icing sugar
Chopped walnuts
Glacé cherries
Angelica slices

Make the basic sweet dough. Sift the flour with the salt into a mixing bowl.

Put the yeast and butter into a separate bowl and warm the milk to blood heat. Stir the milk into the yeast and butter. Stir in the sugar and the eggs.

Make a well in the flour and salt mixture, pour in the liquid and, with your hands, mix until smooth. Put the dough onto a floured board and knead it until it is elastic. Place it in a greased bowl, covered with a damp cloth, then leave it to rise in a warm place for 50 minutes until doubled in size.

Knock down the dough, then cover it again, and leave it to rise once more.

Turn it onto a floured board and roll it into an oblong, about 2cm thick.

Cover the surface with dots of butter, a little sugar and the raisins, then sprinkle over the cinnamon. Roll up the dough tightly and curl it into a ring. Join the ends together and place it on a baking tray. Snip the ring every 3cms with scissors, each snip two thirds deep into the ring. Cover with a cloth and leave to prove for 30–40 mins.

Preheat the oven to 200°C.

Put the Christmas Bread Wreath into the oven and bake for 25 minutes, or until golden. Pierce it with a skewer to test: when the skewer comes out clean, it's done.

Mix some icing sugar with a little water and brush over the ring while warm. Decorate with walnuts, cherries and angelica, then brush again with icing.

39

Gary stared in disbelief at the mess. Spiro Papadakis was already hard at work shovelling debris into a skip. Half of the village came to stare at the damage so Spiro asked them to give a hand while he, Simon, Clive and Youssef cleared away the remains of Ariadne's kitchen. There were broken windows and smoke stains halfway up the stairs. The structure was sound, but the olive garden was strewn with rubbish and the smell of burning hung in the air. It would all have to go to the landfill site, as there was no collection from the mainland. Poor ladies, and just before Christmas, thought Gary, as he helped load a truck to carry away the white goods.

'How can I thank you all?' Ariadne said. 'And how will we get this straight for Christmas?'

'You won't,' said Mel, putting down mugs of strong coffee and a box of homemade biscuits to keep the troops fed and watered. They were sifting through what could be salvaged.

'Nothing will be delivered in time, but thank God it's stayed dry enough to board everything up. Spiro is gathering the locals into shifts and the Began boys are here to help.'

Gary had forgotten there was a group of refugees in town. He saw the women sometimes, with a little boy, walking back from the shops. They looked so thin and weary, but at least the child was settling. Youssef was a hard worker and came with Andreas, the mayor's younger son, to drain and clean Gary's pool when needed. He was polite, with good English, and seemed grateful for any work that came his way.

Someone said Youseff was once an accountant in Damascus but had fled after the troubles there erupted. There was a dignity about him that made Gary feel like a lazy slob, living off cash he had never earned. How different were their fortunes in life. He wondered where the group were living and if the locals resented their presence. Life was hard enough in this recession. Perhaps he would find some extra work for them, tidying up the garden for winter.

Kelly was a little brighter. The reflexology sessions seem to have lifted her bitter mood. She was making preparations for their Christmas, but without the usual London guests, it would be a quiet affair. There would be nothing to distract him from the heaviness he felt inside. If a Catholic priest was available he might find relief in confession. Gary couldn't get rid of the feeling that he was a lazy fraud. They were too young to be retired, sitting around waiting for the English papers to arrive. There wasn't even a golf course, just a little choir of oldies, who had all achieved success in their lives, earning a decent life out here. What had he done, except win a huge lottery pay-out? They were living every working man's dream with everything money could buy, but the only thing they truly hoped for was a family.

If truth were told, he was bored, not with Santaniki or his newly made friends, but bored with having nothing useful to do. If only he could find a cause, a purpose here that might assuage the feeling that his life was over. Was this his punishment for cheating Gran?

There, he had said it, named the cause of his guilt, but even as it raised itself, he pushed it down again. Not now, not here. It can wait.

'Gary!' Spiro yelled. '*Ela!* Come and help me.'

At least he was raising a sweat as he lifted the kitchen fittings out of the house. He stared around the burnt-out kitchen with dismay. The two old ducks would be hard-pressed to replace it. He wished there was a way to help them find replacements, or at least make good the rest of the house. It was then that an idea struck him and he smiled to himself. *Garfield Partridge, you're a genius. Perhaps you have your uses after all.*

40

Ariadne sat in Dr Makaris's little waiting room in the health centre with a heavy heart. He had trained in America and returned to his birthplace to put into practice much of what he had learnt abroad, so she had every faith in his judgement.

'We'll go in together, Hebe. I have some questions to ask the doctor.'

'Why are we here?' Hebe asked. 'My headache is better. I don't want to waste his time.'

'Don't you remember we had a fire last night? There was a lot of smoke, so I want him to check your chest and blood pressure. You've been a bit forgetful lately.'

'Did we burn anything?' Hebe looked out of the window, distracted by a passing truck. 'I wonder where he's going.'

Ariadne saw it was full of rubbish, the contents of their kitchen by the look of it. 'I don't know, dear.'

It was a relief to get into the consulting room and to see the smiling face welcoming them. Dr Makaris's English had an American drawl. 'I don't see you very often, do I? How are things? I heard about the fire. Have you got anywhere to stay?'

'We're at the retreat. They're empty at the moment,' Ariadne replied.

'So, how can I help?'

Ariadne explained her concerns while Hebe stared at the picture on the wall. 'Have we been to Santorini?' Hebe asked.

Dr Makaris watched her intently. 'Tell me, Kyria Hebe, how are you feeling?'

'What?' she replied, not looking at him.

'What happened yesterday? Tell me all about it.'

'Nothing. We went for a walk. I was tired. Ariadne went out somewhere and I went to bed, but my head is better now.'

The doctor looked Ariadne. 'How long has Kyria Hebe been like this?'

'About three months, but lately there's been a few worrying episodes and she's forgotten the fire. She told me she came down to make tea and I think she left a lighted match or something. Thank goodness the gas wasn't on high.'

'I see,' he said. 'I think we should do some little tests.' He brought a pack of animal pictures out of a drawer and asked, 'What day is it today?'

Hebe shrugged. 'Ariadne will know, but it's Christmas soon.'

He placed the pictures on the table. 'Look at these pictures, but take your time.'

Hebe stared at them and smiled. 'I like dogs and cats.'

'Now I'm going to cover them with paper for a minute. Then you can tell me what they all were.'

Hebe looked at Ariadne. 'Why? I'm not a child. Why is he asking me these silly questions?'

'So what pictures did you see?' he asked. 'Can you tell me their names?'

'I like dogs,' Hebe said.

'Good. And the other pictures?'

'What others? I only saw the dog.'

Ariadne felt tears in her eyes. How could such a clever teacher be reduced to this? She shook her head in dismay.

'Can we go now? Why are we wasting the doctor's time?' Hebe stood up. The doctor pressed a button.

'Let my wife give you a little lemonade, while I talk to Kyria Ariadne.' His wife, Caliope, appeared in her nurse's uniform to guide Hebe towards their apartment.

'Is it what I fear?' Ariadne said.

'I'm afraid so, but we must do more checks. Sometimes an underlying cause makes someone forgetful. Does she have double vision or dizziness?'

'You mean a brain tumour? She does get headaches and is sometimes a little dizzy, but she's not herself any more. She can't make decisions and depends on me for everything.' Ariadne began to weep. 'We've been together for forty years and to lose her to dementia…'

'It may not be that. Only scans can show this, but that will mean a trip to Heraklion or Athens for a fuller diagnosis.'

'Wherever,' Ariadne said, with a sigh. 'How soon can we go?'

'As soon as I can arrange it. Prepare to stay for as long as it takes. They will have all the right tests and she will be in good hands.'

'Thank you. We'll wait for an appointment and I'll make the arrangements. Pity it's so close to Christmas. Everything seems to be going wrong for us.'

'The best-laid plans "gang aft agley",' he replied.

Ariadne looked at him in surprise. 'Robbie Burns. How did you know?'

He smiled. 'I roomed with a Scotsman in Boston. He was a Burns fanatic. Now, don't worry, we'll get to the bottom of your friend's problem.'

'That's what I'm afraid of. I fear the worst and what may come next.' Ariadne felt more tears coming.

'All in good time, *siga, siga*… slowly, slowly… We will wait and see.'

Ariadne shook his hand. 'I'll try to take it slowly.' She didn't want Hebe to see her upset, so she straightened her face and took a deep breath. *Onwards and upwards, old girl*, but it was hard when her heart was leaden with despair.

41

Natalie paused to take a breath. 'Della, we've got to help Hebe and Ariadne,' she said, puffing up the steep rocky track. They were trying out a path for a new Fit for Over-50s post-Christmas campaign. Della had suggested a beginners' running class but Natalie felt a Santaniki Strollers group was more realistic. 'The two of them are stuck in the retreat for Christmas, not in their own home. It looks as if the concert will be off too.'

'That's a pity, after all the hard work we've put in. It was going to be a good fundraiser.'

'There's not much cash around at this time of year, not for the likes of the local fishermen or the hotel owners. Perhaps we're targeting the wrong audience. We need sponsors,' Natalie went on.

'Like who?' Della stopped to catch her breath.

'The winery up the hill, some of the expats…' Natalie shook her head. 'We could do a crowd-funding concert online. After all, carols on a Greek island might go viral if we make it funky.' She was thinking off the top of her head.

'Dream on, we're not that good.' Della stopped again. 'But it's a great cause, helping the refugees. Have you looked around here lately? We talk about refugees on the other islands and send clothes, but what about those living among us on handouts and labouring jobs? That should be our first priority – finding them regular work. None of them are work-shy. Youssef and Amir do any odd jobs they can find, and Sammia cleans for anyone who can use her. She's pregnant, by the way. We ought to be supporting them.'

Natalie stood staring out to sea. 'It's a mess, isn't it? Here we are playing at life when Ariadne and Hebe are homeless and there's uncertainty for others. We have to make an effort to do something, though. I was looking forward to our concert and a bit of a Christmas party. I'd even worked out a menu of sorts.'

'Natalie, you're a genius. If we can't do our concert, let's have a great street party, invite everyone in the town to a feast, give something back for living here. It could be what we call a Jacob's join or a faith supper, asking everyone to bring a little dish, a bottle or something.'

'But you don't cook.' Natalie laughed.

'I make the best wine punch. We can rope in the rest of the choir to help.'

'What if the weather's bad?' Natalie had visions of a soggy table and sodden decorations.

'O ye of little faith, think positive, spread the word.' Della was in full flight now, but Natalie wasn't sure.

'Poor Ariadne hasn't even got a kitchen or a home. The choir was her dream. We can't just abandon it.'

'Don't be so negative. They'll be our guests. It'll do Hebe

good to have some fun. She looks so out of sorts and I worry about them.'

'You worry about everybody except yourself,' Natalie said.

'What do you mean by that?' Della was on the defensive and stood, hands on hips.

'Oh, I didn't mean—'

'You mean I drink too much,' Della said.

'That's not for me to say, but you can knock it back.'

'Some of us find comfort in a drink or two… I have my reasons. You cook yourself into the ground, but never eat anything. We both have a knack for punishing ourselves, don't you think?'

'I do eat when I feel like it,' Natalie said, in her own defence. Della was out of turn in making that accusation.

'Oh, yes, beans on toast and an orange or two…'

'I like healthy food.'

'You bake calorific cakes and pastries to feed others, but not yourself. What's that about?'

'Don't lecture me, Della, it doesn't suit you. Kettle calling the pot black.' How dare she?

Della smiled, holding out her hand. '*Touché*… We could make a pact. How about I'll drink less if you'll eat more? There's a challenge.'

'It's not that simple, is it? We both have histories and sadness.'

'Tell me yours and I'll tell you mine.'

'Not now.' Natalie felt panic rising. 'It's private and I'm not ready to share stuff.'

'Why not? I'm no judge. We both have reasons for who we've become, stuff that goes way back. I just think it helps to talk about it, not keep it hidden. I saw a quote in a book once. It said: "I told my fear and it did go. I told it not and it did grow."'

'I don't believe in baring my soul to all and sundry,' Natalie snapped.

'But it's me, your friend. I have fears too, that I can't control myself and I'll end up an old lush, with a withered face and skinny ankles, drinking booze and pissing in some alleyway.'

Natalie hugged her and smiled. 'Never! You're too strong for that and too proud. You're right, though, we all have our weaknesses. It's just that...' she hesitated '... I'm ashamed of what I did. How could I face you all afterwards, if I confessed?'

'Me too. I have a deep shame that I want to blot out with booze. Why are we punishing ourselves?'

'This is too deep for me,' Natalie said. 'I'm sorry, I've got to go.'

'Think about my offer, Natalie. We can help each other move on. I'm sure of that.'

'Bye!' Natalie fled down the path, not seeing anything in her hurry to go home and hide. Della had no right to pry into her eating habits. She liked being skinny and in tight control of what she ate. Baking was her comfort. What was wrong with that?

42

Gary knew it was now or never. It was time to air his idea. 'Kelly, love, sit down. I want to ask you something.' He was shouting from the kitchen.

'I'm busy.'

'No, you're not. This is important. You know the lady who runs the choir and her partner had a fire in the house. It was an accident, but her kitchen is ruined.'

'Don't I know it! Your clothes still stink of smoke and gave me a load of washing. I told you they were lezzies, didn't I?'

Gary ignored her. 'They're good people through and through and I want to get them sorted before Christmas.'

'You're no kitchen fitter. It's up to them to sort it out with their insurance company.'

'But it's nearly Christmas and it'd be good to get them back in their own home, don't you think?'

'I don't care one way or the other.' Kelly picked up her *OK!* magazine again.

'Don't be like that, love. I've enjoyed singing, meeting some decent guys and making friends.' Kelly put down her magazine with a sigh. 'By the pool we have that built-in kitchen area we hardly use. It's got cupboards and a sink, grill, fridge and all that white stuff. It was a great idea at the time, but a waste of money. Now if we removed the fittings and put them in their house…'

'Give away our lovely granite worktops? You must be joking.'

'No, I'm not. I want to give them a kitchen, so they can come home for Christmas. We can decorate and tile it, to give them a surprise.'

'You don't owe them anything. Our pool bar will look ridiculous!'

'Who's to see it in the winter? Come summer, we can replace it. It's not as if we can't afford it. It would be a gesture of support. I like Ariadne – she's a great. You would, too, if you got to know them.'

'It's your money. Nothing to do with me, is it?' Kelly turned to her magazine again.

'Yes, it is, and I did it all for you, so I could give you the moon and the stars, but it all turned sour and changed us into a pair of lazy, selfish gits.' Gary could feel himself stirred up by Kelly's indifference.

'Speak for yourself. What brought this on?'

Gary pulled the magazine out of her hand. 'Some home truths, if you must know, and I think it's about time I told you them. We're living on money that isn't truly ours.'

That made her look up. 'What do you mean not ours? We won the lottery big-time fair and square.'

'Not exactly fair, love.' Gary felt his cheeks flushing, his heart pounding and his knees going weak. The moment of confession had come. 'It wasn't my ticket.'

There was a moment of silence, as Kelly took in what he had said. 'Don't be daft! I saw it and the numbers. You and Gran always used birthdays and house numbers.'

'It was Gran's ticket, not mine. I played online so all we had to do was look them up to see the results. She wasn't that bothered, so I did it for both of us and they were registered to me. Her numbers were different from mine, so when I saw the draw, I declared hers to be mine and claimed it. She often forgot to give me any money over the years. I reckoned they were both mine. She never knew. Besides, you know we never got on, but I did do her numbers out of habit. She was never interested in us and never forgave me for not being her pride and joy. The numbers weren't mine. They were hers, but no one challenged me.'

'How could you? She was your gran and she brought you up when no one else would.' Kelly stared at him.

'I saw her right. We gave her everything she needed to make life comfortable, but she could be an ungrateful cow at times and made my life misery when I was a kid. You have no idea. This was a way to pay her back. She died in comfort and we gave her the best send-off, no expense spared. Besides, I wanted you to have everything we never had, make your dream come true. She was old and frail and I put her in a nice home.' Gary began to cry. 'It's never felt right what I did but I did it for you.' He paused. 'There, it's out now. I'm a fraud, living off someone else's money. We're no better than anyone else, thinking we're one up on everyone cos we're rich. I can't give it back, or make it up to the old cow, but it don't sit easy,

Kelly, and never has. I can't go on living like this. I have to make amends.'

'By giving our pool kitchen to a pair of dykes?' Kelly snapped. 'No one knows our business. It's all in the past. Your gran's dead and you can't change that. You paid for them tickets for years, so what if some numbers were her choice? You've done nothing wrong in my book. You did it with the best of intentions to give us this wonderful life. '

'But it's not wonderful, is it? The one thing I can't give you is a baby. Perhaps God's punishing us for me being a cheat.'

'Hang on, Gary, there's still time and hope, as long as we keep trying.' She nudged him. 'I love you, warts and all. So we've had a bit of luck, that's all anyone needs to know. She ain't here to haunt us. She lived the life of Riley in that home, never seen her so cheerful. You didn't abandon her. You made it up to her, as best you could, and she could be an ungrateful woman. Give those old dears that kitchen, if it makes you happy. I don't care. All I care about is you and me, and I'm glad it's out in the open. I never knew you felt so guilty. But I wish you'd told me before.' Kelly came over to give him a hug. 'We can keep this secret. No one need ever know.'

'But I know and I have to make up for it, do something useful. Perhaps it's time I got a proper job,' Gary said.

'What – here? There are no jobs. Do you want go back home? I suppose we could try another round of IVF.'

'Not yet. I'm staying put and organising that kitchen as a surprise. I have to do something to make amends.'

'You're a deep one,' Kelly said. 'Making me feel guilty for letting you think I'd only love you with money to spend, spend, spend. It wasn't like that, Gary Partridge. You and me were happy enough when we were broke. I suppose we went a bit mad. I felt like a celebrity, not a shop girl from the East End, and all the time you was carrying this guilt on your back like a sack of coal. I'm sorry I've been such an ungrateful bitch, love.'

They sat holding hands and Gary felt as if the burden was shifting. He wasn't a bad lad. He had just yielded to temptation when it landed on his plate. He'd have to live with that knowledge, but from now on he would give, instead of acquiring more and more things. 'You don't mind, then, about the kitchen?'

Kelly smiled. 'You always was the kindest out of us both. I'm just a silly old moo. Perhaps I could help too.'

That was the best thing Gary had heard in months. It felt like an early Christmas present. 'You can be the scrubbing maid on all fours.' He laughed, pushing her down onto the cushions.

'Oh, Sir Jasper, I'm all yours!'

43

Mel watched Sammia bent over the sink, diligently scrubbing the pans. Irini was feeling sick and tired and had agreed Mel could bring in extra help again for the sewing-group meeting tonight.

'Take care where the girls are seated. Maria must not sit by Toula. They haven't spoken since Maria's goats went over the fence and ate Toula's best beanstalks. Katarina must sit by old Praxilla, as she is very deaf and will miss any news. Tonight we make *pastitsio* and I will supervise later.'

Mel had orders for the day, but she was distracted, hoping the delivery of toys would arrive before the big day. Times were hard, but the boys must have their presents. There had been another ferry strike and the seas were rougher than normal. Spiro was helping to repair Ariadne's villa, lending his pickup truck to transport Gary's pool kitchen for the refit. She had underestimated Gary Partridge. This was a generous act, but it had to be hushed up until Christmas.

Sammia was silent. She couldn't be far off her time and Mel

worried about her. 'You'll go to the clinic to see Dr Makaris?' Mel said.

Sammia smiled, shaking her head. 'I am okay. It is not our custom to be seen by a man doctor,' she replied, in halting English.

'But Caliope, his wife, is a midwife, a nurse. She'll help you to deliver.'

'No, my sister will help.' She turned away, not wanting to discuss the matter further

'Where are you staying now?' Mel was curious.

Sammia smiled. 'We have shelter.' Most of the refugee families were given rooms in empty holiday lettings. Youssef and Sammia had a stone cottage belonging to Yannis, the farmer outside the village. At the end of her shift Youssef would call to escort his wife home. Mel hoped the cottage was warm enough for a new baby. She looked out some old Babygros, kept in case there would be another child. Lately Spiro had suggested that two boys to educate would be sufficient. His heir and spare, as the royals had it. Mel would love to have a little girl but, as things were, they needed every penny to keep the taverna in business.

It didn't feel as if Christmas was just two weeks away. After the fire, without rehearsals, the choir had melted away. Della came in for a coffee, full of ideas about a huge street party, with dancing and singing.

Mel had put a dampener on her enthusiasm. 'Nice idea, but Greek families stay home with their families at Christmas and the Brits invite round neighbours and friends. It's a private time.'

'Tell me about it. Everyone hopes the Bartletts will open

their house for their cronies. Not sure if I'll be welcome, after that spat with Dorrie Thorner.'

'That's not fair. Chloë and Simon are very hospitable but they're going to England to see their daughter.'

'No, they're not,' Della said. 'I gather Alexa has other plans. Chloë's upset. I think she tried to go to London to see her, but the storm came and then the strike. Alexa is her daughter by her first marriage, not Simon's child.'

'You seem to know everyone here,' Mel commented. Della could gossip with the best of them.

'So I should. I've been in St Nick's long enough. In my classes I get to hear all sorts of titbits. At least we don't have the Thorners breathing fire and brimstone on us. Why they couldn't let Ariadne have their villa…'

'You know why. There are plenty of people who are prejudiced. It's never talked about in Greek families, so many gays have to go to Athens to be their real selves. I do wish Ariadne would carry on as usual, but I hear Hebe's unwell. The fire has shaken them both.'

'They say she set fire to the kitchen,' Della muttered. 'It was an accident, though.'

'They'll get insurance surely,' Mel said.

'Who knows? Kelly tells me they're giving them a kitchen – even she's come down from her perch to help out.'

'Spiro's on with it now but mum's the word. They want it to be a surprise. Another coffee?'

'Nope. Off to give Julia a hand with some dog walking. The vet's due on the ferry to neuter the latest arrivals No one wants pets unless they're working dogs. So many just get dumped. I'm trying to persuade Natalie to have one. See you…*Yass*.'

Youssef arrived for his wife, his overalls covered with white paint. 'You've been busy,' Mel commented.

He nodded. 'Much to do.'

Sammia had prepared all the vegetables and potatoes for the *pastitsio*, but Mel could see she was tired. 'Your wife needs to rest,' she said. 'But she is such a help to us. Her time is near?'

Youssef smiled. 'Soon, Kyria.'

She watched them walking together, not as they usual did, up the hill to Yannis's cottage, but in the opposite direction, towards the coastal path. How strange to be going for a walk after a long shift.

Irini rose from her sick bed in a foul mood. Nothing was right. The tables were set wrongly, the *pastitsio* was not to her exact recipe. 'I leave you and everything is not as we do it, Melodia, but at least the kitchen is clean.'

Then you sort it out, Mel thought, but bit her tongue once more.

Later the village ladies were seated as directed, all chattering away, complaining about the wet weather, the prices in the minimarket, the threat of more strikes and the loss of jobs.

'Yannis's son and his family have come back from the mainland. He has no work, so he's back on the farm in the cottage,' Toula said.

'But the refugees are living there,' Mel said.

'They had to leave. Family first,' Toula replied.

'So where are they living now?' Mel was shocked at this news.

'Who knows?'

That was why they were heading in a different direction, but where to? Everything was shut up around the harbour.

Perhaps Youssef's brother was settled somewhere. That must be it, but why had Sammia not said anything?

Youssef and Sammia were proud and must find living here so different from Damascus, but all Sammia had said was, 'We are safe here from bombings and soldiers. It is better than in the camp.'

Spiro brought the boys in for a late supper, but Mel didn't feel up to making another meal, so she had set aside a dish for the family. 'How's it going?' she asked him.

'*Etzi-getzi*, so-so, but we will get it done in time. Their garden is in ruins.'

'That can wait,' Mel said. 'Will the kitchen fit?'

'We can make it fit. The floor is okay and the units are good, very expensive. Youssef will finish the decorating soon.'

'Did you know Yannis has had to let them go? Ari is back from Athens.'

'I had heard.'

'Where's Youssef living now?'

'Don't know, he never said.'

'Please find out for me.' Mel added, 'Sammia needs to rest, not work, but work is money. With a baby coming, I'm worried for them.'

'You look tired yourself. Go home and put your feet up. I'll bring the boys back later.'

Mel smiled. 'Thanks, I'm ready for a bath. My ears ache with all that jabbering in the dining room. Please, God, no power cuts this evening. There's a DVD I want to watch if I can stay awake.'

Irini's *Pastitsio*

For the meat sauce
60ml olive oil
2 medium red onions, finely chopped
2 cloves of garlic, chopped
1 tablespoon of tomato purée
700g lean minced beef, lamb or pork
A glass of red wine
1 x 400g tin of tomatoes
1 teaspoon sugar
1 cinnamon stick
1 whole clove
1 bay leaf
Sea salt and freshly ground black pepper

For the béchamel
120g butter
120g flour
900ml milk, warmed
2 egg yolks
A pinch of nutmeg

Sea salt and freshly ground black pepper
100g Parmesan

For the pasta
350g macaroni or penne
110g feta, crumbled
2 eggs

Preheat the oven to 180°C.

Heat the olive oil in a pan. Stir in the onions and cook until they've softened. Stir in the garlic, the tomato purée and the mince. Continue to cook until the mince has browned, stirring. Pour in the wine and let it reduce. Then add the tomatoes, sugar, cinnamon, clove and bayleaf. Season carefully with the sea salt and black pepper. Bring to the boil and cover, turn down the heat and leave the sauce to simmer, stirring occasionally, for 30 minutes. When it's done, remove the bayleaf, the cinnamon stick and the clove.

Meanwhile make the béchamel sauce. Melt the butter over a medium to low heat. Stir in the flour to make a roux, then add the warmed milk gradually, stirring so that no lumps form. Cook until the sauce thickens. Remove the pan from the heat and add the egg yolks, sea salt, black pepper, nutmeg and grated cheese. Stir thoroughly to blend the sauce together.

Cook the pasta for 2–3 minutes, to soften a little, then drain. Stir in the eggs and the crumbled feta.

Butter a large baking dish and assemble the *pastitsio*. Put in half of the pasta, top it with half of the meat sauce, then add the rest of the pasta, followed by the remaining meat sauce. Pour over the béchamel and smooth it to cover the meat.

Sprinkle over some grated Parmesan to cover, then bake for about 40 minutes, until the top is golden brown.

Let the dish rest a little before serving.

44

Ariadne prowled around the retreat's guestroom, unable to settle to anything. What with the fire, and Hebe's possible dementia, she felt the walls were closing in on their life together. Is this what's in store for us? she wondered. She trembled at the thought of Hebe disappearing into the twilight zone while she tried to care for her.

Hebe was fit, had never smoked, did the crossword and was an avid reader. It was a terrible blow to hear Dr Makaris confirm her deepest fears: a body could go on living while the mind was disintegrating. She had seen its effects during her aunt May's last years. She had become wizened, angry, unpredictable, and latterly so violent that, at times, she'd had to be restrained. The sooner the appointment in Athens came, the better, but it would have to be after Christmas.

Christmas. How could she bear to celebrate with all this hanging over their heads? The choir music was destroyed, as was her digital music centre. She wanted to scream in frustration. Not to be in their own home, with no chance of repairs, was unbearable. She did not venture near the villa, and their poor olive garden now was little more than a tip.

The retreat was warm, dry and comfortable enough. She thought of all the famous authors who had been entertained there. Dear Elodie had been a generous hostess. If only she could sit down and share all her troubles with her. Ariadne found herself returning time and time again to the little study where the author had worked. It was a summerhouse overlooking the bay, the perfect writing room away from the bustle of the villa.

Now it felt damp after all the rain. Perhaps it was time to clear out the precious books and manuscripts, in case they were damaged. She was also sure Peter and Alison wouldn't mind her retrieving them. It would be something useful to do.

Elodie's Christmases were always wild, with parties and feasting. She'd had such *joie de vivre*. There was usually a handsome beau, who would toast Elodie and her guests. The champagne flowed, and they'd had such jolly times until ill-health had diminished her appetite, her mobility and her high spirits.

'A writer never dies,' she would say. 'It's a lifetime occupation. Like old soldiers, we simply fade away.' True to her word, Elodie had taken to her bed one day, refused to eat or drink and done just that. Yet here her spirit seemed to linger.

Later on that afternoon, Ariadne began to shuffle books into boxes and collect files of manuscripts and notebooks from the shelves. She couldn't help glancing through the papers, snooping, in fact. The mind of an author must be like a jigsaw puzzle, full of snippets and images, quotes and half-finished sentences. But then she saw a short story, one she'd never read. It was entitled: 'A Memory: Santa Claus and the Chimney'.

I was quite a nervy kid, with fanciful notions and night-mares. Christmas was a time of year when the mills closed and the mucky snow was piled up, covered with sooty bits. We had us all a party of sorts in the school, orange squash, jelly, blancmange, which I hated, and yesterday's iced buns, which were chewy and thick. I loved the idea of Father Christmas bringing presents at midnight.

'Don't expect him to bring much this year,' my mother said. 'He has a lot of hungry kiddies to feed and clothe before coming to our street. Think on, he can't always work miracles.' Nevertheless we went to see Father Christmas, in Whitaker's store. He was a scary man with whiskers and beery breath. I didn't like sitting on his knee, because his hands went up my skirt to tickle me. I didn't like him wiggling his thing at me. The thought of him coming down my bedroom chimney or anywhere else in the house terrified me.

The front room was only used on a Sunday. It was where it all happened at Christmas, with a coal fire, so I decided to make sure Father Christmas didn't use that chimney. I blocked it up as high as I could. He would have to put stuff through the letterbox instead. I went to bed that night, certain that no creepy old man would get into the parlour.

In the morning there was all hell to pay. Mum had left the fire banked up in there so the front room would be warm enough to open presents and receive visitors in. We had paper chains strung across the ceiling, with concertina paper lanterns and a little tree covered with lights, cotton wool on its wiry branches. The card table was spread with Mum's best embroidered cloth, with ladies in crinolines on the corners. Christmas Day was the best day of the year, but not this one.

'Who's the bloody idiot who blocked up the chimney? The smoke's backed up and it's choking in there. Tom, did you do it?' Mum yelled. Smoke had seeped everywhere in the house, stinking out the whole place. The window was sooted up, the cloth covered with smuts, and we could hardly breathe.

'It were me,' I cried. 'I blocked it up, so that old man couldn't come down and steal from us.' That was my excuse and I was sticking to it.

'Well, our Gladys, you've certainly done a good job. Just look at the mess, my lady. How can we have next-door round for a tipple in this stinking mess? Did you not think?'

I knew she wanted to tan my backside, but Dad stepped in. 'The kid was scared. She doesn't realise Santa's the spirit of Christmas who brings Christmas joy. There's no need to be afraid of him, lass.'

'He weren't that nice in Whitaker's. He put his fingers in my knickers,' I said, blushing.

'He did what?' Dad shouted. 'The dirty bugger. Wait till I tell them in the store.'

'It's too late. He's gone back to the North Pole,' I said, in all innocence.

Everyone went quiet after that. They opened windows and the front door to get rid of the smoke.

'We could have choked to death in our beds,' Mam said, calming down. 'Come on, you lot, get stuck in. It's still Christmas morning. We've time to get the worst of it outside and open our presents.'

'How did he get in, then?' I said.

'Never you mind. Happen he left them on the front door-step.'

That was all I was going to get from her.

Ariadne smiled at the story. There was a pile of others to read. Why had they never been published? She realised this must be a file of personal jottings about the real Gladys Pickvance, not the fictional Elodie Durrante, the romantic novelist. How had they been overlooked? The clue lay within the shabby yellow file marked: CONFIDENTIAL.

Ariadne clutched it to her chest with excitement. Peter and Alison must see this. There was still interest in Elodie. Her fans would love to read about the real woman. There was gold to be mined here. She felt almost as if Elodie was still alive. Had she pointed Ariadne in the right direction?

Don't be fanciful, old girl. These memoirs were waiting to be discovered and you were just lucky. Yet it felt more than that, like a gift to lighten her days here. She would read the stories to Hebe after supper. It would help them share their own Christmas memories. She had once read that looking into the past for dementia sufferers could awaken a lot of pleasure: perhaps not all memory was lost for ever.

45

Chloë was trimming the entrance hall with a heavy heart. There was still no word from Alexa and she had no enthusiasm for tarting up the drawing room or the dining room with her elegant collection of Christmas decorations. It felt too soon. The box lay on the marble floor and she wanted to shove it back in the cupboard under the stairs. Every single piece shrieked of past times, with Alexa excitedly decorating the tree. What had she done to upset her? How cruel not even to answer her last email. Simon was no help, whistling away. 'The choir is back on up at the retreat. Rehearsals are starting again. Ariadne has decided no fire will stop us performing and I think she's right. There's a piano there and most of us have copies of the sheet music.' He stopped mid-flow. 'You look like you've lost a shilling and found sixpence. What's up?'

'I don't want to put these silly things up. It's a waste of time.'

'But we always have them dangling everywhere.'

'Not this year. I don't feel festive.'

'What you need is a drink. It'll be okay, you'll see.'

'No, it won't, not without Alexa. I never thought she could be so mean to us.'

'I expect she has her reasons. Have faith in her, darling. Besides, we've always opened our house at Christmas. Think of all the others who have no family to visit.'

'They can go somewhere else this year. I'm not in the mood.' Chloë kicked the box away. 'I'm going for a walk.'

'I'll come with you, then.'

'No, I'd rather go alone.' She paused. 'Perhaps I should fly back and demand an explanation.'

'I wouldn't,' Simon said. 'She might not be there.'

'How do you know? Has she rung you behind my back?'

'Not at all. Just calm down. Alexa will come to us in her own time, when she's ready. It's been a tough year for her. You can't force confidences.'

'We should never have come here, leaving her to live hundreds of miles away.'

'Chloë, just let it go or it'll make you ill. Have faith in her and all the love you've given over the years. She knows you love her and she's your only child.'

Chloë didn't want to hear any more of his platitudes: she was in the vilest of moods. She stormed off to find her fleece, for the wind was chilly and the sky was darkening. Taking Bacchus, their rescue mongrel, she strode out into the fields behind their olive grove. The path rose high onto the mountain track where there was a rocky outcrop. Then she saw a flash of colour.

Was it another hiker? It wasn't the season for tourists to visit the fields. In the spring they were full of poppies, orchids and daisies. Bacchus cocked his ears and, seeing sheep and goats in the distance, she called him back. It was then she noticed wisps of smoke close to the caves. Someone had lit a fire. There seemed to be movement and, for a second, she thought to turn back, in case there was a drug den, but something made her skirt round out of sight and onto a ridge where she could get a better view of what was going on.

A flash of colour again, the distinctive dress of their refugees, the women's black hair no longer covered with hijabs. They were sitting over a fire, cooking, and Youssef's brother, Amir, was coming out of the rock. Good God, they were living in one of the caves! Chloë couldn't believe what she was seeing and bent low to get a better look.

A little child was running around – he belonged to Maryam, Amir's wife. How could this be happening in the twenty-first century? Those families were sheltering in caves, facing winter winds and storms. That wasn't right, not with little ones. They might have a wood fire and water from the stream, but once the mountain snows came, what then?

46

Mel took her break with half of the book group in the taverna, sipping hot chocolate, as Chloë recounted what she had witnessed two days ago on the hillside.

'I don't believe it,' Mel said. 'No wonder I've not seen them passing by. And in those caves, for goodness' sake. We have to do something. Sammia's baby is due soon and she can't deliver it there. I did try to get her to see Dr Makaris, but it's not their custom to have a male in attendance. What if there's a problem? It's her first baby and they can be tricky.' She was thinking of how Markos had had to be sucked out of her in the end.

'We have to find rooms, make someone open up their holiday let,' said Della sipping deep into her mug of chocolate.

'But they cost. Youssef and Amir live from hand to mouth without regular work. It'll be hard for them,' offered Natalie.

'Then we must make sure the tenancy is met by us all chipping in, crowd-funding, if you like.' Della had a chocolate moustache but apparently no one had noticed it.

Natalie nodded in agreement. 'No room at the inn.' She sighed. 'It's a bit of a coincidence being so close to Christmas.'

Mel smiled. 'They're proud people. I'm not sure they would accept our charity.'

'Then we must make it into some sort of trust fund: homes for the homeless, Greeks and refugees alike. Whoever needs a roof over their head could apply for support. Make it an official charitable trust.'

'Perhaps we could buy a property. There are so many on the market, all over the island,' Chloë chipped in.

'But that will take time and would be a bit of a stretch for us,' Della said. 'Better to rent first and see how it goes. I'm sure Father Dennis and the doctor would help. And not just expats, but the whole community.'

'Times are hard for them too, though,' Mel said, imagining how Irini might react to this suggestion.

'All the more reason to include those on the breadline here. At least they have land to live off and big families to support them, but Sammia and Maryam have nothing.' Chloë wasn't going to let them off the hook.

'Then we must make sure our carol concert raises funds,' Mel said. 'We can call it the Christmas Choir Appeal, starting with all the villa owners in the other villages. We'll invite them in person to join in this worthy cause, rattle the tins in their faces.'

'You're right. Between us all, surely we can find an out-of-season rental.' Chloë said, and everybody nodded. 'The Christmas market raised enough to get things started. The pity is we keep drawing from the same old well.'

'Then we can go online, start a Just Giving appeal, make

a Christmas video and stir up some sympathy. I think Gary Partridge might help us. Someone told me he worked in IT before they won the lottery.'

'I bet his wife won't help,' Mel said.

'You don't know that until you ask,' said Della. 'She comes to my Pilates class. I'm sure we could rope her in, as it's such a good cause.'

'Oughtn't we tell Youssef and Amir what we're doing? They must be involved too. If they see the wider project, it won't feel so much like charity to them,' Mel said.

'Good idea, but how do we let them know their secret is out? Should we visit them?' Natalie asked.

'No, we wait until we have something to offer,' Chloë argued. 'Do I take it we have a committee?' Everybody nodded. 'Right then. Mel will ask around, as she knows local families. I'll find out who's dealing with properties, either for sale or to rent, and see if some can be had cheaply. Della can see the Partridges for IT ideas and promotions, and Natalie can visit around the area to get others on board.'

'Who will speak to the Begans?' Della asked.

'I will,' Mel replied. 'Sammia still comes here to help. I'll ask them in for a meal together. I'll insist it's not our custom to celebrate our religious festival knowing others are sheltering in such conditions. They have to know we mean well and that this charity will be for everyone, not just them.'

Later, when they were preparing the evening meal, Mel disclosed their ideas to Irini, who was chopping potatoes. She looked up, interested. 'So the caves come to the rescue again.'

Mel thought she'd got the wrong end of the stick. 'No, we want to find them a safer place.'

'There is no safer place than those caves. In the war they were a hiding place, or so my mama told me. When the Stuka bombers came over the island, strafing houses and people alike, everyone fled to the caves and sheltered there. It was a terrible time. The island was occupied and the troops took all the olive oil, the fruit and the animals for their own use. Little did they know that our uncles hid great amphoras of oil, deep in the caves, where it was cool, along with some chickens and goats, but they were hard times. Look at the war memorial. See how many young men were lost on the mainland, in Crete and here, for the Resistance. They fled high into the mountains hiding in *mitato*, the shepherds' huts.

'I had no idea,' Mel said.

'No, the young forget what a sacrifice it was to stay alive in those awful years and then afterwards, when men fought each other over politics, *popopo*. That was even worse. War tears us apart from family and homeland. Now it happens all over again.' Irini wiped a tear on her sleeve. 'You do right to find a home for the homeless. We Greeks have always prided ourselves on *xenophilos*, the friendship given to strangers, but when things get tight, it can be forgotten. I will ask around my friends to see what rooms might be opened up. Our Lord was born in a stable, after all, but it shouldn't happen in this day and age.'

'Thank you. We must do what is right to help others.'

'And your heart is warm, Melodia. That is good.' Irini patted her hand, as Mel felt tears of gratitude spring to her eyes. A compliment from Irini Papadaki was a compliment indeed.

47

Gary heard the news about the funding appeal while he was at a choir rehearsal, which was taking place with renewed vigour. They were trying to learn a Greek carol to share with the audience, but it was proving difficult to get their tongues round the words. Ariadne conceded defeat, but Mel suggested the local children could bring their triangles and drums and sing it for the congregation. That would make their parents come.

Gary was happy to get involved with the YouTube video about the situation on the island and wondered what angle to take, without offending pride. It needed to have an emotional appeal. The children singing that jaunty Greek carol seemed an ideal backdrop. Perhaps the contrast with the reality of life out there might jerk people into giving.

'You have to help me, Kelly,' he said. 'I need to find locations and images.'

'What about the boarded-up shop fronts and hotels on a wet day?' she suggested. Since his confession of his deceit,

Kelly had been much less prickly and uppity. 'Let's take the jeep around,' she added. 'Della told me about the couples living in the caves. It's dreadful. Someone ought to do something before the weather gets worse… and she's having a baby.'

'It's all in hand. The women are finding somewhere.'

'I could do some knitting,' she offered. Gary knew there was a drawer full of baby wool, all bought in the hope of them having their own child.

'That's a brilliant idea. According to the forecast, it'll be getting colder soon.'

With the help of Peter, they designed a poster for the Christmas concert and Spiro helped with the Greek translation. They found a picture of a ship covered with fairy lights, in the local tradition. Being so busy and involved lifted Gary's spirits. Here was something he could do well, and having Kelly on board was such a relief. Now all they had to do was make a video worthy of the cause. He wanted to interview people. It wouldn't be easy without an interpreter.

Clive came up with the idea of making a pyramid Christmas tree from tins of food that could be shared out like a present from Santa. No one would feel they were being patronised if they were helping themselves to basic foodstuffs. They bought in extra tins from the minimarket, to help the shop increase its business.

He noticed that the atmosphere in the choir was changing. They were taking the concert seriously now, and the project to secure Ariadne and Hebe's villa was progressing well, giving work to a local carpenter, a sparky and builders. It was still boarded-up on the outside, so if Ariadne came to inspect there would be nothing to see. Inside it was a hive of activity as they refitted the kitchen with Gary and Kelly's white goods and granite worktops, making sure that the wiring was safe, the tiles renewed and the paint freshened. It was close to Christmas now and there was still so much to do. Gary smiled as Kelly jumped into the jeep by his side. He had never felt so alive.

48

Natalie was taking her duties to heart. Since the committee meeting at Mel's, she had toured the local villages, putting up posters, finding where the expats were holed up for the winter, explaining their mission over cups of coffee or glasses of wine. The personal touch was paying dividends, with promises of donations, tins for Clive's tree and attendance at the carol concert in support of their Christmas appeal.

Sometimes the old colonel accompanied her because he knew many of the older residents, who were glad of a visit and a chance to catch up on gossip and news from England. 'Good to get out myself, young lady. I'm getting too lazy, these days, and out of puff if I sing too loudly. There's quite a buzz among the locals about the idea of a shelter,' he said.

'We're banking on support from everyone, and so far, so good, with only a little opposition about who should be the recipients. I've enjoyed having your company on these jaunts. I'd no idea there were so many of us foreigners living in the hills, so many interesting artists and retired people, plus some younger families on smallholdings.'

'You can count me in any time.' Arthur smiled. 'Pity old Elodie Durrante is no longer with us. She would have whipped every one of her fans into donating. Such a character... Long before your time, of course.'

'At least Ariadne and Hebe have a place to stay, thanks to her retreat. I hear they've found some memoirs. Simon's a retired editor and keen to help get them in shape.'

'You can't beat a generous northern soul. Elodie had a voice like a rusty foghorn, smoked like a chimney, but never lost her roots. She could drink the bar dry, and had a face leathered by the sun. The old girl was no beauty but quite the philosopher in her own way. I never forgot what she once told my dear wife. "Darling, we go through life with two bags to put most of our problems in. One is for time and the other is for money, but some struggles won't go in either bag. They are the hardest to carry."'

Natalie nodded. Since her spat with Della she'd known only too well that time or cash wouldn't sort out her own heartache. 'It's not easy to get rid of excess baggage,' she said, with a sigh.

'After the war I found it hard to forget the suffering I'd seen, the misery I lived through and the good men I'd lost. It's wearing to drag that sack of grief around, like a ball and chain. Good memories can help us to change, though. If we can dwell on happier times we shared with those we've lost, we honour them. Focusing on the future, not the past, helps us let go of the other stuff.'

'You're quite the philosopher yourself,' Natalie observed. 'Easier said than done.'

'That's where rituals come in handy, you know, honouring the seasons of the year, celebrating with good food and friends, lighting a candle in a church, setting the little boats down a river, seeing off all those demons. It's an act of willpower, but it can be done. It all comes back when I put pen to paper. Now I think of my pals with a smile, remembering the pranks and jokes, the banter and the good times. They aren't lost to me, because they live within me and will do until the day I snuff it. Writing out my experiences helped me. The bad stuff I tore up and burned.'

'Thanks for that,' Natalie murmured. 'You've just helped to rattle all the bones in my own backpack.' Could it really shift her own bad memories and guilt, lessen the sack of coal she was carrying round her heart? If she wrote everything down on paper, all the angst she was feeling, named her shame and put a match to it?

49

Ariadne spent her mornings rearranging the files she had discovered in Elodie's study. There was enough material to make an interesting addition to the novelist's biography. 'Rich pickings here,' Simon said, after he'd read the file of stories. 'Should appeal to a wide audience. What a girl.' He envisaged publishing online and in print, but to do that they would need an ISBN number and someone who could set up the book with a good cover, plus publicity.

It was too near Christmas now for any publication to happen, and Ariadne had the concert and her insurers to manage, as well as keeping an eye on Hebe. Thinking of their future together was heartbreaking. How could she bear to see Hebe decline into a shadow of herself? What was the alternative? To return to England and find a care home? It was too early for that, surely. Hebe was happy spending time with Peter and Alison's children and playing the piano. It was strange how, once she was seated on the stool, she made no mistakes in rehearsals, and preparing her music sheets made her feel useful again. If only they were back in their own home, but it was still boarded-up and Ariadne dreaded to think of the devastation awaiting them when the claim came through.

Perhaps they should take a break in the UK, or wait until the spring and Hebe's assessment before they returned. It would be sad not to spend Christmas in their own home, with Arthur coming for his lunch as usual. At least she had the carol concert to focus on. By now the programme had been established and the readings organised, while publicity had ensured that everyone knew about it. It was such a welcome relief from all her other worries. Including the schoolchildren had been a great idea. Mel was such an asset to the choir, not only for her voice but her links to the local community and her language skills. At least she was happy to sing one of her Sheffield jingles. Ariadne liked 'Sweet Chiming Christmas Bells' best.

She sat on a bench outside the retreat, watching the crystalline bay as the sea shimmered like gunmetal. How she loved this little island with its olive groves and orange trees, the scent of thyme and rosemary always in the air. Could she bear to leave it? Where would they go? It would have to be by the sea – Cornwall, Norfolk or the Yorkshire coast they knew so well, perhaps Whitby or Robin Hood's Bay.

Nothing appealed and this was not the time to make plans. Stay in the moment, one day at a time. '*Siga, siga*, slowly, slowly,' she whispered to herself.

'Teatime. We're making mince pies,' Hebe called from the door. 'It's too cold to have a picnic, so come inside.'

'On my way!' Ariadne shouted, jerked out of her reverie. It was going to be a very strange Christmas this year and possibly their last on Santaniki. Better make the most of it. She shivered, glad to be back beside the warmth of the olive-wood stove.

50

Chloë looked out of the window, hoping for a blue sky, but the clouds were as heavy as her own mood. The house was trimmed – Simon had insisted on it – but her heart wasn't in the usual festive preparations. She kept ringing Alexa's flat, but there was no answer, not even a texted reply. She was more worried than ever.

'I'm going down to the ferry to collect some gardening tackle. Come with me – we can pick up some fish,' Simon said.

'I'm busy, you go,' she replied.

'No, you're not. Come on out. It'll do you good.'

'Don't patronise me. I'm fine.'

'No, you're not, Chloë. You're taking things too much to heart.'

'How can you say that when my daughter won't even speak to me? I wish this Christmas was over. I'm sick of it all. I'd rather forget the whole damn thing.'

'You don't mean that. Christmas is full of surprises and

Ariadne is banking on you and Mel to sing well at the concert. Please come with me, love, just to keep me company.'

'I'm not much company for anyone…'

'Then I'll have to think of ways to cheer you up.'

Chloë put on her Puffa jacket and a silk scarf in a sulk, and they set off. It was chilly, but the winds had dropped. Standing around at the terminal wouldn't be much fun, watching all the relatives arriving off the ferry from Crete, carrying bags full of presents. Still, the fresh air might lift her despair.

They arrived early and she could see the boat chugging slowly into its berth. So many times they had taken the trip across to Crete, to Rethymnon, to the shops or to meet friends for lunch in its ancient streets.

She watched the gangplank being lifted, and one by one the passengers alighted, carrying bags, and cages with chickens or rabbits. Children leapt into the arms of grandparents. How cruel of Simon to make her watch all this. She turned away, with tears in her eyes. 'Let's go,' she croaked.

'Wait a minute. I think my parcel's just arrived. Look over there…'

Chloë turned slowly. A figure was walking towards them, tugging a suitcase on wheels, a figure she would have known anywhere. 'Alexa! It's Alexa! Oh, you came.' Chloë ran forward to greet her, in tears.

'Of course I came.' She hugged her mother tightly, then Simon.

'How was your journey?' Chloë was stunned, almost speechless.

'A long flight to Athens, then Chania and then the ferry, but I'm here now with you.'

'I can't believe it's you. I've missed you so much. Why didn't you reply?'

'And spoil the surprise? I wanted to give you a surprise, when Simon said how worried you were.'

'Simon Bartlett!' Chloë turned to him, wagging her finger.

'Guilty as charged.' He smiled, seeing the look on her face. 'We've been emailing behind your back, making plans.'

'How could you both let me worry so?' Chloë felt her heart leap with delight. 'I forgive you, but only just.'

Alexa's face looked fuller and she was wrapped up for cold weather in a navy coat, with a scarf hugging her throat. Chloë got into the jeep, while Simon took the luggage and Alexa climbed into the back.

'I didn't know what to bring weather wise, but it said cold online. The air is so fresh here after London and the plane. It's good to be away from the crowds and everything.'

'And Hugh?' Chloë asked.

'No idea. He just disappeared, left me the flat, left everything. I think he's having a mid-life crisis – I gather Lover Boy is half his age. Still, if it makes him happy…' Her voice dropped. 'Things happen for a reason, I suppose.'

As they drove up the main street, Alexa saw the huge boat covered with fairy lights. 'Oh, how pretty! It makes a change from all those glaring things in Oxford Street. Will we be having the usual parties?'

'Things are a bit different this year. We formed a choir, Ariadne's Christmas choir, and we're having a big concert to raise funds for refugees, but there will be the usual get-togethers.'

'Don't worry, I've brought my party frock, although it may be a bit tight. I've put on weight.'

'Never mind, you'll soon get it off in January.'

'Not this time, Mummy. It's weight of a different kind.' Alexa laughed. As she stepped out of the jeep her coat flapped open to reveal an unmistakable bump.

'Is that what I think it is?' Chloë gasped.

'Oh, yes, I'm nearly five months gone.'

'Does Hugh know?'

'Not yet. I wanted to keep it to myself and tell you first.'

Chloë hugged her daughter. 'Come in and get warm. I just can't take all this in.'

'You will when you're babysitting and the baby won't settle.'

'But your job?'

'All in good time, Grandma. I need a mince pie and a glug of mulled wine.'

'But you're pregnant!'

'One small glass won't hurt – the alcohol will have burned off – and lots of spice, please.'

Chloë danced into the kitchen. 'Thank you, thank you.' She looked upwards, shaking her head in disbelief. Alexa had returned, bringing with her a gift so precious and unexpected. It felt like Christmas morning. *How could you ever have doubted her?* She wanted to rush out and tell everyone the good news. *Alexa's home for Christmas and not alone!*

Later, when Simon was out, Alexa sat down with Chloë, sipping spiced berry cordial. 'I owe you an explanation. I'm sorry I was short with you when you came to London. It was all a shock about Hugh and me. I thought it was just a difficult patch and we did try to mend things, but the sex got to be less and less. I tried hard to understand why he was leaving, but I was confused. I thought my periods stopped because of the stress, but other symptoms popped up and I just knew. I wasn't sure whether to carry on with it. I'm sorry you came at the wrong time. I had made an appointment at the clinic to… It was a very low point. Then I realised I couldn't go through with it. I felt so ashamed shoving you away, but I had to make that decision on my own. I thought of how you brought me up alone when Dad left, and how you managed and found one of the best husbands in the world. I couldn't let this gift go.' Alexa was crying.

Chloë hugged her tight. 'I'm so proud of you. You've been through hell and I must've made matters worse, pestering you as I did.'

'No, you did what any mother does. You held on, showing you cared, even though I was being a grade-one cow to you.'

'How will you manage? You love your job.'

'I can work from home, freelance. I have the name of a good nursery and lovely friends with children. I'm sure you'll want to play your part too. I'm a big girl, Mummy. I can manage without Hugh, though he'll have to take some responsibility financially. Who knows? He might even grow up enough to take an interest in his little one.' They both laughed.

'Poor Hugh, he won't know what he's missing.'

Alexa pulled a picture out of her bag. 'Here she is… Olympia. Perhaps when he sees this princess…' Chloë saw her grandchild curled up like a frond on the scan. 'So… Olympia Anster…'

'No, Olympia Bartlett. I'm going back to Bartlett. Simon was more of a father than Charlie ever was.'

Chloë was full to the brim with happiness. 'Life gets so

complicated, doesn't it, but there's always a way forward with an open mind. You seem to have it all mapped out. How long can you stay?'

'For as long as you'll have me. I'm due some leave and it will give me time to take stock and firm up plans. I want this little one to love the island and that's why she's going to have a Greek name.'

'A wise and lovely choice.' Chloë smiled, looking at the clock, knowing it was their last rehearsal before the concert, but she was going nowhere tonight, not with her daughter at her side.

51

Clive looked in his shaving mirror, hoping Lucy would appear behind him, but there was nothing and he sensed her presence was fading from him. Until recently she was always bending his ear with words of wisdom. He'd been so busy with choir rehearsals, sorting out Ariadne's kitchen, getting the staging right for the Christmas appeal and helping in the search for a home for Youssef and Sammia that he didn't have time to walk up the path to St Nicholas's chapel but he was going just the same.

The wintry air was cool and there was a dusting of snow at the top of the mountain ridge, but it was not the damp chill of Yorkshire. There were still mornings when the sky opened ink blue and the sea glittered turquoise. It was almost Christmas and hardly a card posted yet. He'd sent a parcel to Jeremy, of course. There was no chance he would come over…

Bella must have a brisk walk along the coastal path, but first he would lay flowers on Lucy's stone. He had bought a wreath of herbs, with bright ribbon for his door, as Lucy always had. He was beginning to neglect her memory and it troubled him.

When would his wretched grief leave him? When would he let her go, put away all the precious objects still lying around the house? Part of him still pretended she would walk through the door at any minute and resume their life together. Clive was cross with himself as he strode out, glad of the chill to chivvy away his grey mood. He would climb to the chapel and light a candle to summon the memories that still gave him pleasure: watching Jeremy opening his stocking on Christmas morning, early-morning swims in the cove, Lucy surrounded by shells and sand in her studio.

Clive bent his head into the wind and climbed up the track, stopping to let Bella sniff and stiffen at anything that might move. He could hear the bells of sheep as they trotted down the mountainside. A sign of bad weather to come? Sheep would come down to lower pasture and take shelter wherever they could. He thought about the family in the cave. They must be brought down to safety soon.

No one had yet found accommodation for them and time was running out. Their arrival had shaken the cosy community, who were now becoming more aware of their own privilege and comfort. All those empty holiday homes, shuttered for the winter, troubled him. Surely someone might open one as a rental.

No amount of carol singing was going to make that happen. They needed a miracle. He entered the little chapel with its fading frescos and peeling plasterwork, glad to be out of the wind. 'So, St Nicholas, what do you make of all this?' he asked aloud with a smile.

Don't be silly. He can't hear you. He whipped round, expecting to see someone in the doorway.

'Lucy, is that you? I thought you'd left me.'

I'll never leave you, dumbo, but it's time you let me loose and started living again.

'What for? What's the point? I can't forget you.'

That's not the point. Loving my memory isn't a life sentence. Don't let it imprison you. Just take me with you on your next adventure. Leave space for new things to happen, new friends and companions.

'You mean Natalie Fletcher?'

Perhaps, but you're not exactly making a decent stab at helping her. Not everyone has our luck in love.

'So what can I do to help her?'

You'll have to figure that one out for yourself. Make yourself available and see where it leads.

'She'll never be you, though,' he whispered.

Don't go looking for another me. Open your eyes, your mind, your heart – and, for God's sake, get rid of all my junk that's lying around. It's morbid and not helpful. Give away my clothes, sell my artwork. Let it go. Keep a photograph or two and a few mementos but not a house full of me. Why would any woman want to live in my shoes? Remember the film Rebecca? *I don't want to be the spectre at the feast. Make this Christmas a special one, my lovely. Then we can all find some peace.* Her voice was drifting away.

'Lucy…' It was then he knew he would not hear her voice again. She had given him his marching orders and they must be obeyed.

52

Mel was surprised but relieved when Sammia turned up at the taverna: Irini was still in bed. Her chesty cold had turned into a fever. Tonight there was open mike, a celebration party for some of the young locals. Mel was on her own, trusting Spiro would grill the lamb ribs and souvlaki while she saw to the stews and salads.

It was getting chilly and she feared for Sammia and her family, living in the caves. Sammia's cheeks were hollow and her belly swollen with her child. 'You shouldn't have come,' Mel said, 'but I'm glad you have. Did you walk?'

'It's not far,' Sammia said.

'Sammia, we all know where you're living and it's far enough. It's not right.'

'It's downhill. I'm fine. I like to work and it's warm in here. It smells of home a little.'

'I wish you could stay here,' Mel said. 'We're trying to find you somewhere to live... I was going to ask you all to come for a supper, Youssef, Amir, Maryam and little Karim.'

'You are kind. We are fine and we can help ourselves.'

Mel shook her head. 'Your English is so good.'

Sammia shrugged away the compliment. 'I went to a good school in Damascus. My father was the principal.'

Mel poured her a coffee. 'Sit down and prepare the vegetables for me. You must rest your feet.' She felt so ashamed to be setting her to work so close to her time. 'Have you seen Caliope, the nurse? Have you got everything, in case the baby comes soon?'

'Yes, she has checked me. You are like my mother, always worrying.'

'Your parents?' Mel hardly dared ask.

'They were killed in a raid, a bombing raid. The house fell on them.'

'I'm so sorry.' What else could she say?

Sammia picked up a knife to peel the potatoes.

'How did you escape?' Mel was curious to know more.

Sammia and Youssef had been trapped in their flat for days since a raid. Eventually Youssef went out to find food. He met some soldiers from the Freedom Army, who accosted him warmly. They asked him to join them, but he said, 'No, I have a family to feed.' He returned to their flat, worried. 'They say next time we meet, you take up a gun and join us, or find someone to take your body.'

There was no choice but to flee. They packed, crossing the border at night, travelling until they came to the city of Izmir in Turkey, where people-smugglers could be found. There was a man in an insurance office ready to help, but they were forced to pay many hundreds of euros, all they could raise. He gave them a secret number to give to the smugglers, whose trade was now a big industry. The man told Amir it was just a short drive, and they were packed into a small bus with black windows. Sammia could hardly stand and breathing was difficult. Some time later, they were pushed out of the bus beside a forest and made to walk for many hours in the dark. At last Sammia smelt the salt of seawater in the air. She thought they were safe, but worse was to come.

Tears filled her eyes, as she spilt out the rest of the story. 'How can I describe to you what we saw?'

They were allowed only one bag. The smugglers stole everything of value, leaving only a few clothes, checking underwear for jewellery, but thankfully not her brassière, where dollars were stuffed into the padding. Maryam was crying with shame.

The boat was a dinghy, already full of many nationalities. They said it was a short crossing but it was at least an hour. The sea swelled and nearly turned the boat over. Karim was terrified and clung to his mother, his eyes full of terror. He was too young to know what was going on, but old enough to sense danger and fear. Sammia saw one woman fall over the side with her baby. Everyone screamed for the boatman to stop, but he motored on, leaving her behind. They threw a rubber ring for her to cling to, but the baby in her arms drifted away and the woman disappeared under the water.

Sammia closed her eyes. 'I can say no more about that, or the camp we were put in, crowded and dirty. That was when Maryam lost her baby. Our life and dignity were taken from us. We were lucky to have people in Crete who let us stay with them.'

Mel touched her hand. 'I didn't mean to upset you, but your story is important. People have to know what is happening out there.' She was weeping.

'We are safe here. As for our future, who knows? My child will not lie in rubble, with planes screaming overhead. He will live in peace. He is our future.'

'A boy?'

'Ibrahim, after my father. I just know it… Allah has blessed us and brought us to this safe haven, but enough of me. There is much to do tonight, yes?' Sammia smiled.

'Irini is sick upstairs, but she will be listening to see if I'm busy. There is an old saying here. "When the moon is rising, sow your seeds. When it is waning, see to your garden and prune, but in a full moon, never get behind the donkey and avoid the mother-in-law." Irini means well. She is a good woman, and a hard worker. The moon is nearly full, so I'm safe.'

'I don't understand.' Sammia looked puzzled.

'Just a joke,' Mel said, with a sigh, knowing she must put her skates on and see to the chores or else. 'Please join us for a meal together. You will be most welcome.'

53

Ariadne was excited. There were only two days until Christmas Eve and the carol service. The community hall was decorated with candles set in greenery. By the entrance was a Holy Santon, a nativity scene with pottery figurines of the holy family and straw for the wooden animals. Everything was ready for the mulled wine, while biscuits, mince pies, gingerbread and Christmas cake were waiting in tins. Ariadne knew the choir was ready to perform, despite a poor show at the last rehearsal. The main street was festive, with little boats lit in windows and wreaths on the doors of the British residents.

She thought about her own house, still boarded-up, looking empty and unloved. They must be patient and wait for repairs to be done. At least they had a roof over their heads, which was more than some. When she returned to the retreat, Hebe was standing at the door. 'Mr Podmore's invited us to supper,' she said.

'Clive? I saw him only yesterday. He didn't say a thing.'

'It's tonight. Look at his Christmas card. Shall I bring my music?' Hebe looked hopeful. 'Perhaps it's another rehearsal.'

'I've not been inside his house since Lucy died. He's been so helpful to us so, yes, we must go.' Ariadne was puzzled. In their close community everyone knew if a social event was happening, but no one had mentioned Clive's soirée. To be honest, she would rather put her feet up or gather together Elodie's papers and jottings. Simon had read them with enthusiasm. The possibility of publishing them online, if the Foundation Trust agreed, was looking good. It was about time the author's life was shared. This was a gem of an opportunity to raise funds.

Going out in the chilly evening meant quite a trek, or begging a lift. She needed a shower, and her hair was a mess, although who cared what she looked like? Christmas in Santaniki was always full of drinking and feasting. There would be news of how their Christmas appeal was doing. It was good that Hebe was excited and looking forward to an outing. She spent so much time alone, looking through the window or playing the piano. There were good and not so good days, and this news had definitely perked her up.

The phone rang and it was Simon, offering them a lift to the party. 'It's all very sudden,' she said.

'I think Clive's been on the receiving end of so much hospitality, he decided to return the favour. Natalie and Della have been helping him with the food, so it'll be a feast. Everyone's going and it should be fun.'

Ariadne and Hebe made the best of their appearance, with layers of woollies, in case it was cold. 'We could almost be in Yorkshire, it's that parky.' Ariadne laughed.

'I like making snow angels and snowballs. We had such fun at school, didn't we?'

'If I lie down now to make a snow angel, I'd never get up, Pilates or not. Come on, we don't want to keep Simon waiting.'

He duly arrived to escort them down the hill. Alexa was in the front seat.

'We heard you were back for Christmas. It's lovely to see you again,' Ariadne said.

'And you, too,' Alexa replied. 'It's getting so cold. Where's the Greek sunshine?'

They drove down the main street, passing the *plateia* and onwards towards the shore. 'Simon, you've missed the turning. It's on the left.' Ariadne knew he was going in the wrong direction.

Simon smiled. 'Got to pick something up first,' he said, and turned abruptly towards Ariadne's villa. Something was happening. She saw a queue of cars and jeeps. The entrance was blocked. 'What's going on?' said Ariadne, in alarm. 'Have we been burgled?'

'Everything's fine, but we'd better go and see.' Simon parked the car on the road, and they got out, Ariadne, holding Hebe's arm, walked into the garden. In the darkness she could barely see the outline of their house. Suddenly the veranda lights went on, revealing their front door, gleaming white. The windows were lit with candles and all of their friends were spilling out of the house. 'Surprise!' they were yelling.

'I don't understand,' Ariadne said, as they were guided up the steps to the open door.

'Come inside,' said Gary Partridge, whose wife was holding out a beautiful knitted Christmas wreath.

The lines of guests parted to let them into their home. It was pristine, painted white throughout, and then they were in the kitchen. Ariadne gasped. What a transformation! Beautiful cupboards with granite worktops, a new cooker and sink. She couldn't speak but Hebe smiled. 'We have a new house.'

'Not exactly,' Simon explained. 'Gary had some spare appliances and Spiro, with his building friends, helped us install them for you. Youssef and Amir decorated the living room. Come and see.'

Ariadne was overwhelmed. 'You did this for us? How can we ever repay you?'

'This is a gift, a sharing from all of us. Please accept it with our love and appreciation,' said Della. 'Look inside.'

The living room was all redecorated, the fireplace gleaming. Their rescued sofa was restored, with new cushions, and bookshelves waited to be filled. The smell of smoke had long gone, almost as if there had been no fire. There was even a little faux Christmas tree in the corner.

'You can come home as soon as you're ready.'

Ariadne sat down, winded. 'It's so wonderful to know we'll be in our own home for Christmas after all. How can we ever thank you?'

'By coming to my place as requested,' said Clive. 'Sorry about the deception, but we wanted it to be a surprise.'

'You can say that again! To think I never came down to revisit the mess…'

'Thank goodness you didn't. We kept the boards up, just in case.'

'Now we really are all heading up to Clive's house. We'll leave you in peace to take stock. Don't worry, there's plenty of willing hands to help you move back tomorrow,' said Father Dennis.

'But Peter and Alison…' Ariadne didn't want to desert them with no notice.

'Rest easy, they know about this. It's all in hand for Christmas Eve…'

Most of their friends slipped away, but Simon stayed with Gary, while Hebe and Ariadne went upstairs to see their redecorated bedroom.

'It's so good to be home,' said Hebe. 'Why did we have to leave?'

'The fire. Don't you remember?' Ariadne said.

'What fire?' Hebe smiled. 'On Bonfire Night?'

'Something like that,' Ariadne replied. It was no use labouring the point. 'Now we have our home restored to us, thanks to Gary and his gang.' Suddenly she felt weak at the knees and very hungry. 'Come along, old girl, let's go to the party. Christmas is coming and I intend to enjoy the fatted goose.'

54

Clive's party was a great success and went on until well after midnight, with impromptu carol singing from the choir. It was good to have a houseful of guests messing up the place, and Bella was a great Hoover, sliding under tables and chairs to sneak any titbits going. He couldn't believe how the idea had come into his head after that walk to the chapel. They were ready to get Ariadne and Hebe back into their own home and the subterfuge had gone to plan. All he needed was an excuse to get them out of the retreat house and down to their home here. Clive had intended to send invitations with his Christmas card, but it wouldn't have succeeded without Natalie.

Two days before, he had called on her with a card and, to his surprise, he was invited in for coffee and cake. The house once again smelt of baking and spices. Natalie seemed more relaxed in herself and suddenly he knew what to say.

'You know about the surprise for Ariadne? Well, I'm going to open my house for the gathering. I wondered if you'd help me clear out a few things first.' He paused, seeing interest on her face. 'It's just that I've never got rid of Lucy's clothes and other bits and pieces – I could never face boxing up her possessions – but I've been thinking lately that it might have been a bit selfish of me. Lucy was a generous soul and wouldn't want stuff hanging around when it could be given to someone in need. I'd like to clear a few things, to make space for the party. I don't know much about girls' stuff, what we should give away or sell on eBay for the appeal. She had a great collection of ethnic jewellery, nothing terribly valuable... I'm a bit lost.'

'I'd love to help. I didn't really know her, but I've heard such a lot about her and that she had such a good artistic eye. I could come over this afternoon, if you like.' That was music to Clive's ears. 'I can bring some meatballs in sauce for supper, and then we can make a start on clearing space for your guests. We are all so excited about giving Ariadne and Hebe their house back, You and Gary have worked wonders in secret, but nothing goes unnoticed in our village, does it? Everyone will want an invite to your party.'

The afternoon had flown by, opening drawers, wardrobes and boxes. Natalie laid out Lucy's dresses on the bed. 'We could hold a sale, or perhaps you'd like to keep some special items.'

'All the woollen stuff must go to the refugee appeal. It's no good it sitting there in the wardrobe when it can keep someone else warm,' he said.

The jewellery made Natalie gasp. 'Wow, these are fantastic! Earrings, torques, pendants. She certainly had style.'

Clive showed her a photograph of Lucy on their wedding

day, in a long, white velvet draped dress, with a bright red cape edged with swansdown. 'I've missed her so much, but giving away these bits isn't as painful as I'd thought it would be, not with having someone to help me.'

Natalie sat on the bed with a sigh. 'I didn't have your luck. Rick and I rubbed along, but he was always on my case, checking up on me, not letting me speak or do separate things. It was so bad that I got fed up. I played along, making him jealous. I never thought it would end as it did.' Then she told him all the details of Rick's suicide. 'You can never make it right. I tortured myself with it until the old colonel put me straight. He told me I didn't need to carry this burden. I could choose to put it down. I've made a promise to forgive my weakness and guilt, to start afresh, to stop punishing myself. Does that make any sense?'

Clive touched her arm in sympathy. 'We both seem to have made a breakthrough, in our different ways. Thanks for helping me out.'

'By the way,' Natalie added. 'I'm going to collect a stray puppy from Julie's rescue. I'm calling him Bertie. He'll be good company.'

'Then we can walk Bella and Bertie together,' Clive replied.

'I'd like that. Bella might teach him how to behave.'

That was the moment Clive knew something had shifted between them, but he didn't want to push his luck: slowly slowly catchy monkey, and all that. Yet his heart leapt with hope. It was going to be a good Christmas after all.

55

Arthur Templeton Brown stared at the dwindling Christmas cards on the mantelpiece, with a sigh. What do you expect, when you've outlived almost all the friends you ever had? He was looking forward to the carol concert. For once he had abandoned his old linen suit for something more in keeping. They were going to wear Christmassy colours, red, green and white, or a funny jumper, if they had one. He rummaged in the back of his wardrobe for his old dress uniform. He could never part with it, despite Caroline saying it stank of mothballs.

He tried on the scarlet jacket. It hung loose on him, but with a thick shirt underneath, it would do. As for the trousers, he would need braces to hold them up. Time to polish his black shoes and spruce up his moustache.

The past months had given him a purpose, with rehearsals, the drama of the storm and Ariadne's fire. It was good to see the girls back in their own home, even if Hebe was looking a bit fey and forgetful. 'Yonderley', his mother used to say of people of a certain age, whose eyes wandered away from conversations. Hebe couldn't be much over sixty.

Who was he to talk? He'd be creeping up the stairs, only to find he sometimes couldn't recall why he was there. At ninety-five he supposed that was par for the course. Maria, who came to clean and see to his meals, was good company and kept his Greek up to scratch. He loved the kind, generous souls who had passed food to him and his men through the prison-camp wire during the war. Caroline and he had enjoyed their retirement in the sun. Now, in the winter of his life, he found he was looking back more and more and wondered how long he had left to enjoy being in this world. His breath was shorter going uphill, his appetite smaller, his afternoons spent napping over the *Telegraph*. Tonight's concert would be fun, if only he could remember the words.

Outside the window, he sensed the temperature dropping. Darkness came so early, although he had only to step out down the lane to the *plateia* and the community hall. Simon had offered a lift, but he was glad of the fresh air and a chance to loosen his stiff limbs. 'Sharp to it,' he ordered himself, as he collected his music sheets together in an attaché case and shut his door. No need to lock it. One of the joys of village life here was the trust between neighbours.

The hall was already half full with everyone milling around, plastic cups of mulled wine in their hands and kiddies racing about in their best outfits. The Greeks knew how to dress their children for traditional parties. Maria's girls were puffed out like pink meringues, triangles ready for the children's carol. He was looking forward to hearing their pure, sweet voices, reminding him of how, as a boy, they were allowed to go from door to door singing 'Here We Come A-wassailing'. There was always a bun or a sweet for them, and a noggin of something stronger for the adult members of the choir.

Ariadne, in conductor mode, was dressed in a bright scarlet shirt and black velvet trousers that shimmered in the candle-light. All the choir ladies were dressed to the nines and the men wore red shirts with bow ties.

'You look magnificent, Colonel,' said young Gary, admiring his uniform. 'Have you met my wife, Kelly?'

In front of him stood a pretty girl dressed in a scarlet trouser suit. 'I hope it's going to be a good show, after all the effort you've put in. The hall looks very Christmassy,' she said. 'Let me get you some mull.'

'What a lovely young lady, you lucky chap...' Arthur whispered to Gary, with a wink.

Soon it was time to gather on the platform, which had been erected specially for the occasion and decorated with tinsel. Arthur was feeling nervous and a little breathless, glad there were chairs to sit on between carols. Yannis, the mayor, was sitting with his wife, plump as a capon, in the front row, and behind them there was a solid core of locals and international residents. Their publicity push had come up trumps. Ariadne rose to introduce the concert. Costas, the local schoolteacher, translated for those with little English.

'In Britain on this night, people will be gathering in churches to sing these ancient carols, celebrating the birth of Our Lord. We wanted to share our tradition with you and to let your children sing your tradition to us. We hope you enjoy the readings, a translation of which is on your hymn sheet. It is our joy to come together in the darkest time to remember also those who, like Mary and Joseph, through no fault of their own, find themselves without home or country. That is why we have a bucket by the door for our refugee appeal. Thank you.'

She turned to the choir and the concert began. One by one they told the Christmas story through carols and readings. Arthur found tears in his eyes, thinking of past times and how he would miss the choir after this evening. He had met so many nice folk he'd never really known before: the couple from the retreat; Greg and Phil, whom he no longer thought of as nancy boys but as a kind couple who had helped out after the fire. Then there was young Gary, Duke, the jazz player, and his girlfriend Pippa. He hoped Elodie Durrante was watching from above. She would be heartened to see how the villagers of all nations had come together to share in this night. All too soon, the last carol was sung and everyone stood for the Greek national anthem, then 'God Save The Queen'.

'Well done, not a bad sound,' Ariadne said, looking radiant and flushed with success. 'Thank you, that was wonderful. We pulled it out of the bag and the children did us proud. Mel's solos were just perfect.'

'This can't be the end of our choir,' Natalie said, and everyone was nodding. She clapped her hands.

'Well, we shall have to see,' Ariadne replied.

Arthur turned to see Yannis, who had been out for a smoke, rushing back into the hall. He was covered with what appeared to be white dust. 'It's snowing!' he shouted. 'Come and see!'

'But it doesn't snow on Santaniki. We're too near the sea,' said Irini. Everybody rushed to the window to watch the flakes, which were floating down like feathers.

'My mum used to say it was the angels shedding their wing feathers,' said Della. 'And I believed her.'

'It's beautiful and so Christmassy,' Hebe added.

'It won't last,' sighed Chloë.

'So let's enjoy it while it's here,' her daughter replied.

Arthur was tired. He didn't fancy walking uphill in the snow, but it was pretty. No one seemed in a hurry to leave, except those living in the outlying villages and the family from the retreat. 'We'll walk you home,' announced Greg. 'We don't want you slipping and spoiling that magnificent uniform.'

Arthur didn't refuse their support. Singing had taken more out of him than he'd expected. He felt his chest tighten. 'Such a grand evening, with icing on the top,' he said, as the snow swirled around them. 'We could be in England.' How the houses sparkled. The branches of the Christmas pine tree were decked with snow. What a wonderful end to the night. Chloë was right: it wouldn't last for long, but it was rather special.

They left him at his door and wished him a merry Christmas. Arthur made his way to his sitting room, where the fire was just about out. He piled on the logs and flopped into his armchair, smiling to himself, tired but content. The choir had given him company, music, memories and purpose, but he was shattered now, bone weary and ready for bed. Tomorrow, Christmas Day, there would be church and lunch with friends. Not a bad prospect, he thought, but first he must sleep.

56

Sammia woke from her rest with backache, and the blow-up mattress was like a bed of nails. It was the Christian festival tomorrow and tonight was their concert. Youssef suggested they should make an appearance, as a gesture of goodwill, but the thought of a bumpy ride, on the back of a scooter along the dark track, made Sammia shiver.

Last night they had shared supper with the Papadakis family, delicious chicken in lemon sauce with roast potatoes, followed by crisp baklavas in a honey syrup with ice cream. Karim played with their boys, who showed off their Christmas tree. As they were leaving, Melodia gave Maryam a little present for Karim. 'St Nicholas comes to all children,' she whispered, as she hid the gift in a plastic bag out of his sight.

Sammia was embarrassed that they had nothing to give in return, as was the custom. How kind the family were to invite them and how concerned they were to get them housed again, but nothing had been forthcoming. It was hard not to look back on their life in Damascus and at the international school, where Christmas was celebrated with singing, dressing up and parties. A Christmas tree festooned with baubles had stood in the school hall and there were invitations to gatherings from fellow staff members.

'You go,' she said. 'I've got a stitch.' Maryam gave her a funny look.

'Are you in pain?'

'No, not really, just aching. I can watch over Karim.'

'Then I will stay too,' Maryam replied, waving the men off, as the scooter spluttered down the track. It was getting colder. They lit more lamps and the Primus stove to boil water for spiced tea, and hot-water bottles.

When Sammia rose to relieve herself, outside in their make-shift pit, she felt snow on her cheeks. 'Look!' she shouted. 'The world is turning white.' The flakes were swirling around them and the hillside fell silent as they settled.

Maryam was always a worrier. 'How will they get back here if it sticks? They will wander into a snowstorm and be lost.'

'I should think they know the way blindfold by now. Don't worry. Karim will have fun in the morning, playing in the snow.'

'But I do worry. It is not right to be here in midwinter, with you almost ready to give birth. You must go into the clinic, when your time comes. This is no place to have a baby.'

Sammia retired back onto her bed, content. They were snug and wrapped in rugs and blankets, as the candles flickered. She woke early in the morning with a searing pain in her back, one she could no longer ignore, and as she stood up, she felt warm liquid trickling down her skirt. It was starting: the baby was impatient to be born.

'Wake up! Youssef!' She shook him hard to rouse him. His eyes opened and he saw her face twisted in pain. He shot out of bed.

'I didn't hear you come in last night,' she said.

'We had to walk back. The snow was blinding and our scooter stopped halfway up the hill. It will have melted by now.' He went to pull back the plastic sheeting, to reveal total whiteness with drifts of snow piled by their entrance. The blizzard was still swirling around them.

Sammia hobbled over to see for herself, as another pain made her bend over in agony. No one was going anywhere in this, she thought, trying not to panic. They were trapped, isolated, with a child eager to arrive in this bleak wintry world.

Chicken in Lemon Sauce

125ml olive oil
3 garlic cloves, crushed
1 teaspoon dried oregano
a pinch of chilli flakes
1 teaspoon dried thyme
3 lemons, 1 cut into wedges, zest and juice of 2
Sea salt and freshly ground black pepper
6 chicken thighs, with bone and skin

Preheat the oven to 190°C.

Combine the oil, garlic, oregano, thyme, lemon juice and zest, sea salt and chilli flakes in a bowl and add the chicken thighs. Cover and leave in the fridge to marinate overnight, if possible. If not, leave it for as long as you can, but at least 2 hours.

Take the chicken out of the marinade and place it in a roasting tin, skin side up. Toss the lemon wedges in the marinade and add them to the tin.

Roast for 30–40 minutes until the chicken skin is brown and crisp.

57

When Mel woke at dawn on Christmas morning, snow lay thick on the ground. The children were opening their stockings, excited at the little bits she had foraged – bubbles, chocolate coins wrapped in golden paper, cars, table games and a book each. The main presents lay under the tree, except for two children's bicycles in the hallway at the taverna. Her first thoughts were for Sammia's family, huddled in a cave. It wasn't right, not in this weather. 'We have to do something before they freeze to death, Spiro. We have to bring them down here.'

He was half asleep and not really listening. The men had stayed up late in the taverna after the concert and Midnight Mass. Irini was not fully recovered from her flu and had gone to bed early. The boys were as high as kites, with the singing, and the excitement that St Nicholas was on his way with gifts.

'I didn't know you could sing like that,' said Irini, after the concert.

'My wife is a woman of many talents,' Spiro said, hugging her. 'With the voice of an angel.'

Mel had blushed. Singing solo had brought out a new confidence in her and, thanks to Natalie, even her cooking had passed the critical palates of Irini's knitting group. The power was off, but they had oil lamps, candles and a Calor gas stove, plus the old bread oven if things got worse. The turkey would be cooked, come what may.

'Can we take the pickup truck to the cave and invite them down for a meal? We've enough turkey to feed half the village.'

Spiro rubbed his eyes, still hung-over. 'Give me time for a coffee, love, and to see the children with their presents.' They were doing Christmas English-style for once.

'They're fine. Your mother can watch them. We can't let people freeze on Christmas Day, can we?'

'It's not their day. They're Muslims.'

'I don't care what they are! It's too cold, and Sammia is due any day. The snow's sticking and the track will disappear, if we don't go soon.'

'Slave-driver!' Spiro groaned.

'Better take blankets, just in case,' she ordered.

Soon they were crawling along the white street, as neighbours shovelled up the snow on their paths and waved. Merry Christmas! It was much worse as they drove uphill past the track to the retreat. Mel had put on boots and her thickest coat and scarf. The snow was still falling and there were drifts. Spiro ground the gears. 'I don't like this, Mel. Visibility is poor. Better to turn round now. I'm not used to driving in snow.'

'We can walk from here – it's not that far. We have to see if they're okay. I won't settle till I know.'

Together they tramped towards the cave, the icy snow biting their lips and cheeks. The path was invisible and their jeans soaked in the drifts, but Mel would not be defeated. She had known much worse drifts on the hills outside Sheffield where they used to go tobogganing and snowballing. Thick snow had lain for weeks in the Peak District. She had blankets on her shoulders and struggled with the weight, but soon the entrance was in sight and she could smell smoke.

'*Ti canete*? How are you doing?' she shouted.

A worried face peered out of the entrance. It was Youssef. 'Allah be praised. You have come for us just in time. Sammia is not well. It is too wet and cold for her. Thank you… thank you.'

Mel saw them huddled around a weak fire, shivering. Sammia was lying on bedding. 'It is my time,' she whispered to Mel.

'You can't stay here. We must get you all down to safety,' Spiro said.

'She has pains, big pains,' Maryam said.

'Then we have to get her to the health centre to see Mrs Makari.'

The men gathered up their belongings, doused the fire, then carried Sammia and sleepy Karim slowly down to the truck Sammia lay groaning in the back on a blanket. Mel, Karim and Maryam were squashed in with Spiro. He backed up slowly but the wheels were sticking. 'I need something to put under the wheels.'

Youssef had brought his prayer mat, some towels and their rug. He rolled out a towel on the ground, and Mel laid another blanket over Sammia as Spiro revved the engine. At first it refused to budge, while Amir sweated, trying to dislodge the wheels. Then it suddenly jerked into life. The snow was coming thick and fast.

Sammia groaned. 'I have to push.'

'Not yet, Sammia! Oh, Lord, she's not going to make it to the village. Where's the nearest house?' Spiro said, with a worried look on his face.

'The retreat. Go there,' Mel ordered. The windscreen wipers were sticking and it was misty, but Spiro drove slowly. There was silence in the back.

It seemed miles to the retreat house, but eventually they reached it. Mel jumped out to open the gate, raced to the door and banged on it. Peter came to answer, still in his pyjamas.

'Mel?'

'We've got Sammia in the truck, about to give birth. Sorry, no time!'

'Alison!' Peter yelled, and she came running.

'Merry Christmas!'

'Not now, Ali,' Mel snapped. 'Have you got a spare room? It's really urgent.'

Youssef was already carrying in his wife, Maryam behind them with Karim.

'The guestroom is empty, now Ariadne and Hebe are back home, but it's cold. Bring her into the warmth.' Peter and Alison's two children stared in amazement at the crowd of snow-covered visitors. They were playing by the fire. 'Archie, take your sister upstairs to play, and you can show this little boy your toys.' She gestured to Karim.

'Is Baby Jesus being born?' said Katy.

'No, darling, that was a long time ago.'

'But it's Christmas Day.'

Mel cleared the room. Alison brought cushions and blankets, hot water and towels. The men went with Peter to open up the guestroom, get a fire going in there and prepare it.

'Have you ever delivered a baby before?' Alison asked. Everyone shook their heads. Sammia yelled, as a pain took her.

'Between us we've had four, so we should know the basics,' Mel said, more in hope than confidence.

Sammia was pacing the room. 'I make big pushes now?' She knelt on all fours. 'You must help me!'

'This baby is in a hurry, so you must breathe gently,' Alison advised. 'Like this.' She demonstrated. 'Push and then rest.'

Mel knew this was easier said than done. It brought back all the panting and pain of the last few moments of childbirth.

They didn't have to wait long.

'Good girl! It's coming! The head is almost here!' Alison shouted, while Maryam was soothing Sammia, speaking in Arabic.

Slowly, slowly, the baby slid onto the waiting towels, purple then pink, taking a lungful of air and howling. Mel gathered him up, wrapping him carefully, then handed him to Sammia. 'Ibrahim is here. Look, just as you thought.'

'We have to cut the cord,' said Alison, turning to Maryam. 'You can do this bit while we sort out the mess. Lots of newspaper to wrap it in. Oh, hell, there isn't any. We need something to bind the cord, something clean.'

Mel fled into the kitchen and tore up a clean tea towel to make a bandage.

There was a pile of ripped wrapping paper in a basket. 'That'll do. Now we must cut the cord, then lay Sammia down and press her stomach so that she delivers the placenta. I saw that on *Call the Midwife*.'

Maryam and Sammia were admiring the baby when the placenta released itself. 'Look to see if it's complete,' Alison said.

'*Call the Midwife*?' Mel laughed with relief, as Sammia put the baby to her breast, tired but beaming with joy.

'My son is beautiful.'

'Let's get you tidy and clean put all the stuff away, then Youssef can come to see his son. He will be anxious to know all is well.' Mel felt tears of relief come to her eyes. Thank goodness she'd followed her instinct and brought the families to safety. 'I won't forget this Christmas in a hurry,' she said. 'Congratulations, Sammia. A Christmas baby – who'd have thowt it?' She'd put on a broad Yorkshire accent to great effect.

They opened the door to the waiting father, leaving Sammia to show Ibrahim to Youssef in private, before the others came to admire the new arrival.

'I think a cup of tea is in order and something stronger for me,' Peter announced. 'And for Mel, by the look of her. The snow's stopped for the moment. The Begans must stay here. Caves are no place for winter, or a baby.'

Mel was limp with exhaustion and relief. Spiro hugged her. 'Time for us to go home. We still have a dinner to cook – and what a tale to tell the village.'

Mel took one last glance at Sammia, the baby cradled in her arms. It was like a scene from a Christmas card come to life, a mother with her baby. All was well with the world.

58

Chloë noted that the Christmas-morning service was thinly attended: older members of the congregation feared falls on the ice and snow. She, Alexa and Simon had arrived with Gary and Kelly, who had stayed the night after the carol concert, not wanting to make the trek to the Bunker. Ariadne and Hebe had made it, too, with Clive and Natalie.

Father Dennis kept it brief, for the church was cold, and he invited them all back to the vicarage for hot drinks and mince pies. Chloë was in a rush to get her dinner going, but stayed to be polite. 'I've got the colonel coming. I don't suppose he'll want to venture out on foot. I hope he's warm in that old stone house. Simon will give him a lift later.'

'He'll be on his first noggin, if I know him. Didn't we all do well last night?' said Father Dennis. 'And now, with no lights or power, we'll have to fall on our own initiative. I'll light the barbecue for grilled turkey steaks this year.'

Thank goodness for the wood-burning stove. It's not quite an Aga, but it'll pot-roast the turkey and trimmings given time, Chloë thought, as they plodded through the lanes. But on second thoughts, maybe the vicar's idea was a good one… The snow was slushy and slippery so she held onto Alexa in case she fell. It would be a bigger gathering than usual, with Alexa, Clive, Natalie, Gary, Kelly, Ariadne and Hebe, but Chloë loved a houseful of friends old and new. It was made all the more special by having her daughter with her to help prepare the table and entertain the guests.

She was bursting to announce the secret that she would become a grandmother in the coming year. All those months of anxiety had evaporated with Alexa's news. Chloë would take on her duties with joy because Alexa, for all her independence, would need her support. However, if she had learnt anything these past few months, it was that Alexa was a grown-up, with her own ideas and plans. Chloë must step back and wait to be asked, not barge in uninvited.

This was turning out to be one of the best Christmases ever and there was still New Year and Epiphany to come. How glad she was that they had persevered with the Christmas choir. Ariadne had done them proud, after all the dramas of the fire and the snow. No one could accuse island life of being boring. Ariadne had told them how she had discovered Elodie's private notebooks and that Simon and Gary had plans to put them up as an ebook, to raise more funds for the appeal. Gary had ideas for marketing and planned to contact Elodie's publishers with a view to reissuing some of her best novels and reviving her profile with new readers.

Even Kelly was coming round to the idea of joining in, thanks to Alexa. She had brought some of her lovely knitwear for babies and toddlers to sell for the appeal. Not the usual pink and blue but colourful, jazzy designs, which Alexa said would sell well. She had squirrelled away some for herself, with a generous donation to the fund.

As they relaxed in front of the fire, Simon looked at the clock. 'I'll collect Arthur and bring him over,' he said.

'Can I join you?' said Ariadne. 'I have a plant to give him and I want to thank him for supporting us. He asked me to call in, said he had something private to discuss, but I never got round to it.'

'Don't be long – I've just decided to cut up the turkey and cook the pieces on the barbecue, like the vicar. It'll be quicker and the veg can go on the stove. Make sure the old man wraps up well.'

Alexa served champagne with canapés, while Hebe helped prepare the vegetables and Chloë dealt with the turkey.

'Did you enjoy the concert?' Chloë asked, as they chopped.

'What concert was that?' Hebe replied, smiling.

'Last night's carol concert in the hall. You were playing the piano,' Chloë said.

'Did it go well? I heard it on the radio. The carols from King's College. We always listen to the World Service,' Hebe replied.

Chloë said nothing. Poor Hebe had forgotten that she was at the front, playing her heart out. Ariadne must be carrying this burden alone. No wonder she looked so grey and exhausted. Chloë glanced at the clock. They had been gone nearly half an hour. Had they got stuck in the snow or had an accident? What could be keeping them?

59

The journey downhill in the jeep was slow and hairy, but Ariadne clung to her plant. It was good of the Bartletts to entertain them so royally. She took back all the mean remarks she had made about Chloë being bossy and patronising. She was a good egg, and her daughter was a delight.

How different it all looked, caked with snow, the square silent and empty. The taverna was shuttered, but she knew that behind the doors a feast was in preparation. The Greeks had been making more of Christmas Day in the past few years, decorating trees with lights, shops filled with music and festive decorations.

Simon parked in the square, where the trucks and pickups were parked. Clive's tins had all but disappeared from their makeshift pyramid tree – those that were left were covered with snow. It was only a short walk to the stone house, which was still in darkness, its curtains drawn. Simon pressed the bell, but Arthur didn't come. He was usually ready and waiting, so Simon banged hard. Still there was no reply.

'Perhaps he's gone out to meet us,' Ariadne said. 'He's usually so punctual.'

'And the curtains are still drawn. Who has his key?' Simon asked.

'Maria does for him. She'll have one, but he won't have locked the door.' Ariadne tried the handle and it opened. 'Arthur? Merry Christmas! We've come to collect you.' The house felt chilly, with no heating, so she went into the sitting room to open the curtains, while Simon went upstairs to check that he was in.

Ariadne drew back the curtains to let daylight flood into the room, and saw that Arthur was still in his armchair 'Arthur, there you are,' she said. 'Arthur?' He was pale and silent. Then she knew. There was no sign of life in his face. 'Simon!' she shouted. 'He's in here.'

Simon came downstairs, to find her holding Arthur's cold hand. 'I'm afraid he's gone,' she said. 'What do we do? He's still in his uniform, bless him.'

Simon checked his pulse and nodded. 'We leave him here to rest in peace. Arthur wouldn't want us to spoil Christmas Day, would he? The concert must have worn him out. We shouldn't have asked him to sing.'

Ariadne was weeping. 'It's my fault. I should have known better.'

'Arthur volunteered and enjoyed the chance to join in. Don't be sad. This is how all of us would wish to slip away, relaxed by the fire after a good night out. Don't worry.'

Ariadne sat down, shocked.

'Close the curtains and shutters. We'll lock the door behind us and let the doctor know.' Simon was taking control.

'I wonder what he wanted to talk to me about.' Ariadne sighed, reluctant to leave the old man alone.

'That we'll never know, but his affairs can wait. Time to head home now. Chloë will be worried.'

'He was such a lovely man. I shall miss him.' Ariadne wiped away a tear.

'We'll all miss him. I don't think they make the likes of him any more.'

60

Della was helping Irini in the kitchen. All the Papadakis relatives were gathered around the big fire in the taverna. Every member of the family had brought goodies to add to the feast, Christmas breads and pastries, rice side dishes, vegetable stews, so the table was laden with food.

Irini was not in the best of moods. 'Where's she dragged him out to in the snow? Will we find them frozen in the morning? Why go looking for trouble?'

Della had no answers. Something must have stirred Mel to make that trek to the cave. 'I know she was worried about Sammia, especially in this bad weather,' was all she could offer.

Della was looking forward to Christmas Day Greek-style. The chapel bell had rung out early doors, waking her. Its three loud sets of three and seven bell tolls always made her laugh. There was an icy trail up to the church steps, swept clear of snow for the faithful, but she would give both churches a miss today.

Last night's concert had taken her back to those Christmas mornings when she'd woken as a child, to a Cadbury selection box in her stocking, a copy of *Jackie*, a colouring book and a pink sugar mouse. Her mum had saved all her coupons and tokens to give them a proper Christmas dinner, with tinned ham, roast potatoes, a Co-op Christmas pudding and a packet of trifle mix, with Carnation cream. Then there was TV with Morecambe and Wise. It had been a world away from celebrations on a Greek island.

Last year there was a picnic barbecue on the beach. Now they were hunkered down by candlelight, but she had kept her promise to Natalie.

It was strange waking up sober, with a clear head and a glass of water. She must watch it tonight, though, as the wine and raki would flow like a river. Two glasses and one raki, out of politeness, and that would be it. She needed to keep her wits about her around Giorgos, who was eyeing her up out of sight of his wife, Elefteria.

The smells wafting from the bread oven were appetising, and by four o'clock they were laying the dishes on the table. Markos and Stefan were stuffed with chocolates, tearing round on their new bikes, frustrated that the snow outside was turning into rain, much to everyone's relief. Then in burst Mel and Spiro, cheeks flushed and soaking wet.

'What time is this?' Irini shouted. 'Where have you been?'

'Watching a child born, Mama, a beautiful little boy, Ibrahim,' Spiro announced.

'Not in that cave?' Della said. 'And on Christmas Day?'

'We got them to the retreat house, just in time. Alison, Maryam and I were the midwives. Mama and baby are both doing well, safe in the retreat's guesthouse. It was amazing, but without Spiro's truck, things could have been very different. So sorry we're late, but we had to tell Dr Makaris. Good thing he lives next door to his surgery. I'm starving!' Mel plonked herself on the nearest chair, while everyone took in the news. A baby born on Santaniki, on Christ's birthday, was surely a good omen.

Della was sorry to have missed such an experience. She would never get over her own mistake but it was time to let go and make changes in her life. Maybe she should return to the UK for a fresh start. Where there's life, there's hope. A fresh start, she mused, where no one would see her as a hopeless drunk. It had been her crutch for so long but not any more. She deserved a brighter life, the chance of a decent relationship. Suddenly she knew the new year would be different, not the same old, same old. *I'm worth more than that.*

She would miss Santaniki and her friends, but somewhere over the horizon, a new life beckoned. This time she was not running away, but running forward.

61

Ariadne let Simon tell the guests the news. No one spoke. 'It was peaceful,' she added. 'I don't think he suffered. He just fell asleep.'

Chloë sat down, winded. 'Such a character. I shall miss him and his stories. Perhaps the choir was too much for a man of his age.'

'Nonsense,' said her husband. 'He enjoyed the music and the company. He wouldn't want us to sit around moping, so let's toast his passing and enjoy the rest of the day.'

Kelly Partridge nodded. 'My uncle Jeff was watching the Cup Final when Arsenal won. He went out like a light, with a smile on his face. I thought the old gent looked dapper in his uniform.'

'I'm glad we sang "Silent Night". It meant so much to him. Simon's right – he will be missed, like all our absent friends,' said Clive.

Natalie saw a tear in his eye. He was thinking of Lucy.

'At least Lucy will have company now,' he added, smiling.

'I can smell something burning.' Natalie jumped up. 'Can I help, Chloë?' The women rushed into the kitchen and saw the roast potatoes sizzling on the barbecue. Natalie whipped them off the heat, while Kelly found the plates to warm them.

Alexa was sitting down, feeling faint, the colour drained from her face.' It's hot in here.'

Chloë was by her side. 'Into the hall – it's cold there. She's just a little dizzy. It's her condition.'

'You mean…' Natalie smiled

'I'm going to be a grandmother in the spring. I was saving it up to tell everyone but Arthur's passing skittled my exciting news.'

Kelly left the room in a rush. Natalie could see she was upset, so she followed her.

'What's wrong with me and Gary that we can't have one?' She sniffed into her handkerchief.

Natalie hugged her. 'Give it time, your turn will come.'

'Are you psychic, or something? It's making me feel sick with envy and I know that's not right. Santaniki's nice and all that, but maybe it's time to go back to the smoke and see a specialist again,' said Kelly, wiping her eyes.

'That's for you and Gary to talk over, but being tense and anxious won't help. Remember what Della said about relaxation?'

'I know, but it's not done me any good, just made me tired and tearful. What's wrong with me?'

'Dry your eyes and have a drink, for Arthur's sake. That cushion you knitted for Chloë in those colours was a super present. Who taught you?'

'My gran. She could crochet and make shawls that thin

they'd go through a wedding ring. I like knitting – it takes my mind off things.'

'With your talent, you could sell online or in a craft shop. Such an exquisite blend of colours too. No one can teach you that sort of eye for colour.' Natalie was trying to comfort her.

'Do you really think so? I just do it to pass the time.' Kelly sniffed and smiled. 'Thanks. You've cheered me up. I shall be jealous, but I get that way. Then I'm mean to Gary, who don't deserve it. He's going to do this novelist's stuff that Ariadne found and enjoy the challenge.'

'So both of you will be busy.' Natalie looked across the drawing room towards Clive.

Kelly said, 'My turn to give you my advice. Mr Podmore's very nice. He seems to look your way regular and really fancies you.'

Natalie blushed. 'I know, and I like him too. He's so very kind.'

'What you waiting for, then?'

'Not sure, the right moment, I suppose.' Natalie laughed. 'Kelly Partridge, are you matchmaking?'

Kelly clutched her arm. 'I think it's past that stage, don't you?'

'Cheeky!' They returned to the kitchen, as Chloë called everyone into the dining room, with its table decorations, crackers and beautiful flower arrangements.

'Blimey! *Homes and Gardens*, eat your heart out,' Kelly whispered, as they sat down for the feast.

Afterwards Ariadne leant back in her chair. 'That was what our daily in Yorkshire would have called "a right belt-loosener". What a marvellous repast, Chloë. Thank you for inviting us all into your home again, and I'm glad you left the empty chair in Arthur's honour.'

Natalie had never eaten so many delicious dishes and, for a change, she hadn't made them. She was learning to enjoy food again, to taste flavours instead of shoving anything into her mouth to keep her energy flowing. Dear Arthur had given her good advice and she would ever be grateful to him for showing her the way to greater peace of mind.

Suddenly there was light and a hum of electricity back on. 'Praise the Lord,' Ariadne said. 'I don't think the freezer food would last much longer.'

'I've rather liked having no TV or internet,' said Alexa. 'It feels good to be cut off from the world for a few days.'

'It'll come and go for the next few days, but the temperature's going up,' said Simon. 'It will soon thaw.'

Natalie smiled, feeling at one with the world, knowing it was time to accept new things into her life, new friends and a future. She saw Clive across the table winking at her. He, too, was learning to let go of the past, but was it too early yet to think of anything more than friendship?

62

Arthur's funeral was a village affair. The local veterans of the Cretan Resistance came out to honour him. The mayor and half of Santaniki stood outside the little Anglican church, saluting him, as they made their way slowly to the cemetery. Father Dennis gave a good eulogy, Simon read a lesson and they sang again his favourite 'Silent Night', with hardly a dry eye.

At the end of the ceremonies, they retired to Irini's taverna for a spread of cakes and pastries, washed down with a case of champagne Gary had been saving for a future party. 'I'm glad we didn't go away for Christmas,' he said. 'We'd have missed all the drama.'

Ariadne was pleased that they were becoming part of the community. 'Without you, we'd not have had a home to go back to. You're a real asset to the village.' She gave him a kiss. 'I wish you both the best for the New Year.'

'I've nearly got the complete memoir online for you to check,' he said. 'Miss Durrante was quite a goer, wasn't she?

What a life she lived, and so much of it here on the island. I'm sure the book will sell well. How's the appeal doing so far?'

'Not enough to buy a property, but enough to rent somewhere,' Ariadne said.

It was at this point that the vicar slipped in to join them. 'Ariadne, I have something to show you. Please excuse us, Gary. I just need a word in private.'

Ariadne stepped out onto the covered veranda. The snow was melting fast, but it was still cold. Father Dennis pulled out an envelope. 'Read this,' he said.

Ariadne recognised Arthur's spidery handwriting.

Dear Dennis,

I am writing to inform you that I have notified my attorney in Crete and given them a copy of my will, just in case the good Lord calls me home sometime soon. It can't be a long wait.

As I have no family, there will be no dispute about its contents: a donation to Help the Heroes and something for Maria. I have been aware of the Christmas appeal to raise funds to shelter homeless families and refugees, so it seems sensible for me to donate my house here on Santaniki for just such a worthy cause. I have known what it is like to have no roof over my head, to be at the mercy of cruel elements and beholden to others for refuge. It must be at the disposal of the village council to use as they see fit, not as a holiday rental but to house any family in need.

I would like the first tenants to be our own local refugees, Mr Began and his charming wife, Sammia.

'The dear, dear man! How generous, and how typical of him.' Ariadne was choked by this welcome news.

News had spread quickly of the Christmas baby's arrival, and gifts arrived daily for the family. Kelly had made little cardigans and caps. There were toys, blankets and offers of a crib and buggy. His birth was bringing people together, but Arthur's gift was beyond anyone's expectation.

Ariadne now observed the Thorners, recently returned from England, having missed the wonder of their concert, the drama of a white Christmas and the coming together of so much love. She sensed them standing on the sidelines, not knowing what to say.

She could forgive their ignorant prejudice against her and Hebe. Every village had its oddballs, dissidents with cold hearts. She felt sorry for them, missing all the fun, not having been part of their little choir. Singing together was such a leveller. The choir was a team built by practice and the love of music. Singing was good for the soul. Together they were bigger than the sum of their parts.

63

The feast day of the Epiphany brightened into one of those sunlit mornings that hinted of better weather to come. The snow still lay on the mountain ridges, but its magic had melted away, leaving little clumps of gritty residue. It was as if the white-out had never been. Washing hung on balconies, and villagers gathered beside the path that passed for a promenade to watch Father Mikhalis paraded in his finest robes with his acolytes, followed by widows in their black and grey Sunday best. Village dignitaries formed a vast procession, as he intoned the liturgy of the age-old ceremony, blessing the waters of the New Year. He then threw the gilded cross, attached to a rope, into the icy water.

Chloë shivered, as plucky local boys dived in to retrieve the holy cross while the flotilla of little fishing-boats and yachts blew their horns and the men let off fireworks once more. The mayor's second son, Andreas, brought up the cross, waving it in the air. Custom said he would be blessed with good luck and health for the rest of the year.

Perhaps it was as well. Chloë smiled, knowing how he raced over the place on his scooter, minus a helmet, usually with some girl riding pillion. Alexa was watching, wrapped in her Puffa jacket. Her three-week stay had brought colour to her cheeks. 'I'm going to miss all this.' She sighed.

'You don't have to go back yet, do you?' Chloë said.

'I must, to sort out my work and a nursery for Olympia. I'll be due maternity leave when the time comes, though.'

'We must pop over soon. You know we'll do anything to help.'

'Of course, but nearer the time perhaps.'

'You have only to ask.'

'Don't worry, I'll bring her here as soon as I can. I want the island to be her second home. She'll love the sea and the beach, and meeting your friends. It's been a super break, but it's time to head back to reality. It's not going to be easy, but I will make sure Hugh gets a look in. She is his child, whether he likes it or not.'

Chloë clutched Alexa's hands. 'Thanks for coming. You made this Christmas so special.'

'It's been quite a time.' Alexa laughed. 'And to think I almost missed your choir, the snow and the Christmas baby. It's me who should be thanking you and Simon for a wonderful time.'

Della was standing beside them lost in thought. She had seen an advert in the local English newspaper for a Pilates-cum-yoga teacher, needed at the NATO airbase on the big island. She had all the qualifications and it fitted her need to find pastures new. Perhaps she could fill in an application and give it a chance. In her heart she was ready to move on. Her new-found sober self was eager to find more opportunities, perhaps to retrain in another sphere. There was nothing to hold her here, and the ferry meant she could keep in touch with her friends. A New Year and a fresh start. Santaniki had been a bolthole, but soothing her wounds with vodka no longer held any appeal. *One day at a time*. She repeated the mantra. She was learning to forgive herself. I'm still young enough to make a new life, she thought. Who knew what might be waiting for her across the wine dark sea?

Clive and Natalie stood holding hands, watching the ceremony from a discreet distance. This new closeness felt strange, but Clive knew Lucy wouldn't begrudge it. She would always be part of him, but on New Year's Eve, at Kelly and Gary's house, when they had all joined hands to sing 'Auld Lang Syne', Natalie had clasped him in a kiss, no longer in friendship but desire, and his whole body had responded.

Walks were no longer lonely affairs, but full of chatter and plans. Bella even had a friend in little Bertie. There was so much to talk about. As they were watching the boats honking and blaring across the bay, Clive knew it was time to strike. 'I haven't explored many of the Greek islands. Have you?'

Natalie shook her head. 'Just family holidays in Zakynthos, then Corfu when I left college, and Crete, of course, with the children.'

'It would be interesting to go island-hopping, before all the tourists arrive,' Clive suggested. 'Would you be interested?'

Natalie turned to him, smiling. 'Sounds great. Are you asking?'

'I'm asking.' Clive tried to mimic a Liverpool accent.

'Then you're on.' She squeezed his hand. 'I'd like to see more of Greece.'

'I was thinking more of a honeymoon cruise than a trip. Now that I've found you, I'd like you by my side. I know Lucy won't mind…' Clive delved in his pocket 'I've been meaning to give you this. It's from the jeweller you admire.' He opened a tiny box to reveal a gold ring, with little diamonds dotted into an N shape.

Natalie beamed with pleasure. 'It's beautiful and, yes, a cruise sounds wonderful.'

He kissed her gently and put the ring on a finger. 'I hope you don't mind but I took your measurement on the sly, when you tried on Lucy's ring.'

Natalie was staring at her left hand. 'Mind? I can't believe this is happening.'

A horn blew as the fireworks shrieked into the sky but neither of them heard a thing, lost in the excitement of their future together.

Gary felt Kelly clinging to his arm. 'You all right now?'

'I feel dizzy,' she whispered. 'It must be the noise and the prawns we ate last night. It was a good party last week,' she added. 'Did you see Natalie and Clive get it on at last?'

'Very cosy.' Gary winked. 'Looking very loved up.'

'I'm glad. Natalie's a nice woman and Clive is a decent bloke, for his age.'

'And you seem happier.' Gary hugged her to him. 'Your knitting's going down a treat. How many orders so far?'

'Enough to be going on with. I forgot to tell you that, while you were at the appeal committee, Sammia came to thank me for the layette. Her baby's beautiful, with such dark eyes. I'm glad they're out of the cave. Fancy Arthur letting them live in his house. Mel said some of their neighbours aren't too happy, but she'll sort them out, given time.' Kelly shivered.

'I think we should be going. You look so pale.'

'I'm feeling out of sorts and need to go back on a diet. My boobs are like balloons.'

'I like your boobs.' He squeezed them.

'Ouch! Get off!' she said. 'Let's go and watch that DVD you brought.'

As they made way their way back up to the house, Gary paused. 'Hang on, girl, when did you last have the curse?'

'You know me, never know when. It'll be on me soon enough, judging by the signs.'

'So, no period, sore boobs, feeling faint… Do you think…?'

'Don't go there, Gary. It's just the PMT I always have.'

'All the same, I think you should do a test.'

'No, we've done too many of them. It's not going to happen. Forget it. I've got my knitting.' She strode out ahead of him.

'You sound just like my gran! Knitting indeed! Let's go home and do something a little more vigorous than knitting…'

'Garfield Partridge, I don't know what you mean.' Kelly giggled.

'Up them stairs and let's be having you…'

★

Mel rushed back to the taverna, which was filling up fast with Irini's friends and villagers on their way home. It was going to be a busy lunchtime for a change. Spiro was back in his post, grilling lamb ribs. She'd come back early from the blessing of the water, knowing they would soon be rushed off their feet. There was just time to call in to see the new family up the street, but Sammia was out. Little Ibrahim was making Mel broody. She felt a special connection to him, after helping to bring him into the world.

Youssef had been alone, busy decorating the living room. They were grateful for some of Arthur's furniture, but all his personal effects had been removed discreetly by the vicar.

The two couples were sharing the house for the time being, but their presence had caused comment from some of Irini's sewing group earlier in the week. 'They said it should go to a local family, not strangers,' Irini reported.

'They're not strangers, and Kyrie Arthur wanted them. It's in his will,' Spiro yelled. 'Tell them, Mama, you know how hard-working they are...'

'Strangers indeed,' Mel added. 'I, too, am a stranger, so what do I know? In the war this township opened its heart to strangers.'

'They were soldiers, and it was different then,' Toula argued, listening in to their conversation. 'They do not worship as we do.'

'In my eyes it's the same God for Jews, Christians, Muslims. At least they make time for worship, not like many others on this island,' Mel responded. 'They're good people, with good hearts and that's all that matters... not like some folk I could mention, who sit around in their dirty shirts, smoking like chimneys, playing cards and drinking, so their families go hungry while the women do all the work.'

'Enough, Melodia. Let's get on with our work,' Irini said. Of course she wouldn't want to offend any regular customers.

Subject closed. Mel sighed. She would have to tread carefully with her neighbours. Only time would prove her right, she hoped. Thank goodness for her children, her husband and her compatriots in the book club and the choir, if it continued. Marrying a foreigner was never easy, trying to fit in with a strange culture and opinions, but this was the life she had chosen and she had no regrets. Well, perhaps just a few, she thought, as she cleared the plates ready for more hungry hordes to descend.

Sammia watched the boats in the harbour, bobbing on the water. The wind was warmer, the daylight a little longer, and she was filled with hope and gratitude. Ibrahim was a citizen of this island, her husband ready to take on any job he was offered. They had a proper roof over their heads, thanks to the generosity of a stranger. At times it was all too much to take in.

How life had changed since they first stepped off the ferry on to this blessed place. Allah, the Compassionate One, had heard her plea and answered in a way only He could.

The baby stirred at the sound of the horns, his eyes open with wonder. She was determined to do everything in her power to keep him safe and well. She watched Karim throwing pebbles into the water, jumping as they splashed. The sea that had brought only fear and death now brought laughter and pleasure to the child. Long may it continue, she prayed.

★

Ariadne sat in the olive garden, feeling the welcome sun on her cheeks while Hebe busied herself in the borders. Ariadne had bought her a kneeling pad with handles for Christmas, so Hebe could ease herself up and down as she weeded. It was good to see her content, her restlessness calmed by touching her precious plants.

What a strange few months since they had all gathered on that book-club night, sweltering in the September heat, when she had thought up a little choir. So much had happened, for the better, she hoped. Elodie would be proud of their efforts. Without her generosity, none of this would have happened. It was also giving Ariadne time to come to terms with what lay ahead. The appointment in Athens loomed, and the decision as to whether they should stay on Santaniki or return to Yorkshire was keeping her awake at night.

How could they ever leave the olive garden? All the work they had done together to create this little paradise, could they yield it up to someone else?

Spring came early here. Hebe was at her best in the garden, among the flowers and tending their olive grove. How could they think of letting it go? Here, indeed were green thoughts in a green shade. There must be a way through the coming difficulties and, after all, she would not be alone. The Olive Garden Choir, begun so light-heartedly, was now a community of new friends and old, who had come to their aid when the fire threatened to destroy their home.

Arthur's gift topped everything. It would seal the future for so many good people who, through no fault of their own, found themselves stranded without hope. From little acorns grew mighty oaks. Who knew where their venture would lead? It was a journey forged through friendships and generosity. Surely only good could come from that.

Extract from Elodie Durrante's
Journal and Jottings

1. Writing for publication is a steep learning curve. You have to master your trade, put in the hours and be prepared to fail.
2. Success can unhinge the unwary. It can make monsters of some. Remember, you are only as good as your last sales.
3. Starting the second novel is like the climb to Everest's summit. You trek round the foothills, knowing what lies ahead.
4. The beginning is exciting, but somewhere in the middle comes the soggy bit, the Slough of Despond. Climb out of the mire of doubts, and let your characters guide you ever upwards towards the climax. Then it's full speed ahead to the finish.
5. Nothing ever comes out as you first hoped. It is distilled through a funnel, sifted into the final essence.
6. Don't talk about your new work, just write. Don't give away your fire.
7. Failure to finish a book is no shame. Perhaps its legs were just too short to run the distance. Writers are like athletes:

some are natural sprinters, some middle-distance runners and other prefer marathons, slow and steady to the goal.

8. A writer once told me the process of writing was better than sex! I told him perhaps he wasn't doing it right.

9. I set off on my journey, like David Livingstone in the jungle, with only hope and faith that it will lead me somewhere worth visiting. It's the characters who open the way forward.

10. Don't be fooled by all the flummery of attending writerly events, lectures, parties, launches. They're not real. You are a writer only when you sit down and write. The rest can be just time-wasting and distracting – unless, of course, you're promoting your own work.

11. Watch out for the wet blankets in your life, who dampen your dreams and ideas. Avoid them while you're busy with your project. Choose enthusiasts who believe in you and cheer you on. Be prepared, though, to listen and take note of genuine and positive criticism. We never stop learning.

12. Finally, be generous to other authors. Celebrate their successes and do not give in to bitterness and envy. There will always be writers more accomplished or successful than you, prize winners with great talent. Don't let the thought of them detract from your own worth.

Elodie Durrante, 1999

Acknowledgements

You will not find Santaniki on any map of Greece. It is a product of my imagination conceived after a boozy lunch sitting under my favourite olive tree one summer afternoon on Crete. It is a breakaway from my usual historical genre and I must thank Rosie de Courcy and her team at Head of Zeus for embracing this new venture and to Hazel Orme for her vigorous copyediting.

Many thanks also for the snippets and observations of my dear friends, resident on Crete and for their continuing support. They know who they are. Any mistakes are my own.

The recipes are drawn from ones I have gleaned over the years with special reference to Elizabeth Cradick's *Cretan Village Cooking* and to Susanna Harris Kokotsaki's wonderful Baklava.

Many writers will understand how hard it was to leave my imaginary island and its characters behind. Already there are a sequel or two of ideas marinating in my notebook. I can't wait to return there.

A letter from the publisher

We hope you enjoyed this book. We are an independent publisher dedicated to discovering brilliant books, new authors and great storytelling. If you want to hear more, why not join our community of book-lovers at:

www.headofzeus.com

We'll keep you up-to-date with our latest books, author blogs, tempting offers, chances to win signed editions, events across the UK and much more.

@HoZ_Books

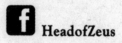HeadofZeus

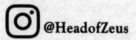@HeadofZeus

HEAD *of* ZEUS